Also by Sam Mitani

The Prototype (2018)

Red Mist (2023)

KEYS TO THE EMPIRE

A Carrara Book

Published by Carrara Media, LLC

carrarabooks.com

First Edition: 2024

Keys to the Empire, Book III of The Prototype Trilogy

ISBN: 979-8-9916226-2-2 (print); 979-8-9916226-6-0 (e-book)

Designed and printed in the United States of America

KEYS TO THE EMPIRE

THE PROTOTYPE TRILOGY
BOOK THREE

SAM MITANI

CARRARA MEDIA

empire, *noun,* \ *em̩ pī(ə)r* \

—*an extensive group of states or countries under a single supreme authority. The name of a luxury crossover vehicle produced by Kamita Motors.*

PRELUDE

The Golden Triangle Special Economic Zone, 2014

WITHIN THE INTIMATE confines of Revere Bar situated inside the King Waterfront Hotel, a middle-aged Chinese man sat alone at the polished wood counter, caressing a classic martini glass. Dr. Linghu Ning, draped in a wrinkled blue suit that loosely hung upon his frame, wore his necktie gently loosened, suggesting that his work for the day was done. A pair of Clubmaster spectacles that partly concealed his bushy eyebrows sat on his flat nose, and his thinning hair was streaked with strands of silver. Mired in thought, he failed to notice a gentleman with a clean-shaven face, dressed in a snug gray W.W. Chan suit, enter the room until he claimed the seat immediately next to him.

He pointed to the Chinese professor's martini.

"I'll have what he's having," he said in English to the bartender, a dark-skinned female in her thirties with wavy brown hair.

"One Bombay Sapphire martini coming up," she responded.

The man then turned to Linghu. Staying with English, he said, "Your lecture last month at MIT was truly inspirational."

Linghu smiled and tilted his head in appreciation. "You were there, were you?"

"My name is Charles Qiang Hu. I lecture at MIT in my spare time. Radar engineering."

"Then, I take it you aren't here for the Energy Conference. What brings you all the way to this accursed part of the world?" asked Linghu.

"Other business," Charles replied.

Linghu's suspicions were immediately aroused. The Golden Triangle Special Economic Zone, or GTSEZ, was a sprawling development nestled in Laos near the borders of Myanmar and Thailand. In the seven years since it was established, the GTSEZ had rapidly transformed into a notorious hub for criminal enterprises; a breeding ground for illegal activities ranging from drug and human trafficking to money laundering. While officially part of Laos, its governance lay in the hands of a dubious Chinese businessman, making it a near-autonomous entity in all but name. Simply put, anything was possible in the GTSEZ.

Linghu made a swift appraisal of Charles. His black hair was slicked back, framing a handsome, square-jawed face. He appeared to be in his mid-forties, standing in the neighborhood of five-foot-eight, and in good physical condition, evidenced by wide shoulders that accentuated a lean, athletic build.

"Where did you study, Professor Hu?" Linghu asked.

"Peking University," Charles replied proudly.

"Ah, I still have quite a few friends there. I'm surprised I've never heard of you. Are you sure you're not a *Guóānbù* (Ministry of State Security agent). You certainly have that kind of swag."

"You're quite observant," Charles responded. He then seamlessly transitioned to Mandarin. "In fact, professor, there's an MSS agent in the lobby lounging on the sofa with his head buried in an iPad, and yet another watching the rear exit."

"You *are* MSS, aren't you?" Linghu asked in Mandarin, a tinge of accusation in his tone.

"I'll leave that for you to decide."

Linghu took a swig from his glass. "You're all wasting the party's money, sending so many men to watch me. Sorry to disappoint you but the thought of defecting has never crossed my mind. I'm quite happy in Beijing."

Charles paused as the bartender delicately placed a fresh Bombay Sapphire martini before him.

"That's very reassuring to hear," he said in English after she left.

Showing disinterest in prolonging the conversation, Linghu casually glanced at his Casio timepiece and swiftly polished off the remaining contents of his glass. "It's late. It was a pleasure meeting you, Hu *Jiaoshou* (Professor Hu), if that's even your real name. Enjoy your martini."

Without waiting for a response, Linghu stepped off his highchair and made his way out of the bar, leaving Charles Hu alone with his drink. As Linghu traversed the lobby, a small crowd had gathered near the main entrance, many of them wearing nametags affixed to their clothing. On a tripod near the front counter sat a large cardboard sign that read "Welcome to the East Asian Blockchain Conference." Suddenly, the piercing wail of the hotel's fire alarm echoed through the hotel's speakers, stopping everyone—including Linghu—in their tracks.

One of the hotel staffers behind the reception counter, a tall African-American woman, stepped forward.

"I'm the hotel manager. Please stay calm and make your way to these doors," she announced. "The concierge will direct you."

The crowd around Linghu began moving in the direction of the front entrance, prompting him to follow the flow, when he felt a firm grasp tighten around his right arm. He turned and saw the bartender, the very one who had just served him his martini.

"I'm with the Central Intelligence Agency," she said in a hushed voice. "Come with me, Dr. Linghu."

His first reaction was to pull away, but when he noticed a firearm tucked underneath her vest, he relented and nodded in acknowledgement. Acting decisively, the bartender steered him in the opposite direction, against the flow of the crowd, back toward the kitchen.

"This place is crawling with Chinese agents," Linghu said softly.

"We know," she replied. "We have a boat out back. There's an agent standing by who will take you to safety."

Amid the blaring fire alarm, Linghu and the female agent entered the kitchen, where the cooks hurried to the hotel's emergency exit. The two followed them closely, hastening their steps until they emerged outside, onto the River Walk that hugged the bank of the Mekong River. The sticky, humid air greeted them like a slap on the face. But before they could reach the River Walk, a young Asian man, his hand nestled within the recesses of his light blue jacket, blocked their path.

"Shit," the bartender muttered.

With Linghu's arm still firmly in her grip, she swung on her heels and retraced her steps. However, she didn't get far, for another Chinese man, donning a black sportscoat, stepped out of the hotel, obstructing their way back into the building and forcing them to hold their positions.

Sandwiched between two MSS agents, the bartender reached into her vest and pulled out a Glock 9mm handgun, pointing its barrel at the man in the black sportscoat in front of her.

The MSS agent raised his hands in a calming gesture, signaling everyone to stand down.

"No need to get dramatic," he said in accented English. "Simply give the good scientist back to us, and we can all walk away."

"He came to us," the bartender shot back. "And you have no jurisdiction here. It's you who needs to back off."

The lead MSS agent gestured to his partner in the blue jacket to stow his weapon—a command the colleague dutifully heeded. He then addressed Linghu in English.

"Professor Linghu Ning, this woman is lying, is she not? You were, in fact, abducted by her. You're being detained against your will, isn't that correct?"

As Linghu hesitated, another figure joined the standoff, this one materializing from the direction of the boat docks. He was Caucasian, his head topped with short blond hair, and his gun was already drawn.

"Drop your weapons," he exclaimed in English.

The young Chinese operative placed his hand on his gun nestled in his holster as the newcomer approached slowly from behind. With a swift glance over his shoulder, he fired through the fabric of his blue jacket. Sensing danger, the American agent dove to his left, unleashing a shot in the process. The air crackled with the sound of gunfire as they emptied their magazines in a relentless, deadly volley. Within moments, both men crumpled to the ground, their bodies pierced by bullets that had torn through their clothing.

Shaken by the sudden violence, the female agent unleashed a round at the lead MSS agent; however, her bullet sailed wide, allowing her counterpart to drop to a knee and retaliate with three quick rounds. Two of them ripped through her chest, knocking her back dead.

Witnessing the bloody death of the woman next to him, Linghu sank to his knees, his body hunched, his hands placed over his head as his body trembled with fear.

Nearby, a small crowd of people on the walkway scattered in disarray, releasing a cacophony of panicked screams. Amid the tumult, the lead MSS agent advanced toward Linghu, a smile fixed on his face. But his progress was abruptly halted by the sharp crack of another gunshot, a lone bullet finding the middle of his forehead.

From his hunched position, Linghu watched as the man dropped to the ground next to him with a loud thud.

An eerie silence descended over the walkway, when Charles Hu emerged from the shadows, gripping his recently discharged firearm. He walked to Linghu.

"Are you hurt?" he asked in Mandarin.

Linghu looked up. "I'm not going back to China," he cried emphatically.

Charles gently pulled Linghu up to his feet. "Don't worry, professor. I'm CIA. I'm what you would call a double agent."

～

THE RENOWNED CHINESE scientist stared blankly at the night sky, the words having no effect on him. It was clear to Charles that the good professor had entered a mild state of shock. A lifelong scientist confined to the tranquil walls of a laboratory was ill prepared for witnessing several people being fatally shot up close.

"We're going for a boat ride, professor, and I guess I'm driving," Charles said casually, glancing at his downed CIA colleagues.

Before he could take another step, another gunshot echoed across the river. Reacting on pure instinct, Charles immediately dropped to the ground and shouted for Linghu to do the same. He dove to the first place that offered some semblance of cover, an open space beneath an elevated walkway. He returned fire blindly, and peering cautiously over the edge of the walkway, he spotted another MSS agent hiding behind a bench, pointing a gun in his direction.

The agent called out to Charles in Mandarin. "Since when have you joined the Americans, Hu Qiang?"

Charles responded with a bullet, but it missed its mark.

The agent continued, "Why? You're revered by many back home. You're practically a legend."

"I made my choice long ago, and it was the right one," Charles countered.

Charles was never notified about a third operative. Perhaps the higher-ups at the MSS had become suspicious and deployed an extra set of eyes to watch over him. But none of that mattered now. It was imperative that he neutralize the threat, praying that the agent hadn't yet relayed what he had discovered to his bosses.

Aiming carefully, Charles steadied his gun and unleashed two precise rounds. A distinct yelp of pain confirmed that one of the bullets met the target. The force of the impact sent the man falling backwards.

Crawling out of his hiding place, Charles hurried to Dr. Linghu, who was lying face down on the ground.

"Are you all right?" he asked.

Linghu didn't respond.

Kneeling beside him and turning him over, Charles saw the front of Linghu's shirt stained with blood. Rapidly peeling off his own jacket, he pressed it against the wound, before pulling out his cell phone and punching in four numbers.

"I'm behind the hotel," he said. "Two of our agents down, three of theirs neutralized. Package has been hit and requires immediate assistance."

Professor Linghu groaned, his eyelids slowly lifting.

"Stay with me. Help is on the way," Charles said in Mandarin.

"It's no use," Linghu murmured. "I'm losing too much blood. I need you to do me a favor."

The scientist slowly reached into his pocket and produced a gold medallion, about the circumference of a compact disc and an inch thick. Engraved on one side was an image of a dragon with a small emerald stone set in the place of its eye. On the other side was the Chinese character, "王."

"Stay still, professor," Charles urged.

Ignoring the advice, Linghu held the medallion up. He spoke in a hoarse voice. "I have secretly perfected a technology that will change the course of human history. The information is..."

Charles gently shook Linghu, attempting to keep him awake; however, after seeing the vacant gaze of the renowned Chinese scientist, he knew there was no point in attempting to converse with him further. He gently lowered Linghu's head to the ground and passed his hands over his eyes, closing his eyelids. The medallion, smeared red with Linghu's blood, remained in his lifeless hand. Prying it loose, Charles jammed it into his jacket pocket. He then rose to his feet and proceeded toward the bench where the MSS agent he shot earlier had fallen. However, upon reaching it, he found no trace of the man. A diminutive splash of blood at the base of the bench served as the only indication that he was there at all. In a state of panic, Charles scanned the vicinity, fervently seeking any sign of him. The vibration of his cell phone interrupted his actions. Retrieving it from his pocket, he noticed that the incoming call was from Nigel McKeen, the CIA's deputy director.

"What happened?" asked McKeen.

"Two agents down. The package was eliminated as well," Charles replied.

"Shit," McKeen blurted.

Unable to contain his mounting frustrations, Charles let loose. "I agree. This entire operation has been a shitshow. His death, as well as your agents' deaths, are on you."

McKeen remained even keeled. "The local police and Chinese agents are en route. I suggest you get out of there now."

"Can't. My cover's been compromised. An MSS agent spotted me and escaped. I need to find him and..."

McKeen cut Charles off.

"Then it's time to come in," he said.

"What about my family?"

"You can't go back," McKeen answered. "We'll keep watch over them. You know the deal."

An extended silence stretched between them, until Charles finally broke it.

"Unfortunately, I do, and it sucks," he said, abruptly ending the call.

With cell phone in hand, he walked to the brink of the River Walk and leaped onto an unmoored, unattended motorboat, promptly firing up its twin Yamaha engines. Tears welled in his eyes, as he flung the phone overboard. After taking hold of the vessel's controls, he guided the boat into the blackness of the Mekong River, leaving a heap of dead bodies, and his life in its wake.

ACT ONE

THE COINS OF WEI

魏的獎章

CHAPTER 1

Los Angeles, Present Day

STEPPING out of his modest two-story home, dressed in a gray Magnis & Novus suit, Charles Qiang Hu, now going by the name Dalton Lang, casually slipped into the driver's seat of his silver Acura MDX, one of three similar models in the quiet residential neighborhood. With a population of roughly forty thousand—nearly half of them made up of Chinese and Taiwanese residents—the city of San Gabriel in the greater Los Angeles area served as the ideal place for a fifty-something Asian man to blend seamlessly into the background, evade notice, and lead a quiet, simple life. The only remnants of Lang's past were his collection of impeccably tailored Hong Kong suits and a cache of weapons he kept hidden in the garage.

Under the glow of a Southern California winter sun, Lang guided his vehicle from his driveway onto South Granada Avenue. The morning air retained a slight chill, yet the forecast promised a week of sunshine with occasional scattered clouds. He sank into the plush seat, the gentle strains of *O mio babbino caro* by Giacomo

Puccini playing softly through the car's sound system, when he caught sight of a black Lexus ES sedan in the rearview mirror, trailing about three car lengths behind. It made the same right turn onto South El Molino Avenue as he did. He remembered seeing a similar vehicle during his daily jog the evening before, parked roughly a block and a half away from his home. It was the first time he'd seen the car in the neighborhood.

His thoughts were interrupted by his smartphone, its ringtone resonating through the MDX's speaker system. The dashboard monitor revealed the caller's identity as Eva Maston.

"Well, if it isn't my favorite attorney," Lang greeted after pressing the phone button on the steering wheel.

Eva replied in her usual sweet voice. "Good morning, Dalton. I'll be dropping Ruth off in a few minutes. Is that okay?"

"Of course, but she doesn't need to help out."

"It'll be good for her, but she might want to be paid, though," Eva said with a chuckle.

"I hope you're not negotiating on her behalf because I don't have the resources to go against a highly paid public defender like you."

"Hah, says the man with his own restaurant. But I can't believe it's already been eight years, Dalton. I remember when 'The Den' first opened. You barely had any customers."

Lang recalled those early days vividly, when he made the bold decision to invest the money he received from the U.S. government into a restaurant venture. Owning and running an eatery had been his dream ever since setting foot on American soil. Determined to keep his identity under wraps, he enlisted Eva's expertise to form an LLC to purchase and manage the place. The higher-ups at the CIA were far from pleased with Lang's new venture. "Too much risk of exposure," they warned. But Lang asserted he knew how the game worked, and he would take every precaution. "Let me enjoy life a little, will you?" he told them, and in the end, they reluctantly agreed, albeit with plenty of reservations.

"Yeah, it was touch and go there for a while," he replied to Eva. "Honestly, I didn't think it was gonna make it."

"You worked hard. See you in a few."

As Eva ended the call, Lang checked his rearview mirror for the fifth time. The black Lexus was still there, maintaining the same discreet distance, following him onto East Colorado Boulevard, part of historic Route 66. When he pulled his MDX up to the curb in front of Bistro Densetsu, the Lexus, its windows darkly tinted, continued forward, taking a right turn at the first intersection and disappearing from view.

Lang took a moment before stepping out. When he felt sure that the vehicle wasn't returning, he eased himself out of the Acura and tossed the key fob to the valet before heading into his restaurant.

Nestled within the chic confines of Old Pasadena, Bistro Densetsu had evolved into one of the most popular dining establishments in the area, specializing in fusion cuisine that blended Asian and South American fare into a distinctive gastronomic experience. The place quickly developed loyal regulars and, before long, the patrons began referring to it as simply "The Den." Lang would have preferred to give his restaurant a Chinese name; however, Eva decreed that Japanese cuisine was in vogue and drew more high-end customers. And she was right.

Opening the glass door for Lang was Demetrio Garcia, the manager of The Den, holding a clipboard and pen.

"*Buenos dias, jefe*," he said. "I need you to sign off on this."

Lang looked at the order sheet on the clipboard and stopped. "Five grand? For ten bottles of whisky?"

Garcia shrugged. "Don't look at me, Yuna's the one who ordered them."

Lang half-heartedly scribbled his signature on the document and entered the premises. In contrast to its rustic outdoor appearance, the interior of the Bistro Densetsu featured a meticulously designed international theme, with a blend of contemporary elegance and traditional Asian decor. The carpet shone in a deep red, signifying good fortune and prosperity in the Feng Shui tradition. Ornate wooden statues decorated the corners, and the walls were adorned with artwork by Hokusai and Chinese calligraphy. Off to the side of the main dining room was a fully stocked bar, where Yuna Kim was already busy preparing aperitifs for the evening's event.

"Good afternoon, Yuna," Lang greeted.

Yuna smiled. "Hi boss. Big day today."

Dressed in a collared white shirt and black stretch trousers, Yuna's slender five-foot-six frame moved about the bar exuding the grace of a ballerina. Her shiny black hair cascaded in a ponytail, framing her small yet attractive face, accentuated by large brown eyes that always seemed to sparkle under the dim lights. Her English was slightly accented, having spent most of her life in South Korea, where she served as an intelligence officer in the Korean Army. She reminded Lang of his daughter, whom he had not seen for more than a decade.

"I just signed off on your order," Lang said. "But a bit excessive, no?"

"Yamazaki Whisky is the 'in' drink now, and trust me, we don't want to run out," Yuna said. "It's our eighth anniversary. Eight is a lucky number in Korea."

Lang sighed. "In China too, but not five grand..."

At that moment, a white Range Rover pulled up to the curb in front of the restaurant.

"I'll be right back," Lang said, making his way to the front entrance as Ruth Nguyen stepped out of the passenger side of the vehicle.

Clad in a casual pink hoodie and weathered jeans, Ruth's jet-black hair was cut close to her head, and her complexion bore the unmistakable hue of a person with half Asian, half Caucasian heritage. Because of that, she was often mistaken for Lang's daughter. In fact, the thirteen-year-old girl had seemed to adopt him as her surrogate father, frequently texting him for life advice after her parents' divorce two years prior.

"It's wonderful to see you," Dalton greeted, guiding her toward the bar. "Allow me to introduce you to Yuna, the most talented and free-spending bartender in L.A."

"Nice to meet you," Ruth greeted with a smile.

"The pleasure is mine," Yuna replied.

"Now, let's get busy," Lang declared, leading Ruth into the kitchen.

At six p.m. sharp, the first guests of The Den's "Eighth Anniversary Soiree" began assembling in the bar. In a mere twenty minutes, the venue reached its saturation point, hosting an eclectic mix of the establishment's loyal regulars and several local politicians and celebrities. Ruth helped wait on tables, while Yuna meticulously ensured libations found their way into the hands of every patron. When the festivities drew to a close, departing guests were presented with a small gift at the door—a commemorative pen—a subtle reminder of the special occasion as they headed home into the night.

Long after the last patron had departed and all the tables cleared, Lang remained ensconced in his office, staying out of public view. He meticulously reviewed the images recorded by the security cameras on his laptop, when a sharp knock on the door interrupted his concentration.

"Who's there?" Lang asked.

The door slowly opened, and Ruth stepped inside, holding a handful of crinkled ten-dollar bills.

"Is something wrong, dear?" Lang asked.

"I didn't know I could make so much in tips," she replied with a twinkle in her eyes. "You know, I've got nothing going on tomorrow."

Lang chuckled. "We're serving brunch in the morning. What do you say I pick you up around nine?"

"Kinda early, but I'll be ready."

"Interesting. You won't wake up for church, but you do wake up for cash. Turns out you're more Asian than I gave you credit for," Lang remarked playfully with a wink.

"Wow, that's not racist at all," Ruth said, a tinge of sarcasm and disbelief in her tone. "And please don't play that opera stuff on the stereo in the car. It hurts my ears."

Lang frowned. "Young lady, opera is life. I'll have Demetrio take you home now."

As she stepped away from the office, oblivious to the staff, a lone figure slipped through the side entrance. Concealed beneath his belt was a handgun. He moved with purpose, navigating the vast, dimly lit space until he settled into an unoccupied booth at the rear, his eyes surveilling the room with trained precision.

CHAPTER 2

No one saw Guo Jianlian enter the building. Clad in a sleek black suit, his elongated face marked by pockmarks and a slender goatee, he sat alone, sipping tea from a small cup that was left unused on the table. His hair was cropped tight on the sides, and although he was still in his late forties, he had the aura of someone much older.

Noticing him from across the room, a restaurant staffer approached. The name tag on her chest read "Yuna."

"I'm sorry, sir, we're closed now," she informed him.

Guo remained absorbed in his tea, unfazed by her words.

"The owner is expecting me," he said casually.

Yuna shot him an inquisitive look.

"You know the owner?" she asked with a tinge of skepticism.

"Old friends."

"Okay, I'll let him know," she said, casting a final glance toward Guo before heading for the kitchen.

Guo took a measured sip from his cup when a familiar voice suddenly sounded from behind.

"It's been a while, Jianlian."

The unexpected interruption nearly caused Guo to spit out his tea. Swinging his head around, he saw the familiar face of the MSS agent he knew as Hu Qiang, comfortably settled inside the booth behind him. Guo moved from his booth to join him.

"I see you haven't lost your talents in stealth," he said in Mandarin.

Lang responded in the same language. "There must be a good reason why you're sitting here sipping tea, and I'm not lying face down with a bullet in my head."

Guo smiled. "You look well. You haven't changed a bit."

"Please use my current name, if you don't mind. I'm sure you know it."

"Of course," acknowledged Guo. "So, tell me, Mr. *Dalton Lang*, how does one live with himself after betraying his own country and joining forces with her mortal enemy?"

"Let's skip the small talk, Jianlian. Why are you here? Or better yet, why didn't you try to kill me on sight?"

"You never were one for chit-chat," Guo responded disappointedly. "Fine, let's get straight to the point. This is what brings me here."

He slid his hands into his trouser pockets and retrieved a gold medallion roughly the size of a compact disc. Adorning one side of its surface was a meticulously engraved depiction of a tiger, with a small yellow sapphire as its eye. On the flip side was the Chinese character "蒙."

"Do you know what this is?" Guo asked.

Lang scrutinized the piece closely, then responded with a simple shrug.

Guo erupted in a hearty laugh. "Oh, I think you know exactly what this is. It's the enchanted Tiger Coin, but not the real thing, a very fine replica of one. The real one has been lost for centuries."

"How does that explain why you're here?" asked Lang, shifting impatiently in his seat. "What is the deputy minister of China's notorious Ministry of State Security doing in Old Pasadena asking me about some counterfeit coin?"

"Patience," Guo demanded. "The genuine Tiger Coin was one of three coins given by Qin Shi Huang—the first emperor of China—to his top generals after the Battle of Wen. The others were the Dragon Coin and Monkey Coin. Together, they're known as the Coins of Wei."

"They're quite large to be classified as coins," Lang noted.

"I suppose it was his version of presenting a 'key' to the city, only in this case, it was to his empire," Guo responded. "The coins, or medallions, if you will, were separated after the Qin Empire fell. They are rumored to have mystical qualities, unlocking supernatural powers to anyone who brings them together again. About fifteen years ago, Professor Linghu Ning had exact copies of these coins made. We found two of them, but the Dragon Coin has been missing since the professor met his unfortunate demise."

"I still don't see what any of this has to do with me," Lang said.

"The Dragon Coin was in the possession of Dr. Linghu Ning when he was tragically killed in America—what was that, fifteen years ago?" Guo paused, anticipating a reaction, but Lang merely averted his gaze, feigning disinterest. But Guo knew better. "You were with him when he died, were you not?"

Before Lang could answer, Yuna returned, wearing a look of concern on her face.

"Can I get you anything, boss?" she asked.

"Could you give us a few minutes in private, dear? He's an old friend, and we're just catching up," Lang replied, flawlessly transitioning to English.

"Sure. The bar is all cleaned up, and we sold out of Yamazaki."

"That's great. You called it, didn't you?" Lang said with a warm smile.

"So, I'll see you tomorrow?" Yuna asked.

"You bet. Good night."

Yuna pivoted and, as she untied her apron, exited the room.

"Attractive young woman," Guo observed.

"By the way, how *did* you find me?" Lang asked with genuine curiosity, switching back to Mandarin.

"Let's just say that the U.S. government's witness protection program isn't all that it's cracked up to be," Guo answered with a tinge of self-satisfaction.

"Apparently not."

Guo's face suddenly turned serious. "I think you know where the Dragon Coin is, and I want it."

"I don't know of any Dragon Coin. Sorry you had to come all this way for nothing."

Resting his elbows on the table, Guo spoke the next words softly yet clearly. "Do you still keep tabs on your family? You know, the one you left? Although it seems like you've managed pretty well without them."

Lang's body tensed, his voice morphing into an ominous growl. "Keep them out of this. If I find out that you've harmed them in any way, I'll gut you."

Guo clapped. "Now, that's the Hu Qiang I remember. You needn't worry about your wife and daughter. We have no interest in them...at least not yet. By the way, did you know that your little Beth is now an FBI agent?"

"I'm going to tell you for the last time, Jianlian. I don't have what you're looking for," Lang repeated wearily.

"That's unfortunate. Then how about you do a favor for me, for old time's sake? Find the fake Dragon Coin and bring it to me. And while you're at it, get me the fake Monkey Coin, too."

"You lost two coins? What has happened to the mighty MSS?"

Guo let out a sigh. "The Monkey Coin was stolen from us recently—an inside job—and while we were able to detain the culprit, the cursed thing had already been sold on the black market. The buyer was the Aikawa-Gumi."

"The Japanese yakuza?"

Guo nodded. "Sho Aikawa is an avid collector of ancient Chinese relics, and he's been after all three coins since he found out about their existence. The fool thinks they're the real deal."

"I get it now," Lang said with a bob of his head. "You want someone totally unconnected to the government to do your dirty work. The MSS can't be seen sticking their noses into gang business, especially gangs outside of China."

"That's the general idea, and it's the only reason why you're still breathing."

"But why me? Why not recruit a mercenary? There must be a long list of former operatives for hire out there, much younger and more motivated than me."

"Too risky. The chances of it getting back to us are too great," Guo replied. "And besides, you were the most lethal killer the MSS had ever produced, the legendary Phantom Assassin."

"And if I refuse?"

"Trust me, Agent Hu Qiang, you don't want to hear the answer to that question."

Lang leaned in, his eyes narrowing with suspicion. "But there's something else isn't there? I can't see the MSS getting all worked up about a bunch of counterfeit coins. What's the real reason you want these things, Jianlian?"

"All you need to worry about is getting the two coins for me," Guo said.

"And if I do as you ask?"

"For starters, we'll leave you, your family and your friends alone. Heck, I might even forget I ever found you."

Lang chuckled. "Like you'll hold up your end of the bargain. Sorry, Jianlian, not interested."

"That's really a shame. I hope you realize what the consequences will be."

"Do your worst," Lang said.

Guo scoffed at the dare. "Still, we're old friends, so I'll give you a day to think about it. I'm on a plane back to Beijing tomorrow. Call me at this number if you change your mind."

Reaching for a paper napkin, Guo hastily scribbled a slew of numbers on it, placing it on the table as he slid out of the booth. He then rose from his seat and headed for the exit.

Leaving the napkin undisturbed, Lang followed Guo as he made his way across the main dining room and out the door. Lang stopped at the doorway and watched his former colleague head to a waiting black Mercedes-Benz AMG G63.

"Next time," Lang called out as Guo stepped into the vehicle. "I would appreciate it if you kept your goons away. I don't like them loitering around my shop."

With a laugh, Guo stepped into the rear cabin of the G-Class. Then, out of the shadows, three darkly clad figures materialized and slipped into another Mercedes-Benz SUV. As the vehicles drove away, not a soul noticed a black Lexus ES sedan stopped along the street, a block away.

CHAPTER 3

In the sanctity of her second-story master bathroom, Eva Maston embarked upon the daily morning ritual of preparing for her workday. Appearing a decade younger than her actual forty-five years, she exuded an aura of professionalism and charm in both her attire and demeanor. She hardly wasted words, and her face seamlessly transitioned from alluring to formidable with the slightest provocation, making her one of the most feared public defenders in the city. Her choppy-bobbed blonde hair brushed the top of her broad shoulders, complementing the sleek lines of her form-fitting beige Prada business suit.

Bathing in the soft glow of a lighted vanity mirror, she carefully applied various cleansers and tonics to her face, followed by the application of a palette of cosmetics, enhancing her facial features with subtle strokes. When the process was complete, the mirror reflected a visage that exuded professionalism, a certain level of sexiness and plenty of self-assurance. Satisfied by what she saw, she made her way to her daughter's bedroom down the hall.

"Wake up, honey," Eva said, opening the door and standing in the doorway. "Dalton'll be here any minute."

Taking refuge under the futon blanket, Ruth murmured, "Let me sleep for a few more minutes."

The chime of the doorbell interrupted their familiar morning routine.

"Angela, can you get that?" Eva called out. She then turned back to Ruth. "You see? He's already here. Get up or he'll leave you behind."

Eva was halfway down the rounded staircase when her maid opened the front door. Fixing her earrings in place, Eva watched in curiosity as Angela staggered backwards, then fell to the wooden floor with a gruesome thud, a black hole in the middle of her forehead.

"Angela!" Eva exclaimed, her voice echoing against the walls.

In the next instant, two men, their faces concealed by Japanese Kabuki masks, entered the home. They brandished pistols fitted with suppressors, moving with practiced intent. With her mind entwined in a haze of confusion and terror, Eva sprinted frantically back up the steps toward the sanctity of her bedroom.

One intruder spotted her and promptly gave chase, the other pulled the maid's limp body further into the recesses of the house.

Having no time to fetch her phone on the nightstand, Eva returned to the master bathroom, immediately locking herself in; however, within seconds, the door handle exploded with a pop, leaving behind a ragged hole.

Eva felt a searing pain in her chest. She looked down and noticed a scarlet stain spreading on her dress. The last thing she saw was the bathroom door slowly swinging open, as the terrifying sight of two Kabuki faces approached unimpeded.

~

LEAVING the Acura MDX parked in the driveway of his San Gabriel home, Dalton Lang hailed an Uber for an early morning commute to GT Performance & Storage in Orange County. The sun had just ascended over the eastern horizon, and the congestion on the freeways remained relatively light, allowing his hired Mazda CX-5 to complete the trip in an hour. After stepping out of the vehicle, Lang, dressed in black jeans and a Henley shirt, entered the facility through the side gate, passing an array of specialty vehicles stopped along the building, including a couple of Skyline GT-Rs and an M100 Lotus Elan. He made his way to an open warehouse door, where inside the vast indoor space, the owner of the establishment—a Japanese man in his late-forties wearing a *GT Channel* T-shirt, surfer shorts and an oversize baseball cap—wiped down the windshield of a Bayside Blue 2002 Nissan Skyline GT-R, known as the R34. Also inside the warehouse was a pristine Porsche 959 and a Ferrari Daytona, their priceless presence providing the establishment with an air of high-end automotive diversity. A wall-mounted flat-screen television broadcasted the morning news.

"Good morning, Taro," Lang greeted. "How's my baby looking?"

Noticing the arrival of a valued customer, Taro removed his working gloves. "You're early Lang-san. Man, I'm gonna be sad to see her go."

"Three years in storage is more than enough. It's time I let her run a bit," Lang said, shaking Taro's hand.

Taro held out the key to the car. "Remember, be careful when the turbos come on, it can bite you in..."

"Can you turn up the volume?" Lang cut him off, his gaze fixed on the television.

Displaying surprise by the sudden request, Taro picked up the remote that rested atop a nearby workbench and pointed the device to the TV.

On its screen, an attractive Latina woman reported live: "...a fiery crash in Bel Air believed to be the result of a carjacking gone wrong. Sources say that one of the victims was a Chinese diplomat named Guo Jianlian. He and his driver were killed, their bodies badly burned."

A grainy photo of Guo flashed on the screen.

The reporter continued: "Mr. Guo Jianlian was a member of

China's security council. The Secretary of State is expected to hold a press conference..."

"That's enough. Thanks," Lang said.

Lowering the television volume, Taro remarked excitedly, "That can't be good for Sino-American relations."

"Probably not. Anyways, thanks for having the car ready on such short notice."

After shaking Taro's hand again, Lang ducked into the driver's seat of his Nissan, inserted the key into the slot and fired up the twin turbocharged inline-6 engine. It came to life with a melodic whir, and after giving it a couple of revs, he guided the car out of the shop and headed for Pasadena.

Lang had forgotten how enjoyable the R34 was to drive. The glorious aria of the engine sang of the raw power at its disposal. Once the turbochargers kicked in with its unmistakable whine, the car surged forward like a rocket, delivering forceful acceleration that didn't let up until deep into the speedometer. The car also possessed world-class handling, provided by its high-tech all-wheel-drive system.

While traveling north on I-605 through Whittier, Lang pulled out his cell phone to dial a number he hadn't thought about in years. The absence of a Bluetooth system in the right-hand-drive Nissan forced him to perform the long-lost art of operating a handheld device while manually changing gears with his off hand.

On the third ring, the familiar voice of Nigel McKeen, now the Director of the CIA, greeted him through the phone's speaker.

"Contacting me out of the blue after ten years of silence means this probably isn't a social call, is it, Dalton?" he said.

"My location was compromised, by the MSS no less," Lang replied.

McKeen's response was immediate. "Are you in danger? Do you need assistance?"

"Negative, but there've been some odd developments in the last twenty-four. For starters, it was MSS Deputy Chief Guo Jianlian who found me. He visited me at my restaurant last night. And now, I just saw that..."

"He's been killed in a carjacking incident in California," McKeen completed the sentence for him. "What a coincidence. It wasn't you, was it?"

"Negative."

"Why didn't he take you in, or shoot you on the spot?"

Taking a brief pause to decide how much he wanted to disclose, Lang answered, "He asked me to search for some counterfeit coins. Seemed important enough for him to look the other way concerning me. But now that he's gone, I should be in the clear."

"Why do you think that?" McKeen asked.

"If he had told anyone else in the MSS that he found me, they would have a sizeable team hunting me down right now, and I haven't seen a soul. And besides, whatever Jianlian was working on seemed like it was off the books, and the men he was with didn't seem like MSS agents, they dressed and moved more like mercenaries or gangsters."

"We may never know. We'll look for whoever leaked your location. Only a handful of people knew about it, so it shouldn't take long. And we'll need to relocate you again, so..."

"Let's hold off on that," Lang interjected. "There's some important business I need to tend to. I'd like to see what Jianlian was up to."

"Fine, but be careful," McKeen said. "The sooner we provide you with a fresh identity and location, the safer you and everyone around you will be. In the meantime, if anything new or suspicious comes up, contact me immediately. We'll let you know what we find on our end. McKeen out."

The phone call concluded with impeccable timing, coinciding perfectly with Lang's arrival at the curb of Eva Masten's residence, nestled in a swanky neighborhood seven blocks from Rose Bowl Stadium. As he parked his Nissan along a tree-lined sidewalk, he noticed Eva's white Range Rover still sitting in the driveway.

Must be a late start for her today, Lang guessed, making his way to the front door.

Pressing the doorbell button, he expected the maid, Angela, to immediately greet him with her customary warm smile, but to his surprise, no one came. He waited and pressed the button a second time. Still nothing. Then, noticing that the door was unlatched, he gently nudged it open.

"Hey Eva, hey Ruth, it's me," he announced.

He stepped into the home and immediately noticed Angela's lifeless form sprawled on the tiled floor; a trail of blood smeared behind her.

"Angela," he exclaimed, rushing to her side.

Noticing the solitary bullet hole in her head, Lang didn't bother to check for a pulse. Her body was still warm, indicating that whatever had transpired here had occurred within the last few minutes. Having left his firearm in the car, he rushed to the kitchen, extracting a carving knife from a wooden block knife holder. Noticing that the rear door was slightly ajar, he exited the kitchen and stepped into the living room. He ascended the staircase slowly, holding his weapon at the ready, poised to strike at any presence that might emerge.

"Eva? Ruth?" he called out again.

Still no response.

Advancing into the master bedroom, Lang gravitated toward the bathroom where he noticed that the door handle had been blasted away. When he pushed the bathroom door open, he was confronted by a scene straight out of his worst nightmare. Eva sat slumped against the sink cabinet, her once vibrant eyes now shut tight. A crimson stain had covered most of her dress. Rushing to her side, his fingers searched for the faint flicker of life beneath her skin. Relief flooded through him as he detected a feeble pulse, then noticed the swelling of her chest with shallow breaths. Without wasting another moment, he pulled out his phone and dialed 911.

"There's been a shooting," Lang said as soon as a female operator's voice sounded. "Send help right away."

After providing the operator with the address, he carefully lowered Eva's body to the cool tile floor. He then turned his attention to his surroundings, his eyes scanning every corner of the room for any shred of evidence that could shed light on what had transpired. His gaze landed on an unfamiliar object resting innocuously on the bathroom counter, an item that he'd never seen inside of the home. It was a *hanafuda*, a Japanese playing card intricately adorned with the vibrant depiction of a white sun against a dark red sky. He promptly placed it into his pocket.

"Shit, Ruth," he gasped, suddenly aware that she might still be in the house. Rushing from the master bedroom, he burst into her bedroom, his weapon ready to strike. He immediately noticed that the closet door was closed. Gently sliding it open, he found Ruth huddled in a fetal position, her body quivering as tears streamed down her cheeks.

Dropping to his knees beside her, he enveloped her in a comforting embrace. "There, there. I've got you. You're all right now."

Lang refused to believe in coincidences. That someone had attacked a close friend precisely on the day after the MSS compromised his location left no doubt in his mind that the two events were somehow linked. And then there was Guo's untimely death. The wheels of something sinister had been set in motion.

As he held Ruth tight, a familiar anger surged within his soul, an emotion he hadn't felt since the wrenching moment he had to leave his family more than a decade ago. Although he was powerless to change the past, this time there would be no running away. This time, he vowed to track down those responsible and mete out a just retribution, alone and with extreme prejudice, if necessary, just like in the old days.

CHAPTER 4

Considered among the most picturesque medical facilities in the city, Huntington Hospital boasted structures reminiscent of a luxurious hotel resort. Multiple towers stretched skyward, a grand driveway welcomed visitors, and a lavish lobby provided a welcome setting, befitting its status as one of the area's foremost care facilities. The emergency waiting room was larger than average, its space filled with guest chairs clustered in several rows beneath harsh fluorescent lights. Here, the air reeked of antiseptic, while the general atmosphere was heavy with anticipation and concern. Among a dozen guests and patients, Dalton Lang and Ruth Nguyen sat in silence, awaiting news of Eva Masten, who'd been rushed in by ambulance over an hour ago.

From the corner of his vision, Lang spotted two men clad in dark blue jackets and non-matching trousers entering the facility. As expected, they stopped immediately in front of him, each of them flashing a police badge.

The younger of the two spoke first. "Mr. Dalton Lang? We're with LAPD. My name is Detective Albert Barris, and this is my partner, Rex Fedorak. I'm so sorry to bother you at a time like this, but we need to ask you a few questions."

"Are you serious?" Ruth snapped. "We just answered a bunch of questions at the house. My mom has been shot and fighting for her life, and our maid was killed. Shouldn't you be out looking for the ones who did this?"

The other patrons of the medical facility cast uneasy glances their way as Lang placed a reassuring hand on Ruth's forearm.

"It's all right, dear. Let me take care of this. You wait here," he said. Then, turning toward the officers, he gestured toward the door. "Let's step outside."

Upon exiting the waiting room, Lang wasted no time cutting to the chase. "What do you want?"

"We're investigating a couple of incidents in downtown L.A. that may be connected," Detective Barris said, taking out a notebook and pen. "Do you have any idea who could've done this?"

Lang shook his head. "As I told your Pasadena PD colleagues earlier, I haven't the slightest idea. I went to the house to pick up Ruth at about nine, and I found the maid fatally shot. Then I called 911."

Barris scribbled in his notebook. "What is your relationship with Ms. Maston?"

"She's my lawyer."

"Just your lawyer?" asked Fedorak, whose weasel-like face was adorned with wire-rimmed spectacles and a bushy, white mustache. His head was topped with disheveled gray hair.

"Excuse me?" responded Lang, bothered by the insinuation behind the question.

"Well, which is it?" Fedorak asked. "Are you two bonking or what?"

Thoroughly offended, Lang poked his index finger into the detective's chest. "Look, you son of a..."

Barris raised a conciliatory hand in an attempt to defuse the tension.

"Rex, pay a little more respect, will ya?" he said. Then, turning back to Lang, he uttered in a softer, more diplomatic tone, "Sorry about that, sir. We'll be back in touch soon. In the meantime, if you think of anyone who might have even the slightest connection to this, please contact us."

Reaching into his back pocket, Barris pulled out a business card, presenting it to Lang. When the detectives walked away, Lang returned to the emergency room and took his seat next to Ruth.

"I want you to stay at a hotel for a few days," he said. "You should call your father."

Ruth met his gaze with a fiery stare. "Why? He doesn't care about me or mom."

"Where is he now?" asked Lang.

"Last I heard, he was living with some bimbo in Thailand, so I wouldn't know how to get in touch with him anyways."

"I'm sorry. Your mother never really mentioned him to me. I didn't know."

Their conversation was cut short by the appearance of a doctor of Indian descent. She walked with purpose, heading straight to where Ruth and Lang sat. The name badge identified her as Belvinder Mahindra.

"I'm sorry, we did all we could," she said in a heavy tone.

Ruth screamed painfully from the top of her lungs.

Lang held her tight.

"May we see her?" he asked the doctor.

Mahindra nodded. "Of course. Again, I'm so very sorry for your loss. If you can follow me."

As they followed the doctor, Lang and Ruth's footsteps sounded softly down the hallway. Mahindra guided them to a spacious room, where Eva lay peacefully on a large hospital bed.

Lang's breath caught in his throat at the sight of her lifeless form. With his hand trembling, he reached out to touch her cold skin. But before he could make contact, Ruth rushed to the side of the bed and placed her head onto Eva's body, her cries echoing off the walls of the room. Lang laid a comforting hand on her shoulder, offering silent reassurance that she was not alone in her pain. Eventually, her sobs began to subside, replaced by a deep, heavy wheezing.

"Is there anything I can do?" Lang asked.

"I want to be alone with her," Ruth replied without looking up.

"Of course. Then, I'll be right back," Lang said softly. "I called Yuna. She said she'll be outside if you need anything."

Ruth didn't respond. Her gaze remained fixed on the still form of her mother. Lang knew that her silence spoke volumes, her grief too raw for words. With a heavy heart, he turned away and exited the room.

Once he was outside, Yuna Kim approached from the direction of the guest parking lot, her eyes expressing a mix of concern and urgency.

"I left as soon as you called," she said. "Who could have done this?"

"I have no idea, but whoever it is will pay a heavy price."

"Count me in too, boss."

Lang responded with a look of gratitude, his hand gently resting on Yuna's shoulder. "That won't be necessary. I'm going to take Ruth and stay at the Hilton Doubletree in Little Tokyo. Tell no one and bring the 'Widowmaker' to me there tomorrow morning. Also, have Demetrio double our security at the restaurant."

"Of course," Yuna replied.

"I need to make a quick trip home, so stay here for Ruth until I return."

Yuna nodded. "Is she inside?"

"She's with her mother," he replied, heading to his Skyline GT-R.

Once inside his car, Lang's knuckles whitened as he clutched the steering wheel, the leather squeaking under the pressure of his grip. He did his best to hide his emotions in front of Ruth, striving to project an illusion of strength and stability on what was sure to be the darkest day of her life. But the weight of Eva's death cut deep into his own soul, and he found it impossible to restrain his anger. With a primal scream, he unleashed his frustration upon his prized car, smashing his fist into the hard leather dashboard while Mandarin expletives spurted from his mouth.

Eva's death was his fault, plain and simple. If they had never met, she would still be alive.

Lang was accustomed to dealing with death, but never before had he been forced to confront the stark reality of being responsible for the demise of someone who he held so dear. Perhaps it was because he had kept his distance from most people, always opting to work alone, but this time, he had let his guard down, become too comfortable, and the consequences were tragic.

Never again, he whispered to himself. *Never again.*

When he arrived at his San Gabriel home, he grabbed an overnight bag and garaged the Skyline GT-R, opting to travel in the more inconspicuous Acura MDX. He then hurried back to the hospital.

When he returned to the emergency room, he found Ruth where he had left her, at her mother's side, sitting frozen in her seat, tears still streaming down her cheeks.

"Are you ready to go?" Lang asked gently.

Ruth nodded. Her movements were slow and deliberate as she rose from her seat. She leaned down and pressed a kiss to her mother's forehead, a final farewell to the woman who had given her life, love and guidance.

With a slight nod of the head, Lang dismissed Yuna Kim, who had been standing by in the lobby, and guided Ruth to his vehicle. Once she was belted securely in the passenger seat, he steered the Acura westbound on the I-10 freeway in the direction of downtown Los Angeles. Ruth gazed blankly into the distance, not uttering a single word, while Lang occasionally cast glances her way, worried about her mental state. Unlike him at her age, she had never encountered such profound violence and the loss of a parent, and the experience would no doubt leave lasting scars on her psyche. Despite his desire to offer comfort and reassurance, words eluded him.

As the sun began its descent under the western horizon, the Acura MDX exited the freeway at Soto. Lang stuck to side streets while casting cautious glances into the rearview mirror. Content that he had no tail, he eased into the driveway of the Hilton Doubletree, the largest hotel in Little Tokyo.

Lang instructed Ruth to wait on the sofa in the lobby, while he walked up to the reception counter alone. Greeting him there was a young Japanese woman whose nametag read Yui, no doubt one of many aspiring actresses who worked in the area as waitresses, receptionists or hostesses.

"Welcome to the Doubletree. May I help you, sir?" she asked.

"I made a reservation a few hours ago. The name is John Lee," Lang replied, pulling out a Nevada driver's license.

False identification, don't leave home with it.

"And, I'll be paying cash," he added, knowing that this particular establishment accepted hard currency because of its many Asian clientele who preferred not use credit cards.

"Very good, Mr. Lee. I see here you requested two rooms next to each other for three nights."

Lang nodded. "Is there anything on the fourth or fifth floor that faces the southeast? Feng Shui, you know. We don't feel safe unless we follow the karma."

Yui chuckled at the remark. "Of course, let me see what we have."

After pounding her keyboard for a full minute, she presented Dalton with two card keys. "Your room number is written here, and Wi-Fi is complimentary. Enjoy your stay."

With card keys in hand, he beckoned Ruth over, and together they made their way to the guest elevators. Their rooms were on the fifth floor, and upon entering hers, Ruth made a beeline for the bed, burying her face in the pillow.

"I wish I could take back all the bad things I said to mom," she cried.

Performing a quick visual sweep of the space, Lang responded in a comforting tone, "She knew you didn't mean them. Now, try to get some sleep."

"Can you stay with me for a bit?" Ruth asked.

"Of course." Lang replied, dimming the light. He then settled into an armchair and embarked on a still form of Qigong meditation.

When he meditated, fragments of a past that he could barely recall danced through his mind. His origin remained shrouded in fog, but he knew he was born in Hong Kong, to a Chinese father and Japanese mother, who met an untimely end in a "traffic accident" when he was still a toddler. He couldn't recall the faces of his parents, nor was he sure of their real names—their identities were completely expunged by the Chinese government as if they had never existed—but if the CIA were to be believed, his true surname was Mori or Sen, depending on the Japanese or Chinese pronunciation. His father was purportedly an agent for British Intelligence, and his mother a nurse. But beyond that, details were scarce, for the CIA told him the British government refused to release any names of operatives working in Hong Kong, both past and present.

Following their deaths, the toddler without a name was dispatched to Beijing to reside in an orphanage where the directors there methodically erased all traces of his past, leaving only one shameful detail intact: his half-Japanese ethnicity. With no one willing to adopt a baby with "contaminated" blood, he was soon transferred to a military school, where he bore the brunt of relentless bullying. They called him *Hunxue'er*—half-breed—and every day was a struggle for survival. But from a tender age, he exhibited a prodigious talent for both problem solving and marksmanship, which led him to become the youngest recruit in the history of the Ministry of State Security. During his training at the People's Republic Security Academy—the MSS equivalent of the CIA's "Farm"—he scored the highest points ever for a trainee, surpassing many of the instructors' abilities.

After his sixteenth birthday, the MSS enrolled him into the prestigious Peking University, and by the age of twenty, he earned a doctorate in radar engineering. It was at the university where he developed a keen interest in operatic music after listening to a CD of Wolfgang Amadeus Mozart's *The Magic Flute,* given to him by a visiting English teacher. Upon graduation, the MSS began sending him on assignments to discreetly eliminate enemies of the state. He was extremely efficient at his job—no one ever discovered his identity —and the legend of the Phantom Assassin was born.

The muffled rumble of Ruth's snoring brought Lang back to the present. Checking his Hublot watch, he quietly eased himself out of the armchair and made his way to the window. Peering through a slit in the curtains, he looked down onto Second Street, where he noticed a black Lexus ES driving slowly down the road. It then made a turn into the parking lot with a sign that read "Club One." He was sure it was the same black Lexus that he had seen before, and it was time to find out who its owner was.

CHAPTER 5

Being one of the most popular Japanese hostess clubs in Los Angeles, Club One frequently buzzed with patrons, especially during the late-night hours. Inside the lavishly furnished and well-lit establishment, a multitude of Japanese women—most of them in their twenties—sat beside older men, sipping expensive drinks, and providing them with playful banter.

Because most of the club's customers were Asian businessmen, the host of Club One, dressed in a neat tuxedo, expressed surprise when he noticed a tall, husky African-American gentleman in his mid-sixties enter through the front door. Clad in a blue polo shirt under a loose-fitting black leather jacket, Melvin Patterson approached the reception desk with a determined aura.

"I'm here to see Joe," he demanded in an unwavering tone.

"Ah," the host said. "I was told to expect you."

"You were?" asked Patterson.

"I'm Taku. Please, come this way."

Leading Patterson past a dozen tables, each of them occupied, Taku gestured for Patterson to take a seat at a discreet booth nestled at the back of the club. He clapped twice, summoning a pair of alluring young women dressed in enticing cocktail dresses. They gracefully took their places on each side of Patterson.

"This is Shizuka and Yumi, our two most popular girls," Taku announced.

"I didn't ask for any girls. I asked to see Joe, and..."

Taku swiftly interjected. "I'm so sorry, but the manager is tied up with other business this evening. He asked if you could visit him tomorrow at his office."

Patterson leaned forward in his seat. "Now, listen to me, I..."

Taku cut him off again. "He told us to make sure that you are taken care of tonight. Drinks are on the house."

Glancing at the VIP table across the way, Patterson spotted Joe Nakajima—a gangly forty-something man, who sported tattoos on his arms and a small scar on his cheek. He was sharing drinks with several other rough-looking Asian men. When their eyes met, Nakajima offered a subtle nod in Patterson's direction.

After Taku bowed deeply and took his leave, Patterson found himself alone in the company of the two young women.

"What's your name?" inquired Yumi, while Shizuka expertly stirred a drink using the house shochu and water.

"How old are you girls?" Patterson asked.

Yumi answered with a smile, "I'm twenty-one, and she's twenty-six."

The two women slid closer to Patterson, pressing themselves against his body.

"Will you buy us champagne?" Yumi asked with a hint of subdued innocence. "We do almost anything for champagne."

Yumi gently rubbed Patterson's thigh, flashing him a smile and a wink.

"Apparently, the drinks are on the house, so knock yourselves out," Patterson replied, gently removing Yumi's hand from his leg and placing it back on her lap.

Raising her arm high in the air, Shizuka called Taku over. When he approached, she said, "Dom Perignon Pink, *onegaishimasu.*

Taku nodded and did a one-eighty back to the bar.

"The boss told us to take special care of you," Yumi said in a sweet voice, placing her hand back on Patterson's thigh.

"Yeah, what else did he tell you?" Patterson asked, once again removing it.

"Why do you ask to see the boss tonight?" asked Shizuka.

Patterson let out an amused chuckle. "Oh, I get it. You two are his little spies, squeezing information from horny old men. Well, just tell him I'll visit tomorrow morning, and I won't take no for an answer. Thank you for the company."

Fully extending his stocky six-foot frame, Patterson stood and made his way to the exit, leaving the two young women to savor their coveted bottle of champagne alone. Once outside, he inhaled the refreshing chill of the L.A. night, retrieving a box of Marlboro Reds from his jacket. He tapped a cigarette loose, but before lighting it, he discarded it to the ground, smashing it with his boot.

"I gotta quit," he said to himself.

Unlocking his black Lexus ES, he swung the door wide and plopped himself onto the driver's seat. As he reached for the Engine Start button, he felt something cold and hard press against the back of his skull.

"Put your hands where I can see them unless you want a hole in your head," a voice hissed from the darkness behind.

Patterson deliberately placed his hands on top of the steering wheel. "Look man, I just spent all my money in there, so I'm flat out of cash."

"What are you doing following me around?" the voice asked.

Turning his head ever so slightly, Patterson caught a glimpse of Dalton Lang. "Hey brother, I'm not following you. If I'm not mistaken, you're the one holding me up."

"Eyes forward," Lang directed. "You're with the Japanese yakuza. I know they own this joint."

"Do I look like I work for the Japanese yakuza?"

Lang took a moment before answering.

"They may be outsourcing," he said.

"Well, they ain't outsourcing from Africa, I can tell you that much."

"Then, who the hell are you?"

Patterson remained silent, but the cold steel barrel pressed harder into his head.

"Talk," Lang demanded.

"Okay, okay. I'm FBI."

"Bullshit."

"It's true," said Patterson. "I'm a special agent. Let me show you my badge."

"Move slowly, or I'll blow a..."

"Yeah, yeah," Patterson interjected, slowly sliding his hand into his jacket pocket and pulling out a small leather wallet, which he held over his shoulder.

Swiping it from his grasp, Lang scrutinized the credential under the illumination of a nearby streetlamp that penetrated the cabin through the rear window.

"What are you doing driving around in a Lexus?" he asked. "I thought you Fed types drove domestics."

"It's called blending in, man."

Lang tossed the wallet onto the front passenger seat of the car. "I hate to break this to you, but it's not the car that needs blending in. So, what were you doing in front of my restaurant yesterday?"

"Following Jianlian Guo."

"Jianlian? Why?" asked Lang.

Patterson glanced into the rearview mirror. "I'm sure you know that he's a high-ranking member of the MSS, but he's also been involved in some really bad shit recently, like dealing fentanyl, ordering hits all over Asia and smuggling underage girls to work at suspect massage joints."

"Not Jianlian. You're mistaken," Lang said.

"He's been in cahoots with the Blue Dragons for a few years now. It seems that his bosses at the MSS recently got wind of his, um, extra-curricular activities and were about to bring him in."

"Jianlian on the take from the Blue Dragons? Impossible."

"Believe what you want. Listen man, I know who you are, too. You're the Phantom Assassin, right?"

Lang's eyes open wide.

"I knew it," Patterson exclaimed. "I remember you back when I was assigned to the CIA Hong Kong Station. Although we only had fuzzy photos of you, when I saw you the other day, I knew it was you."

Shifting his position away from the mirror's reflection, Lang said, "I have no idea what you're talking about. And, you still haven't told me what you're doing *here*. You don't seem like the Japanese hostess club kind of guy."

"There's been bad blood between the Blue Dragons and the yakuza recently, and Guo seemed to be right in the middle of it. And the fact that he's been killed in a car accident seemed a bit too convenient, you know what I mean?"

"No, I don't. The Blue Dragons and the Aikawa-Gumi have had a truce for the past fifty years."

"Well, that truce has been seriously severed," said Patterson.

Lang placed the *hanafuda* card he found at Eva's house on the center console.

"Does this have any meaning to you?" he asked.

Picking it up, Patterson replied, "Yeah. This is the calling card for the Aikawa gang. In Japan, they leave it behind after a hit to let everyone know it was them. Don't tell me you found this..."

"I'd appreciate it if you keep out of my business from here on, Agent Patterson," Lang said.

"I'd appreciate it if you just let law enforcement handle this. And, holding up a federal officer's a felony. Hell, maybe I'll take you in myself."

Receiving no response, Patterson swung his head around, only to find the rear cabin of his car empty, save for a large, steel ballpoint pen on the seat, one whose thickness was similar to the barrel of a pistol.

CHAPTER 6

Dalton Lang drew open the curtains of his hotel room, allowing the soft glow of the early morning Southern California light to filter in. A thick formation of clouds shrouded most of the Los Angeles sky, a marine layer that lingered all the way to the Pacific Ocean. The overcast conditions would provide ample cover, Lang mused, sensing a tinge of nervous anticipation for the task that lay ahead. After a quick shower, he slipped into a black sweater, matching charcoal Levi jeans, and a pair of lace-up combat boots. He inspected himself in the full-length mirror when a knock sounded on his door.

"It's me, boss," Yuna Kim said from the other side.

Lang undid the lock and allowed Yuna to enter.

Dressed in a knit beige halter top and Lululemon joggers, a small fanny pack hanging from her slim waist, Yuna stepped inside with a black travel golf bag slung over her shoulder.

"Did anyone see you coming to the room?" Lang asked, taking the golf bag from her.

"Negative," Yuna replied. "Even the reception counter was empty. So, do you want to tell me what you're up to?"

"Just going to have a quick look around. That's all."

A second rap on the door prompted Yuna to go into immediate black ops mode. Instinctively, her right hand darted behind her back, her fingers closing around the cold handle of a DPx Hest fixed-blade combat knife concealed in her fanny pack. With seamless fluidity, she moved to the side of the doorway before gripping the doorknob with her other hand.

"Who is it?" Lang asked.

"It's me. I woke up way early. Are you decent?"

It was Ruth.

Yuna eased the tension in her body, returning the knife to her fanny pack and swinging the door open.

"Good morning," she greeted.

Surprised by her presence, Ruth hesitated. "What are you doing here, Yuna?"

"Just dropping a package off for the boss."

Ruth offered a casual wave to Lang. "Hi Dalt."

"How are you doing, dear?" he asked concernedly.

"I still can't believe she's gone," Ruth replied as tears began welling in her eyes.

"I know, dear. It will take time. Just stay indoors today. Yuna is here to get you anything you need."

"I didn't know you played golf," she remarked after noticing the hefty bag on Lang's shoulder.

"Um, yeah," Lang responded awkwardly. "I thought I'd go to the driving range and clear my head. You know, 'spank whitey,' as the Australians say."

"Wow, that's not racist at all," Ruth responded. "But golf at a time like this? You said yourself that it's dangerous out there."

"I did, didn't I? Yeah, well..." Lang hesitated.

Ruth placed her hands on her hips. "You need to stay here with me."

Then, without warning, she reached out and seized the golf bag, pulling it forcibly toward herself.

Realizing too late that he should have let the shoulder strap go,

Lang clung tight, causing the zipper at the top of the bag to become undone. This only encouraged Ruth to keep tugging, which she did until the handle of a Sako TRG M10 sniper rifle popped out.

Ruth gasped, "Oh my God. What's this? What are you doing?"

With haste, Lang reclaimed the bag and pushed the rifle back inside. As he zipped it shut, he noticed Yuna wearing a look of defeat, her palm placed on her forehead. Turning to Ruth, he said in a calm voice, "There are some bad people out there. I'm just trying to find out who they are. That's all dear."

"Are you crazy?" Ruth shot back. "You're a restaurant owner. You're not a Chinese John Wick. Yuna, say something."

Yuna, with her hand still on her forehead, remained silent.

"Listen, Ruth. Yuna will stay with you until I return. Do as she says," Lang commanded.

"But..." Ruth uttered, but Lang cut her off.

"I'll be back before you know it. Please, just be a good girl and stay put."

Before she could respond, he threw the golf bag over his shoulder, donned a black Nike golf cap and walked out the door.

⌇

RUTH TOOK pride in always endeavoring to do what was right. At school, she diligently studied to maintain high grades while making a concerted effort to avoid associating with the wrong crowd, especially the riffraff who dealt with drugs. Her mother instilled in her an inherent sense of justice and a strong moral compass, emphasizing the importance of never cutting corners and adhering to the rules. Therefore, she was unwilling to ignore Dalton's apparent venture into vigilantism. She cared for him greatly, so she was determined to stop him before he did something that would land him in jail, or worse, get himself killed.

She hurried to follow him out the door, but her path was promptly blocked by Yuna.

"I wouldn't worry about Mr. Lang. He's capable of taking care of himself," she said coolly.

Attempting to push Yuna out of the way, Ruth exclaimed, "He's lost his mind. We need to go to the police. I've already lost my mom. I don't want to lose Dalt too."

But Yuna stood resolute, not allowing her to pass. "I can't let you leave. It's the boss' orders."

At that moment, Ruth realized that the head bartender of Bistro Densetsu wasn't the charming creature that everyone made her out to be. She sensed something dark and foreboding lurking beneath the surface of the Korean woman, exuding an aura that she was one not to be messed with. It was also the first time Ruth noticed a tattoo of a heart pierced by a sword on the inside of her forearm.

Ruth decided to take a different tact. Taking a step back, she said, "How long will he be, you think?"

"Probably an hour or two. So, what do you want to watch?" Yuna asked playfully, switching modes instantly. She turned on the television with the remote.

"Anything...and nothing," Ruth retorted, settling into the armchair with a defiant pout.

With the television showing CNN, the two sat in awkward silence for several long minutes when the stillness was broken by the sound of Ruth's growling stomach.

"I'm not feeling so good. I haven't eaten since the day before yesterday," she said.

Yuna reached for the hotel phone. "I'll order room service for you."

"They'll take too long. I'm hyperglycemic, so if I don't eat now, I'll get ill."

"They have hamburgers on the menu," Yuna pointed out.

Just then, Ruth's body began to jerk and shake in a rhythmic manner. Her eyes rolled back into her head, making only the whites visible. After a few seconds, her eyes returned to their natural state and her shaking subsided.

"I'm not feeling so good..." Ruth murmured.

"Oh, my goodness," Yuna said, her expression showing concern. "There's a store downstairs with premade sandwiches. I'll get you a ham and cheese croissant."

"Hurry," Ruth pleaded.

Casting a glance Ruth's way, Yuna snatched her fanny pack and exited the room. After the door had closed, Ruth waited a minute before rising from the bed. When she sensed the coast was clear, she opened the door and discreetly made her exit.

CHAPTER 7

Detective Albert Barris didn't enjoy taking orders from anyone—not from his parents, his boss and especially not from his wife—but he decided about a year ago that if he had to play by someone else's rules, he was going to get paid for it.

With the "protection racket" being a concept as old as time—where the protector promises security from outside threats in return for financial payment—he chose to broaden his financial avenues through this dependable yet ethically ambiguous business model. He started by exploiting the owners of suspect massage parlors on the fringes of legality. After discovering that their rendered services extended beyond a simple back rub, he offered to not only look the other way, but convince others at the station to leave them alone...all for a nominal fee to be collected at regular intervals, of course.

A few months prior, he received a cryptic message from a "Mister Fuji," beckoning him to a discreet tea house in Chinatown. Lured by the promise of "great financial compensation in return for specialized services," he attended the meeting solo, but instead of a person named Fuji, he was greeted by a lieutenant who called himself "Sato." Curiously, Sato wasn't Japanese, but a Caucasian in his mid-fifties with wavy red and gray hair, a full beard and deep wrinkles marking a sullen face. But to Barris, it mattered little who sat on the other side of the table, as long as the money was good, and it found its way into his wallet on schedule. Half an hour later, he strolled out of the teahouse a couple of grand richer and as the newest member on Fuji Enterprises' unofficial payroll.

As was his custom on "collection day," Barris ditched his partner, citing personal reasons. Sitting behind the wheel of his Chevy Blazer EV, he cruised down Second Street, when his gaze caught a teenage girl strolling alone on the sidewalk—she looked familiar.

Barris hurriedly extracted a photograph of Ruth Nguyen from his breast pocket and held it up for comparison. A perfect match. Immediately, he pulled his Blazer to a stop along the sidewalk and retrieved his cell phone. Dialing a number committed to memory, Sato answered on the third ring.

"This better be an emergency," Sato said.

"You're not gonna believe this, but Eva Maston's daughter is all by her lonesome in Little Tokyo. No sign of Papa Bear."

"You're sure it's her?" asked Sato.

"One hundred percent."

"What's she doing?"

Barris observed Ruth's movements. She initially headed in one direction, only to abruptly turn around and walk the opposite way.

"She looks lost. What do you want me to do?" asked Barris.

"Nothing. Just provide me with her location."

"Coming your way now," Barris replied, sending a dropped pin in a text message.

"Oh, and the boss wants to speak with you," Sato said. "I'm sending you an address. Be there in one hour."

The line went dead.

∾

STUDYING the tourist map that she received from the hotel receptionist, Ruth thought she was headed in the direction of the nearest police station, when instead she found herself in the middle of a large courtyard. The sign on the nearest building read "Aratani Theater."

Realizing that she had made a wrong turn, she retraced her steps back to Second Street, when she noticed two men wearing Japanese Kabuki masks rapidly approaching. They were headed straight for her.

As she turned around and sprinted back to the courtyard, the masked men swiftly closed in. One of them grabbed her around the waist, while the other muffled her screams for help by covering her mouth with his hand. They moved in total synch, fast and coordinated, hoisting Ruth off the ground and carrying her in the direction of a windowless gray van stopped along San Pedro Street.

Ruth resisted, but the men were too strong, their relentless grip rendering her attempts to break free impossible. Then, oddly, she felt her legs released, followed by a scream of pain from one of the men. When she turned to look, she saw that one of her captors had a dagger embedded in the back of his shoulder, a large splotch of blood staining his shirt.

A few feet away stood a woman, a bandana covering the bottom of her face, and a combat knife clutched tightly in her grasp.

"Yuna?" Ruth mumbled under her captor's hand.

∼

UPON RETURNING to Dalton Lang's hotel room with a cold ham sandwich, Yuna Kim found it empty, eliciting a sharp Korean curse word from her lips. She was not one to be easily fooled, but instead of wallowing in the humiliation of being outsmarted by a 13-year-old girl, she couldn't help but admire Ruth's sheer audacity and acting skills. The girl had nerve—and talent.

She will make a good agent someday, Yuna thought.

Not bothering to search the premises, Yuna descended the stairs to the lobby and headed outside. She was familiar with the Little Tokyo area, frequenting its shops on weekends to savor Japanese cuisine. She sprinted toward Japan Village, a lively collection of eateries and stores offering delicacies and trinkets from the Land of the Rising Sun.

Quickly making her way along Second Street, Yuna spotted a commotion near the Aratani Theater. Her heart raced as she saw Ruth being dragged away by two men in Kabuki masks. There was no time to think—instinct and adrenaline kicked in—her hand immediately going for the knife in her fanny pack. Ruth and her abductors were still too far to engage directly, so to slow them down, she sent her blade flying. The steel found its mark, embedding itself in the shoulder of one of the hoodlums. The man cried out in pain, staggering back and releasing his grip on Ruth.

"Let go of her right now, assholes," Yuna demanded.

She closed in on the masked men, a second knife already in her hand.

Undeterred by his fresh wound, the injured gangster pulled the knife free from his shoulder and pointed it at Yuna.

"I'll cut you up," he sneered.

Yuna, who didn't so much as flinch, responded, "I could have put that in your neck, but I spared you. Move out of the way, or you won't be so lucky next time."

The masked man responded by lunging forward, the knife going for Yuna's midsection. Sidestepping the attack, Yuna countered with a skillful swing of her six-inch blade, narrowly missing his head by inches. Her movements then seamlessly transitioned into a reverse roundhouse kick, connecting solidly with the side of the man's head. The force of the impact sent the Kabuki mask flying, revealing an Asian face of a thirty-something male, who was now missing a couple of teeth. He stumbled sideways, giving Yuna more than enough time to score a flying front kick to his chin, knocking him unconscious as he fell to the ground.

She then set her sights on the second captor who continued to drag Ruth across the courtyard. But before she could launch an attack, the side door of the gray van slid open, and from inside the cabin, a man wielding a semi-automatic rifle appeared. He aimed his weapon at Yuna and unleashed several quick rounds. The sharp sound of the gunshots echoed through the square, sending the few onlookers nearby scrambling for cover. Yuna hastily sought refuge behind a large tree as another barrage of bullets followed in her wake.

Peering from her hiding spot, she watched helplessly as the thugs loaded Ruth into the van and slid the door shut. Yuna rushed after them, but the vehicle was long gone, vanishing into a sea of traffic down the road.

Amid the fading sound of its screeching tires, the growing wail of police sirens filled the air.

"*Ssibal*," Yuna cursed, a wave of dejection washing over her.

Mired in defeat, she retraced her steps back toward the hotel.

CHAPTER 8

A Tesla Model 3, adorned with an Uber decal on the windshield, maneuvered into an empty alleyway near the intersection of Second and Vignes. The vehicle crept to a stop beside a derelict office building, its facade a ghostly relic of forgotten companies.

"Is this really the place?" the Uber driver named Nate asked.

"Yep, right here is fine," Lang replied, stepping out of the Tesla's rear cabin and retrieving his black golf bag stowed in the vehicle's trunk. Staying in place until the Tesla was out of sight, he climbed a short concrete stairway that led to the building's rear entrance. Carefully placing the golf bag on the ground, he produced a set of lock picks from his pocket and went to work. In thirty seconds, the door was unlocked. Avoiding the watchful gaze of the video cameras mounted to the walls, he pulled the brim of his Nike cap down and headed up the stairwell with the golf bag on his shoulder.

Slightly out of breath, he stepped onto the rooftop, where he took up a position on the north side of the building that afforded him an unobstructed view of a one-story structure approximately five hundred meters away. The sign in front read, "Mitsui Import Services." He grasped the brim of his Nike hat and rotated it, wearing it backwards. He then unzipped the golf bag and extracted the Widowmaker, his Sako TRG M10 sniper rifle. He meticulously cleaned the scope with a microfiber towelette before fixing a suppressor to the barrel's end. He also pulled a specially crafted carbon-fiber bipod from his bag and attached it to the rifle, aligning the sights toward the Mitsui building. Nearly everyone in the underground community knew that Mitsui Imports served as a front for the Aikawa gang's L.A. operation.

Surveying the building's surroundings, Lang noted a Bentley GT and a late-model Nissan GT-R in the parking lot. Someone was undoubtedly home. Then, from the corner of his vision, he noticed a black Lexus ES sedan racing down Temple Street, recklessly tearing into the parking lot of the establishment.

Well, what do we have here?

The Lexus screeched to a halt, and the driver-side door swung open. Melvin Patterson stepped out of the car and headed toward the building's front entrance. His path was promptly blocked by a duo of rough-looking Japanese men—yakuza.

Unable to make out what was being said, Lang could see through his scope that Patterson was agitated—the FBI agent threw his hands in the air and angrily shouted at the two gangsters. In response, one of them drew a pistol from his pants pocket, but rather than recoiling in fear, Patterson appeared to provoke them further, daring them to take the shot.

What is that idiot doing?

A third yakuza appeared on the scene—a lanky Japanese man sporting a buzzcut and wearing a white tank top with beige cargo shorts that revealed a canvas of tattoos on his arms and legs. It was Joe Nakajima—the head of the L.A. chapter of the Aikawa-Gumi—and in his hand, he gripped a *katana,* a traditional Japanese sword used by the samurai.

Gently, with a soft click, Lang disengaged the safety on the rifle.

~

IF THERE WAS one thing Melvin Patterson detested, it was someone who didn't keep their end of a bargain. He regarded the act of breaking a promise as the darkest betrayal, and in his mind, the Aikawa gang had just shattered his trust, and he wasn't about to let them get away with it.

"We had a deal, and you broke it," he barked at Nakajima. "These murders—Guo and the lawyer—they have your fingerprints all over them."

Unwavering, Nakajima shot back, "You malicious dog, I haven't the slightest idea what you're talking about."

Patterson reached into his pants pocket and extracted a *hanafuda* card—the one Lang had given him the previous night. He flung it into the yakuza's face.

With a quick movement of Nakajima's head, the low-level yakuzas seized Patterson from either side, securing his arms and forcing him to his knees. They then extended his left arm forward, holding it out like a roll cake ready to be sliced. Nakajima unsheathed his *katana*, its silver blade capturing the glint of the morning sunlight.

"You dare try to pin the murder of Guo Jianlian and some lawyer I have never heard of on the Aikawa-Gumi? It's you who have betrayed us, FBI dog," Nakajima said, raising the sword over his head.

Too paralyzed to even scream, Melvin averted his gaze, bracing for the inevitable, yet the anticipated strike never came. Instead, the reverberating *cling* of metal hitting metal shattered the morning stillness, sending Nakajima's sword flying from his grasp. The gangster screamed in agony, clutching his hand and doubling over in pain. The first projectile was quickly followed byanother, this one producing the thud of metal penetrating flesh. The man to Patterson's right went down, a bullet entering and exiting his thigh.

The remaining henchman immediately released Melvin and made a dash for the building. Nursing his injured hand, Nakajima followed him in, leaving his colleague with the wounded leg behind. As Patterson slowly rose to his feet, two black Chevrolet Impalas sped onto the premises, skidding to a stop at the entrance to the parking lot. Three men and one woman—all clad in dark blue wind-breakers bearing the bold inscription "FBI" in yellow—jumped out, their guns drawn.

"We got it from here, Melvin," said the female agent, a striking blonde who Patterson felt could've pursued a modeling career.

"About time, Chelsea," Patterson retorted. "And that was good shooting. Was it one of our boys or someone from LAPD?"

Chelsea leveled a curious gaze his way. "Hold on a minute, you didn't shoot them?"

Patterson paused, then responded, "Of course it was me. Who else could it be?"

Visibly relieved, Chelsea replied. "You had me going there for a second."

Their conversation was halted by an arriving ambulance, where two EMTs promptly tended to the injured gangster. Meanwhile, the remaining three federal agents burst into the Mitsui Imports build-ing, their firearms leading the way. Within a matter of minutes, they reemerged, accompanied by Nakajima and the other yakuza, both in cuffs.

As he was being pulled toward the waiting Impalas, Nakajima offered a stark warning to Patterson: "No one crosses the Aikawa-Gumi. You cannot hide. Our boss will find you."

"I'll save him the trouble," Patterson shot back. "I'll go to him myself, and I'll make sure to give him your regards."

After the Impalas and the ambulance drove away, Patterson remained, standing alone in the middle of the parking lot. His gaze swept across the surrounding area, carefully scanning each building, searching for the elusive mystery shooter who had intervened on his behalf.

CHAPTER 9

With lightning quick precision, Dalton Lang disengaged the bipod attached to his rifle, stuffing the items neatly back into the golf bag. Securing it with a zip, he bent down to recover the empty, dislodged cartridges that fell on the rooftop, when his cell phone vibrated in his pants pocket. Retrieving it, he saw that the caller was Ruth Nguyen.

"Hi Ruth. How are you doing?" Lang asked.

An electronically disguised voice answered in her stead. "We have your girlfriend's daughter. If you want to see her alive, bring us the Coins of Wei."

"What? Who is this?" asked Lang.

"Your worst nightmare if you don't do as you're told."

"Are you the ones who killed Eva?" Lang growled.

"An unfortunate accident. If you don't want the same thing to happen to the girl, bring us the coins."

"I don't know what you're talking about."

"Then goodbye," the voice said. "We'll send her body parts to you in a cooler."

"Wait," Lang pleaded, his mind racing on how they could have taken Ruth. "How do I know you really have her?"

The phone stirred with a subtle vibration, signaling the arrival of a text message. Opening it, he saw an image of Ruth gagged and tied.

Son of a bitch.

"Satisfied?" the voice asked.

"You know they're counterfeits, right? The coins."

"Let us worry about that. You just bring them to us."

"The only coin I know of is the one Guo Jianlian showed me, the Tiger Coin," Lang fabricated.

"There are two more. The Dragon Coin and the Monkey Coin. Bring us those, and we'll exchange them for the girl. You'll be instructed on how to contact us. You have one week."

"Wait, you want the Monkey Coin too?" asked Lang.

"Yes."

That's peculiar, thought Lang. If the culprits were the Aikawas, which he had thought all along, they wouldn't be asking for the Monkey Coin because they supposedly already had it.

So, who was this, if not the yakuza? Who else knew about the coins?

Then, another revelation became apparent, and Lang expressed it out loud. "You didn't ask for the Tiger Coin, did you? This means you must already have it. So, it was you who killed Guo Jianlian. Who are you?"

"The Dragon Coin and the Monkey Coin. One week," the voice responded.

The line went dead.

Without a moment to spare, Lang hurriedly redialed Ruth's number, hoping to establish her location. But instead of a ring, he was greeted by a message saying that the number was no longer in service, a telling sign that the SIM card had been removed or destroyed.

The abductors' objective became unmistakably clear: They were after the coins. But their identity now totally eluded Lang. He mentally envisioned a diagram of the origins and the current locations of the Coins of Wei.

Whereabouts of the Coins of Wei

<u>Tiger Coin</u>
Guo Jianlian → Stolen by ? → Possession of ?

<u>Monkey Coin</u>
Guo Jianlian → Rogue MSS agent → Sho Aikawa

<u>Dragon Coin</u>
Linghu Ning → Charles Hu → Dalton Lang

With each passing moment, the mystery intensified, and the safety of Ruth hung in the balance. One thing he was sure of was that the orchestrator of this deadly game of death and deceit was exceptionally cunning and treacherous, more so than he could have imagined.

He wondered now if he could take on this adversary alone.

CHAPTER 10

For as long as Detective Albert Barris could remember, the brick two-story building on Fifth Street was just another dilapidated apartment complex in the Arts District of downtown Los Angeles. On numerous occasions, he had driven past the structure, noting its walls adorned with a myriad of graffiti, yet not once did he give the place a second thought. Never could he have suspected that within its worn walls lurked the hideout of an illegal money laundering operation.

Pulling his unmarked Chevy Blazer EV to a halt before the main entrance, he exited the vehicle and gave the green, steel door three solid knocks. His gaze tilted upward, spotting three security cameras fixed to the wall; it was the first time he had noticed them. When the door swung open, he saw the familiar face of Sato—the man who had met him at the teahouse a month prior. He stood at an average height, around five feet and ten inches, with a plump build that hinted at a fondness for greasy foods. His hair was red, with streaks of gray, while a matching bushy beard covered the bottom part of his face. Yet, it wasn't his physical stature that caught Barris' attention, but rather, the pronounced limp that accompanied his every step.

"Come in, hurry," Sato gestured.

Upon entering, Barris was greeted by a sight that defied expectations. The interior of the building exuded the ambience of a luxurious English manor, a stark departure from the edifice's weathered exterior. A mini chandelier hung from a molded ceiling, while rich, mahogany wood adorned the walls, complemented by ornate paneling that added a touch of old-world charm.

"I like what you've done to the place," Barris commented lightheartedly.

After shutting the front door with a resounding slam, Sato gestured for Barris to follow him further into the structure. They passed through a narrow corridor, eventually reaching a staircase that branched both upwards and downwards.

"So, what's your story?" asked Barris. "Why the limp?"

In no mood for engaging in conversation, Sato ordered, "Go downstairs."

Sensing a wave of insecurity of being guided into an underground chamber without so much as an explanation, Barris stopped at the staircase.

"What's going on?" he asked. "I'm not going any further unless I get an explanation."

"As I mentioned to you on the phone, Mr. Fuji would like a word with you," Sato replied. "After you."

Appearing as though he had no other option, Barris descended the flight of stairs, which ended at another steel door. A numeric pad was mounted on the wall next to it. Sato punched in a five-digit code that produced a mechanical click from the door lever. He then pushed the door open, inviting Barris to step through.

"No, this time, you first," Barris insisted, gently placing his hand over his holstered weapon.

With a slight chuckle, Sato limped into the basement; Barris followed.

They stepped into a vast and cold concrete chamber. There was a large steel safe against the far wall and a dozen or so wooden smuggling containers stacked in the opposite corner. Two Asian gangsters loomed over a Caucasian man confined to a folding chair at the far end of the room. His hands were tightly bound behind his back, his mouth gagged with a thick cloth rag, and his ankles secured to the chair legs with zip ties. Barris recoiled as he took notice of the captive's face; it belonged to his partner, Rex Fedorak.

"What the hell is going on?" Barris asked.

Sato retrieved his phone and activated the speaker mode, holding it up in Barris' direction. An unfamiliar voice addressed him from the device. "Hello, detective, I'm Fuji. It's nice to meet you."

"If you can call this *meeting*," Barris responded into the phone.

"We assume you know who the man in the chair is," Fuji said.

"He's my partner. Mind explaining to me why he's tied up?" Barris inquired.

"Detective Fedorak forced himself onto one of our girls and became extremely rough with her—one of our best girls, I might add. She's currently being treated at the hospital," Fuji explained.

Barris turned to Fedorak. "What the hell did you do, Rex?"

One thug removed Fedorak's gag, allowing him to speak.

"I went to that massage parlor in Boyle Heights, but it wasn't my fault, Al. The girl said she liked it rough, so I slapped her around a bit, that's all," Fedorak explained.

Another gangster walked up to Barris and displayed a phone to him, swiping through a series of photos depicting a young Asian woman, her face bruised and battered, looking like a poster child for domestic abuse.

"Oh Rex, you dumbass."

"You gotta help me, Al," Fedorak cried.

Fuji's voice resonated from the phone again. "Her injuries are quite serious, but she'll live. However, she'll be hospitalized for several weeks. We also discovered that this girl wasn't the first; Detective Fedorak seems to have a habit of roughing up young, defenseless women. He also uses his position with the LAPD to blackmail them for hundreds of dollars, which means he's ultimately been stealing money from us. We asked Detective Fedorak to compensate for the damages that he's done, but he has refused."

"How much are we talking about?" Barris asked.

"All said, two hundred thousand should cover it," Sato replied.

"Ain't no way I got that kind of cash," Fedorak exclaimed.

"Shut up, scum," commanded one of the Asian gangsters, delivering a forceful backhand to the side of Fedorak's head.

"Can we give him a pass?" Barris pleaded. "I mean, if you torture a cop, you create all kinds of trouble. All kinds. I can make sure he stays in line from here on. What do you say?"

"Who said anything about torture?" Fuji's voice was calm and even. "I deemed it only fitting that you be apprised of the fate that befalls your partner, and also, what we do with those who steal from us."

Fuji then barked something in a foreign language, triggering one of the gangsters to produce a machete. In a single, fluid motion, the gangster sliced the blade across Fedorak's neck, severing the common carotid artery and inducing hypovolemic shock. In a matter of seconds, Detective Rex Fedorak was dead.

Unable to fully comprehend the shocking turn of events he'd just witnessed, Barris sank to his knees. He opened his mouth, but words failed him, rendered speechless by the totally unexpected, and grim, execution.

"I suggest you find a new partner, or better yet, work solo," Fuji said. "We'll dispose of his body accordingly. It'll never be found. Just remember that a similar fate awaits anyone who betrays us. Is that understood, Detective Barris?"

Barris remained silent, his gaze fixed on his dead partner slumped in his chair. He realized now that Fuji Enterprises wasn't just a money laundering operation, but something far more serious and ominous.

"Is that understood?" Fuji repeated, this time with more force.

"Yeah, I understand," Barris responded softly, realizing that he had sold his soul to the devil, with no means of escape.

CHAPTER 11

Perched on a stool at the bar inside Bistro Densetsu and wearing a neat navy suit with his necktie undone, Demetrio Garcia indulged in sips from a bottle of Asahi beer, savoring the smooth finish of the Japanese brew.

"What a hectic night," he remarked. "We came close to running out of tuna sashimi."

"Thank goodness we didn't, or we might've had a riot on our hands," Yuna Kim quipped with a playful smile, briskly wiping down the bar counter.

"I thought the extra security guards would cause some concern for the customers, but none of them seemed to mind or notice," Garcia said. "Still, I can't believe that Dalton's lawyer was killed, and her daughter abducted. How does that happen?"

Yuna couldn't conceal her disappointment, her gaze dropping with a disheartened expression. After a quick moment to collect herself, she said, "You go on ahead. I'll lock up tonight."

Demetrio slid off his highchair. "Thank you, Yuna. And someday, we need to have a drink together. I want to know your story. *Buenas noches.*"

"Good night," Yuna said, accompanying him to the front door.

Remaining in place until the taillights of Garcia's Ford Bronco vanished into the Pasadena night, Yuna ensured the place was vacant before securing the front door lock. After switching off the main lamps, she ventured into the kitchen.

Ever since Yuna Kim was in high school, she had harbored a dream of seeing the world. Growing up near the quaint coastal town of Jangsaengpo, renowned for its whale museum, opportunities were limited for women—most of her childhood friends had embraced the conventional path of becoming dutiful housewives and mothers. But that wasn't a script Yuna wanted to follow. As soon as she finished high school, she fled her small town by enlisting in the Korean military against her parents' wishes. Her exceptional academic achievements secured her a coveted position in the army's exclusive intelligence division.

A few years in, she met Dalton Lang—known then as Charles Hu —on a joint U.S.-South Korea mission to interview a North Korean defector. She was impressed with his resume as a former MSS agent who dissented against the communist regime. In return, he complimented her on her street smarts and excellent combat skills, which included a fifth-degree black belt in Hapkido. Their respect for each other laid the groundwork for a lasting, amicable relationship. When her ten-year tenure in the military was up, she asked to join him in America to start a new life in the "land of the free," to which he acquiesced after serious consideration. She remained the only person to whom Dalton Lang disclosed his new identity after his relocation, a testament to the trust woven between them over the years. Lang helped her get through bartending school and set her up as the head bartender at his restaurant, which had since become her second home.

Yuna continued into the storeroom where nonperishable items were neatly arranged. Walking past cans, plastic bottles, and various cured meats, she arrived at a large bookshelf against the wall concealed behind a vinyl curtain. On the shelves were old cookbooks and cooking utensils, but next to it was an electronic scanner on the wall. Placing her hand onto its surface, a faint light scanned her palm, followed by a satisfying click. The left side of the shelf popped open, unveiling a concealed corridor. She walked through the hidden doorway and descended a curved staircase leading to a hidden cellar. Thinking she was alone in the building; she was startled when she saw Dalton Lang standing over a wooden workbench. He was packing a small suitcase with a blowgun, a box of darts and several vials of liquid.

Noticing Yuna on the stairs, he said, "I'm going out of town for a few days."

The secret basement of Bistro Densetsu resembled an armory, with several rifles hanging from the walls, many of them shrouded in layers of dust and cobwebs. On the opposing side were an array of ancient weapons: swords, axes, crossbows, and even a *kusarigama*—a traditional Japanese weapon with a sickle at one end and a heavy iron weight at the other, linked by a metal chain. Tucked away at the rear of the chamber was a compact shooting range.

"I'll keep watch here," Yuna replied, walking up to the workbench and opening one of its drawers. She extracted a Smith & Wesson 59 automatic, deftly pulling back the slide.

Lang glanced over at her. "I don't want you getting involved, Yuna. You left your military days behind you, remember? That was our deal."

Holding the firearm up and examining it from every angle, she replied, "I guess we can't change who we are."

"Just keep a cool head," Lang ordered. "Don't do anything rash, like today in Little Tokyo."

Shutting the lid of the suitcase, he walked to a wooden Buddhist altar resting on a shelf near the front of the room. A faded photo of a pretty Asian woman occupied its center. Placing his hands together, he uttered a brief prayer, then discreetly flipped a hidden latch behind the stand, revealing a secret compartment. From within, he extracted the Dragon Coin.

"I thought that this coin would bring me luck, but instead..." he let the words drift off.

"I'm sorry about Ruth," Yuna confessed, a hint of shame in her voice.

Lang glanced over at her, offering a reassuring smile. "We'll get her back."

CHAPTER 12

Standing alone on the fractured pavement of a neglected parking lot of the shuttered Marine Corps Air Station El Toro, Dalton Lang gazed heavenward at the gentle purple glow of dawn. Clad in a light fleece jacket that hung over a red Nike polo shirt and white trousers, he looked the part of a golfer, but one who had lost his way, for there were no fairways or greens in the vicinity. No one had bothered to tell Lang that the El Toro Golf Course, which once thrived here, had been shut down years ago, leaving behind nothing but bulldozed mounds of earth, dotted with weeds and gopher holes.

So much for blending in, he thought, reassessing his getup.

From the distant horizon, Lang caught the unmistakable sound of propellers rhythmically thumping the air, growing louder with each passing moment. Following in its echoes was a black Airbus H125 that touched down in the heart of the abandoned parking lot, several yards from where he stood.

The gust from the main rotor blades kicked up thick clouds of dust, as Lang adjusted the collars of his pullover and hurried toward the waiting chopper with his suitcase in tow, hoisting himself and his luggage into its rear compartment. He slammed the door shut, and the helicopter returned to the sky, soaring northward into the gentle light of dawn.

The only occupants of the aircraft were Lang and the pilot—a thirty-something ex-military type with short brown hair and tinted glasses. The pilot turned toward Lang and gestured for him to don the headset dangling from a hook on the back of the front seats.

"Good morning, sir," the pilot greeted when the headset was in place. "I have a call for you from Director McKeen."

He flipped a switch on the center console. After a distinct click, McKeen's voice sounded in the earpiece, loud and clear.

"Greetings again, Dalton. We don't talk for nearly ten years and now twice in as many days."

Lang replied loudly into the microphone. "This affair with the coins, it goes much deeper than I'd anticipated. I'm sure you know by now, but they took another hostage, a thirteen-year-old girl. We need to get to the bottom of whatever's going on ASAP. Have you found who leaked my location yet?"

"Unfortunately, no. But whoever it was, we're fairly confident that they're not inside the agency, at least not anymore."

"Fairly confident? That's not very reassuring."

"Agreed. That's why I'm bringing in an outside team," McKeen said. "Do you remember General Paul Verdy?"

The mention of Verdy stirred memories in Lang. It was a name he hadn't heard in years but one that he would never forget.

"Of course," he replied. "He was instrumental in helping me defect. If it weren't for him, I'd be dead or rotting away in a secret Chinese detention center."

"Verdy now runs a PMC, one that's been a tremendous help to us recently."

"He's gone private?" inquired Lang.

"Yep," McKeen confirmed. "General Verdy's group stopped a plot to blow up the Los Angeles Auto Show a few weeks back, and they're the ones who got Nasim Al-Ahmed."

"Impressive."

"You're on your way to meet him now. And there's one other thing I should probably mention to you. His director of counterintelligence, a fellow by the name of Max Koga, happens to be dating your daughter."

The words caught Lang off guard, not just because his daughter had unexpectedly entered the conversation, but also because the idea of her being romantically involved had never occurred to him.

"Small world," Lang responded nonchalantly, masking any trace of discomfort that he may have felt.

"Good luck, Dalton," McKeen said. "Over and out."

With a faint click, the headset went silent.

Just as the sun breached the horizon, the Airbus H125 touched down in the field of what seemed to be an abandoned winery. Around him, neglected grapevines sprawled lifelessly around weathered wood posts, stretching across the land as far as the eye could see. Meeting Lang when he stepped from the chopper was a man in an electric golf cart. He had short brown hair and an unusually bushy mustache. Clad in a light black jacket, gray turtleneck, and khakis, he introduced himself as Mitch Snowhill.

"Please jump in, Mr. Hu, or would you prefer I call you Mr. Lang?" Snowhill asked.

"Dalton," Lang replied, sliding into the rear seats of the golf cart as the chopper returned skyward.

Snowhill skillfully guided the golf cart along a winding dirt trail that eventually led to a structure resembling a Victorian-style manor. Despite the weathered appearance of the exterior, the scene inside revealed a warm and luxurious living space, complete with a crackling fireplace that added a touch of coziness to the room.

"Make yourself at home, Dalton. It'll be a few more minutes until the support team arrives," Snowhill said, turning around and returning outside.

Peeling off his jacket, Lang made his way toward a cozy lounge chair in the corner of the room and sank into its soft cushion. A nearby side table held an iPad. Eager to pass the time, he picked it up and perused various news articles about the incident at the L.A. Auto Show and the demise of Nasim Al-Ahmed.

It didn't take long before Snowhill returned, this time accompanied by two men, one of whom Lang recognized as General Paul Verdy. His large defensive-lineman frame, his customary attire of a black leather jacket, white shirt and khakis, brought back memories of a time long forgotten. By his side stood a fellow of Asian descent. He was in his early thirties, Lang guessed, measuring about five-ten and carrying a weight of about a hundred and eighty pounds.

So, this is Max Koga, the one who's dating my daughter, Lang mused.

"It's good to see you again, doctor," Verdy said.

"It's good to see you as well, general," Lang replied. "And this is the young man Director McKeen mentioned?"

Verdy nodded.

Lang walked toward Koga and stretched out his hand. "My name is Charles Hu. I've been told you are a friend of my daughter," he said, electing to use his old name for the sake of shock value.

It worked.

Koga's eyes grew wide, and he wore an expression as though he had just seen a ghost. He looked over at his boss and uttered, "Does Beth..."

Verdy shook his head in response.

"I now go by Dalton Lang. By the way, how is Beth?" Lang asked, attempting to ease the tension.

Koga paused before answering, "Actually, she's still looking for you."

The words had a powerful impact on Lang. Ever since the day he came in from the cold, he had attempted to keep tabs on his wife and daughter, especially Elizabeth, but the task proved challenging. Their digital footprint was all but nonexistent, and he was strictly prohibited from contacting them. He had hoped Beth would've accepted his absence and moved on—become a lawyer, get married, have kids—but never did he imagine that she would choose to become a law enforcement officer.

"Let's save all that for later," Lang declared, quickly changing the subject. "The clock is ticking gentlemen, and I'm very eager to get started."

"Couldn't have said it better myself," Verdy concurred. "Let's get this show on the road."

CHAPTER 13

Agent Mitchell Snowhill stepped forward, exuding an air of self-confidence.

"Please follow me," he directed, leading Dalton Lang, Paul Verdy and Max Koga to what appeared to be a cozy dining room.

At its center was a large circular table, surrounded by matching wooden chairs. On top of the table surface were white folders, each bearing the mark "Confidential." The men, one by one, claimed their seats and proceeded to break the seals on their respective folders.

"General, I assume you've been briefed on the situation?" Snowhill asked.

Verdy nodded. "The director filled me in slightly, but Max here is still in the dark. So, if you don't mind, Dr. Hu, er, Dalton, can you give us a quick rundown?"

"Delighted to," responded Lang, launching into a detailed account of the events of the past three days, beginning with the unexpected meeting with Guo Jianlian.

After Lang had finished, Verdy was the first to speak. "What I want to know is why the MSS is so interested in getting their hands on a bunch of fake coins?"

"That's the billion-dollar question," Lang replied.

Snowhill cleared his throat, drawing the attention of the three men. "We believe that the coins are of interest to the MSS because Dr. Linghu Ning possessed all three of them before he was killed in Boston more than a decade ago."

"I know. I was there," Lang commented. "For the record, it was an exfiltration that went completely sideways."

Verdy nodded. "I remember that incident. You've sacrificed plenty since, Dalton."

Once again, Snowhill cleared his throat, redirecting the attention to him. "As I was saying, the coins were in Dr. Linghu's possession because we're sure he was the one who had them made. For those who don't know him, he was a true genius in the field of nuclear physics, the generational kind, comparable to Richard Feynman or even Albert Einstein—the kind that comes along every fifty years or so."

"I've never heard of him," Koga admitted.

"You can credit the Chinese government for that," Lang said. "They kept him under wraps...like a secret weapon."

"Back to the coins," Snowhill said. "Since then, these counterfeit coins have gone separate ways, as if they possessed a will of their own. Our informant inside one of China's government-run labs thinks Dr. Linghu somehow transferred his research onto these coins, one of which he was going to hand to us when he defected."

"Did you just say that these coins might contain data regarding Professor Linghu's research?" Lang inquired with surprise. "Why am I hearing about this only now?"

"It was need-to-know," Snowhill replied. "Now, if you could open your folders."

The men simultaneously flipped open the white folders. Inside were several documents and photos of the three coins, as well as a headshot of Linghu Ning and Guo Jianlian.

"So, the data on these coins...what sort of research are we talking about?" Koga asked.

"Our best guess is that it had something to do with nuclear fusion —maybe cold nuclear fusion, considering Linghu's area of expertise and the fact that he had hinted of this when he was in communications with his CIA handler," Snowhill replied.

"Nuclear fusion? That's just science fiction, right?" Verdy commented.

"Not at all, boss," Koga responded. "It was achieved for the first time a few years back in California, if I remember correctly. And again, in South Korea, not long after that."

"Back up. Can someone explain to me what exactly fusion is?" Verdy asked. "The only fusion I'm an expert on is the kind you can eat."

Tapping into his deep science background, Lang took the lead. "Thermonuclear fusion is the process of generating energy by fusing atomic nuclei. Normally, these atoms resist fusion, which is why we don't experience thermonuclear explosions occurring constantly around us. To achieve fusion, we must overcome the Coulomb barrier, an electrical repulsion that keeps the atoms apart. Depending on the type of atom, this requires temperatures in the order of billions of Kelvin. However, once initiated, the reaction is clean, producing no greenhouse gases or nuclear waste, only a tremendous amount of energy. The challenge lies in generating the extreme heat necessary to break through this electric barrier."

"Let me get this right. Do you mean that with fusion I can essentially get more energy back than what I put in?" Verdy inquired.

"For all intents and purposes, yes," Lang responded, "which means you can have a limitless supply of energy. You'll never run out. Never."

"Bravo, Dr. Lang," commented Snowhill. "And all this time, I thought your PhD was an honorary one."

"As far as I know, I passed all my exams at the university," Lang said.

"What about cold nuclear fusion?" Verdy asked.

"Like the name implies, it achieves the reaction at or near room temperature," Lang explained. "As I mentioned before, it takes an immense amount of heat to break down that electric barrier. Our sun, for instance, is a massive fusion reactor, and you can imagine the heat it generates. Achieving such temperatures to initiate fusion is incredibly challenging; so far, we've only been able to maintain that temperature for about a minute. In theory, cold fusion can overcome that electric barrier at room temperature."

"That would be a total gamechanger," Koga said excitedly. "It would solve the world's energy crisis overnight. Cheap, unlimited source of energy."

Lang nodded. "Yes, but there are many, many challenges that need overcoming before nuclear fusion can become a feasible option, and many including me, don't believe cold nuclear fusion can ever be achieved."

"On the very remote possibility that Dr. Linghu's research did have something to do with nuclear fusion, cold or otherwise, it's vital we get our hands on his data before the Chinese or the Russians," Snowhill said. "Obviously, he didn't share his findings with the Chinese government, or we would've known by now. Whoever possesses advanced nuclear fusion technology can instantly become a dominant world power—politically, militarily and financially. And they can remain the alpha dog for decades, if not centuries, to come."

From the folder, Koga produced a document, containing a brief profile of the Aikawa-Gumi, complete with an organizational chart and photos of the top officers.

"How are the Japanese involved in all this?" he asked. "Are they after the technology too?"

"The Japanese government is not aware of Dr. Linghu's research, but this yakuza organization seems to have a special interest in the coins," Snowhill answered. "The head of the clan seems to think they're the real coins from 240 BCE."

"Do we know the location of all the coins?" inquired Koga.

"Well?" Snowhill said, directing his gaze at Lang.

"Based on what I know, the Aikawa gang has the Monkey Coin,"

Lang replied. "And the Tiger Coin is in the possession of the people who killed Eva Maston and took her daughter. And I believe now that the Aikawa gang had nothing to do with Eva's death or the kidnapping of Ruth because the real culprit asked for the Monkey Coin. Why would Aikawa ask for something he already has?"

"Good point," Verdy said.

Lang continued. "As for the Dragon Coin..." He paused, then slowly reached into the exterior pocket of his suitcase that sat on the floor next to him. From within, he extracted the Dragon Coin and placed it on the table.

A profound stillness gripped the room, every gaze riveted to the gold medallion in front of them.

"Is that what I think it is?" Snowhill uttered.

"Don't ask how I have it, I just do," Lang said. "So, what do you suggest we do next?"

Koga was the first to speak. "Our first objective is to retrieve the Monkey Coin, since we know where it is. The yakuzas have it, right? Once we have the two coins, we can use them to get a better idea of the identity of our enemy."

"Agreed," Verdy concurred.

"Sounds good to me," Snowhill chimed in.

Lang smiled. "I was hoping you would say that. And I have just the plan to get the Monkey Coin."

CHAPTER 14

After entering the Federal Building in Westwood, California, located a few miles from the UCLA campus, Melvin Patterson took the elevator to the seventeenth floor, where the air was thick with the hum of law enforcement activities. Paying no heed to the rows of cubicles clumped in the center of the room, he advanced toward a small office tucked away at the rear, thankful that all his limbs were still attached to his body. If it had been anyone else, the mere threat of an arm being severed by a samurai sword would have induced severe trauma and anxiety, but Melvin took it all in stride, for he had encountered far more harrowing experiences in his life, particularly during his tenure with the CIA while stationed in Hong Kong.

A graduate of New York University with a BA in criminology and a proficiency in Cantonese, Patterson joined the Company as a junior analyst assigned to the agency's Hong Kong Station. Initially relegated to mostly deskwork, within a few years, he began handling mid-level assets, with some of his informants being junior members of the Chinese Communist Party. During his fifth year on the job, he lost two of his most trusted moles to an MSS hitman that Patterson dubbed the "Phantom Assassin." Despite relentless efforts, Patterson and his CIA coworkers were never able to uncover the identity of the killer—the only thing they were certain of was that he was young, highly intelligent, and frighteningly efficient.

A few months prior to the Tiananmen Square protests in Beijing, Patterson packed his bags and returned to the States. Not long afterward, he wanted to start a family, so he made the hard choice of leaving the CIA and embracing a new career with the FBI, where a majority of his assignments kept him inside the country. Three and a half decades down the road and two marriages later, he was still with the Feds, having ascended to the position of senior officer of the Directorate of Intelligence department.

Upon entering his compact office, Patterson seated himself in a reclining chair and casually hoisted his feet onto the desk. He was preoccupied with an assortment of thoughts, when a sharp knock at the door interrupted them.

Clad in a navy suit and tie, Rob Newey, the assistant FBI director in charge of the Los Angeles division, stepped into the room. Sporting a short haircut and an All-American clean-shaven face, he embodied the look of the quintessential G-man.

"Come in, make yourself at home," said Patterson sarcastically, promptly removing his feet from the desk.

Undeterred by the tone, Newey cut straight to the chase. "Care to tell me what that was all about?"

"What was what all about, chief?" Patterson answered.

Newey settled into a seat facing the desk. "Word is that the Aikawa gang was about to slice your arm off in broad daylight. I thought we had a deal with them. They keep us in the loop with gang activity in Little Tokyo, and we let them run their hostess club."

"Yep, that was the deal, but for some reason, they think we betrayed them."

"That's just great," Newey responded with a sigh. "I've got Islamic terrorist cells in San Pedro, the Russian mob running rampant in West Hollywood, and now I have to deal with a gang war in Little Tokyo?"

"I don't think it's a gang war, chief."

"Then who the hell shot them up yesterday?" Newey asked.

"No idea. But let me talk with Sho Aikawa and find out what's really going on."

Newey shot Patterson a surprised look. "You mean go all the way to Japan? Are you high?"

"I'm fairly sure that the Aikawas are connected to everything that's been going on here for the past few days," Patterson explained.

"Look buddy, you're only a few months away from retirement. And the guy you were investigating, Jianlian Guo, is dead. So, why don't you do yourself—and me—a favor and put it on cruise control until the end?"

"And do what?" Patterson fired back. "I have two ex-wives who hate my guts and three kids who don't have time for me. This is all I have left, man."

Newey leaned back in the chair, and after a contemplative moment, he responded, "Okay, fine. Consider this an early retirement gift, but you're flying economy. And do me one last favor: Don't make me regret it."

"No guarantees. Thanks, Rob."

When Newey left the room, Patterson made his way to a steel file cabinet and unlocked the lowest drawer. From its depths, he extracted a thin weathered manila folder, labeled with the words, "Phantom Assassin, Hong Kong." Returning to his desk, he opened it up. From a pile of weathered sheets of paper, he picked up a grainy photograph depicting a young Asian man in his twenties clad in a dark military uniform.

"I thought I heard the last of you thirty-five years ago, but here you are popping up in my world again," Patterson addressed the photograph. "How the hell did you get here?"

ACT TWO
THE PHANTOM ASSASSIN

幽靈刺客

CHAPTER 15

Kowloon, Hong Kong, 1989

UNDER THE VEIL of a cloudy night sky, a lone fishing boat motored toward Kowloon Bay, leaving a soft, white wake past several junks. As the small vessel docked into an empty slip along a private pier, the rolling ripples of the sea reflected the shimmering lights of the Hong Kong skyline like a giant kaleidoscope.

The captain of the boat, Chen Hsin-Yuan, switched off the motor and stepped out of the vessel's enclosed helm.

"Nigel, we're here. Should I get the Gen-Sec?" he asked in English to a Caucasian man, standing on the foredeck.

Dressed in black from head to toe, Nigel McKeen flicked his half-smoked cigarette into the seawater below.

"Don't use that term in the open," he cautioned. "Refer to him as 'Kai.' And make sure he's in his disguise."

Nodding obediently, Chen ducked into the trunk cabin, reemerging a moment later with a diminutive man in his mid-seventies, clad in a loose cotton shirt, baggy pants and a large straw hat.

Thin salt-and-pepper hair framed his wrinkled, weary face, his eyes bearing the traces of recent hardships.

For McKeen, the stakes were high on this operation. It bore the potential to catapult him up the CIA's hierarchical ladder, possibly helping him to secure an executive position within the agency. He was the lone mastermind behind the plan to exfiltrate the deposed political leader from the clutches of the Chinese government. The most challenging phase had gone off without a hitch—smuggling him to Hong Kong through Macau by boat. Now, all that remained was to secretly fly him out of the country from Kai Tak Airport under the cover of night. However, fate had a way of upending even the best-laid plans—their jet had experienced mechanical issues, delaying their departure for at least an hour, forcing McKeen to make a whirlwind of last-minute adjustments.

Disembarking from the boat, McKeen said to Kai, "Sir, please come with me now."

"I thought you said that once we're in Western-friendly Hong Kong, we're in the clear," Kai responded. "Why all this sneaking around?"

"There are Ministry of State Security spies all over the place, sir," McKeen said. "You of all people should know to never underestimate the MSS."

The boat captain, Chen, offered a parting statement, "Good luck, sir. I pray for your safety."

"Pray for China's future," Kai fired back.

As the motorboat departed from its slip, McKeen led Kai along the creaky, weathered dock, their path leading them toward a black Mercedes-Benz 560SEL waiting at the end of a darkened road. As they stepped past the dock gate, a popping sound prompted McKeen to reach for his pistol, holstered at the small of his back. A breath of relief escaped him when he observed a group of children huddled in a circle on the opposite side of the unlit road, their laughter filling the night as they ignited sparklers and roman candles.

McKeen walked toward them, his voice booming, "Scram. Get out of here before I call the police."

The children quickly ditched the scene, leaving their firecrackers behind.

With his attention diverted by the kids, Kai inattentively stepped off the sidewalk, failing to detect a Honda Elite 50 scooter speeding in his direction.

Unable to swerve out of the way, the scooter grazed him on the arm. Although light, the impact was enough to send the elderly man sprawling onto the hard ground, his hat falling from his head.

"General Secretary," McKeen called out, inadvertently shouting Kai's former title.

The scooter skidded to a stop just a few feet away, its thin rubber tires squealing against the slick tarmac. A young woman pulled off her open-face helmet and tossed her long black hair away from her face. Draped in a knee-length coat that exposed the lower half of her slender legs, she possessed catlike brown eyes and a wide mouth with full lips.

"I'm so sorry, but I thought you saw me. Are you all right?" she asked.

McKeen rushed to Kai's side and assisted him back to his feet. The engine of the waiting Mercedes-Benz roared to life, shining its headlights upon Kai's face. The woman caught a glimpse of the old man's features in the glow, and a subtle glint of recognition flashed on her face.

"Do I know you?" she asked. "You look just like..." Her eyes opened wide, and she gasped loudly. "I'm sorry, I'm late for work. Please accept my apologies."

Hastily, she secured her helmet and steered her scooter in the opposite direction, gunning the engine to full throttle. McKeen drew his handgun, fixing his aim on the fleeing woman, but before he could squeeze the trigger, Kai intervened. He grabbed McKeen's arm and forcefully pulled it down, preventing the shot from being fired.

"What's wrong with you? It's just a local girl," Kai scolded.

"The look on her face. I'm sure she recognized you," McKeen said, watching the scooter's taillight disappear around the corner. "She may be a spy, sent to be on the lookout for you."

"Nonsense. She's just on her way to work."

"I pray that you're right, sir," McKeen replied solemnly.

The Mercedes-Benz sedan pulled up beside them, the driver-side window descending. The man seated behind the steering wheel, Agent Scott Tucker, stuck his head out.

"Is everything okay?" he asked.

"Let's hope," McKeen replied, opening the rear door for Kai.

Once the former Chinese Premier stepped into the spacious rear cabin of the German luxury sedan, McKeen slid into the seat next to him. The door slammed shut, and the car headed in the direction of the Consulate General of the U.S.

CHAPTER 16

From the onset of the twentieth century, Hong Kong had evolved into a pivotal financial center in Asia, celebrated for its distinctive blend of Eastern and Western cultures. Under British rule, the city had become a flourishing economic power, vividly illustrated by its picturesque skyline adorned with towering skyscrapers. Although Cantonese was the official language here, English was widely spoken, and the legal and administrative systems followed British practice.

Within a private residential neighborhood on the northern border of Kowloon Tong—a few minutes' drive from Kai Tak Airport—Lo Peng's Club Americain, a members-only jazz bar, provided locals and expats a place to convene and forge bonds over drinks and live music in a distinctly American-style setting. It also doubled as a discreet meeting hub for CIA agents, as well as a place to conceal and manage the agency's assets.

Outfitted in a Navy blazer and Levi jeans, Qiang "Charles" Hu made a conscious effort to project an aura beyond his twenty-two years because the nightclub's regular patrons were generally at least a decade older and predominantly Caucasian. His face was partly obscured by a pair of lightly tinted tortoiseshell glasses, while a newsboy cap was pulled low over his brow.

The front entrance of the club was manned by the usual bouncer, known among the regulars as Yeung. Charles casually approached the imposing figure, taking note of Yeung's robust, muscular build, and cold, intense eyes that instilled fear in anyone daring to contemplate crossing his path.

"Who are you?" Yeung asked in Cantonese when he noticed the unfamiliar visitor approach.

"Good evening. My name is Charles," Hu answered in English. He liked the name Charles because it sounded closer to the pronunciation of his given name of Qiang—*chiang*, not *kiyang*, as westerners often called him.

Yeung rose from his chair, purposefully displaying his intimidating physique.

"What do you want?" he asked in a low, deep voice.

"I'm here to have a drink. May I go inside?"

Yeung shook his head. "This place is members-only. Go to Tsim Sha Tsui. More places for guys your age there."

"That's too bad, but I really want to have a drink here."

Without a hint of warning, Charles delivered a rapid chop to Yeung's Adam Apple. The strike, while not intended to be lethal, was forceful enough to immobilize the bouncer momentarily, causing him to clutch his throat and gasp for breath.

Instantly positioning himself behind his incapacitated opponent, Charles locked Yeung's thick neck in a sleeper hold, and within seconds, the bouncer was unconscious. He then carefully dragged the larger man's body behind a sizable metal trash container behind the building, before efficiently securing the bouncer's arms and legs with plastic cuffs. Finally, he placed a gag over Yeung's mouth, ensuring that even if he regained consciousness, he would be helpless to intervene in what was about to go down.

Dusting off his blazer and fixing his cap, Charles entered the facility through a side entrance and stepped into the main dining room. He was greeted by a handful of wooden tables arranged in a large semi-circle pattern, each one surrounded by a set of four matching chairs, all facing a large, slightly elevated stage. Only a handful of the seats were occupied on this night, the patrons indulging in sips of whisky while taking in the sounds of cool jazz performed by a local trio on stage.

Seating himself in a chair at the farthest corner of the room, Charles visually swept the establishment for every exit door, every potential escape route. He had barely settled into his seat when a waitress made her way toward him. An oval nametag on her blouse identified her as Nathalie.

"Can I get you something?" she asked in Cantonese.

"Nothing for now," Charles answered, his hand moving to the interior pocket of his blazer in search of a pack of cigarettes. However, before he could get to it, Nathalie surprised him by producing an open pack of Benson and Hedges of her own from a concealed pocket in her skirt.

Flashing a grateful smile, Charles pulled out a single stick and placed it between his lips. On cue, Nathalie produced a lighter, its flame already aglow. Charles gently guided her hand toward him, drawing the flame closer until the tip of his cigarette was lit. With a satisfying sizzle, he leaned back and blew out a wisp of smoke into the air.

"Not much of a talker, are you?" Nathalie commented. "I haven't seen you here before. Did you just move to the area?"

"Visiting a friend," Charles answered.

"You must be from the motherland. Your Cantonese has a bit of a twang."

"You have a very good ear, Nathalie. I went to school in Beijing."

"Just let me know if you need anything else, handsome. Be seeing you," Nathalie said in Mandarin with a wink before gracefully sashaying away.

Charles admired her rear view until she vanished behind the "Staff Only" door near the bar's entrance. A minute later, she reappeared on the stage, accompanied by what seemed to be the proprietor of the establishment—a rotund figure dressed in a black suit and bowtie, sporting wire-rimmed glasses and a short, neat goatee.

He announced in perfect English: "Welcome to the Club Americain. I'm Lo Peng, the owner. We'll be closing early tonight, but let's end things with a special performance from our own Nathalie Chow, who's making her singing debut right here and now."

A soft round of applause filled the room as Nathalie took the mic.

With a sweet, high-pitched voice, she addressed the audience in the Queen's English. "Thank you. I'd like to start things off with a request. Does anyone here have a song they would like to hear?"

The bar's patrons, all five of them, returned to their drinks without responding.

"Not the most enthusiastic audience I've seen. All right, I'll start things off with one of my favorites," Nathalie said, looking back to the piano-bass-sax trio. With a one-two-one-two-three, she launched into the song "It Had to Be You," the trio following her lead flawlessly.

Taking in the performance, Charles reached into his navy blazer once again, not to retrieve his pack of cigarettes, but to take out four small photos. Three of them were of CIA agents, the names Nigel McKeen, Scott Tucker and Grant Bricklin scrawled at the bottom of their respective images. The fourth photo was of an elderly Asian man, marked with a red "殺" at its corner, the Chinese character for "kill." Although he had never seen the men in the flesh, he knew the Asian man's face well; in fact, most everyone in China did. Charles examined the four headshots intently before igniting the photos with his lighter and carefully placing them in the ashtray. His gaze remained fixed on the photos until it withered away into a delicate pile of ashes.

CHAPTER 17

As Nathalie Chow worked her way through her three-song set inside Lo Pen's Club Americain, outside the nightclub, the black Mercedes-Benz 560SEL carrying CIA agent Nigel McKeen and his prized package coasted to a stop at the front entrance. Observing their arrival through the main window, Lo Peng rushed outside to greet them.

When he arrived, McKeen lowered the tinted window of the Benz while remaining seated in the rear seat.

"Someone from the consulate just called and told me to expect you," Lo Peng said.

"I'm sorry to drop in on such short notice," McKeen responded in a low voice. "We had to deviate from our original plans. Too many MSS agents reported around the consulate."

"Are you sure you weren't followed?" Lo Peng asked.

"We've been driving around for an hour, and we've been very careful. I'm sure," McKeen responded.

"I haven't yet closed for the evening, but we only have a few customers tonight, and they're all regulars. Would you like to wait inside my office?"

"If you're sure it's secure," McKeen said.

"Follow me," instructed Lo Peng. "Leave the car here, and Yeung will park it. Wherever he's gone, he should be right back."

McKeen stepped out of the German luxury sedan, assisting Kai from its plush rear cabin. Also stepping out of the car were Grant Bricklin, a rookie agent, and the driver of the vehicle, Scott Tucker. The four men followed Lo Peng toward the side of the building, where they entered the premises through an emergency exit. Once inside, Lo Peng guided them into a dim corridor that was separated from the stage by a thick black felt curtain. As they made their way past the stage, Nathalie, having just wrapped up her performance, sauntered through the curtains, a content smile adorning her face. But her expression instantly changed when her eyes locked onto McKeen and Kai.

"You!" McKeen exclaimed, his voice cutting through the back-stage hush. "Stay where you are."

In a panic, Nathalie pivoted, sprinting in the opposite direction and disappearing back through the curtain. She vaulted into the main dining area, ignoring the startled reaction of the patrons, continuing forward until she burst out of the building through the main entrance.

"Don't let her get away," McKeen shouted to Tucker and Bricklin, who promptly gave chase. McKeen then turned to Kai. "It was the girl from the dock. I knew that she recognized you."

~

THE NOTION of grabbing her Honda Elite scooter and making a quick getaway did cross Nathalie's mind; however, she dismissed the idea, recognizing that the time it would take to kickstart the thing would allow her pursuers to catch up. From her previous encounter with them, she knew that at least one of them carried a gun. She couldn't fathom why they were pursuing her, but she had no intention of sticking around to find out. Her instincts told her she had seen something she wasn't supposed to, and they screamed at her to keep moving.

Cutting through the middle of an upscale residential neighborhood, Nathalie decided her best bet was to seek a crowd. Perhaps the presence of people would act as a deterrent and discourage the men from coming after her, she thought. In the late-night hours, the only nearby place where people gathered was the local *pai dai dong*—an open-air street food market that remained open until the early morning hours. Although lacking the crowds of Temple Street's bustling night market, one could usually find more than a few stragglers seeking nourishment there after a hard night of drinking.

It would have to do.

Taking as many secluded side streets as possible, she reached the *pai dai dong* in no time flat. The small road was lined with food stalls where midnight chefs meticulously prepared a variety of local delicacies—from fishballs to egg tarts—releasing an enticing blend of savory aromas into the night air. Casting a quick glance over her shoulder, Nathalie studied the two men pursuing her—one sported straight, brown hair, while the other had wavy, red locks. They navigated through the crowd, callously pushing people aside like rag dolls. Nathalie couldn't shake the feeling that she might have made a critical mistake: These guys seemed unfazed by witnesses.

With no other option than to press on, she blindly stepped into an intersection, causing a Toyota Crown to screech to a stop a few inches from her body. The driver angrily sounded his horn, but Nathalie hardly cared, for she was literally running for her life. Glancing over her shoulder again, she saw the brown-haired pursuer jumping over the hood of a slowing taxi, maintaining his relentless pace. However, the man with the red hair was nowhere to be seen... until he reappeared directly in front of her. He blocked the route forward, cutting off her access to a nearby police station. She turned to retrace her steps, only to find the brown-haired man closing in rapidly. Trapped in the middle, she desperately examined her surroundings. Then she saw it, behind one of the food stalls: a narrow alleyway. Without a second thought, she ran for it, knocking over a small table and drawing vehement curses in Cantonese from the disgruntled stall owner.

About halfway through the narrow passage, she felt a pair of arms seizing her shoulders from behind. They pulled her into the shadowy depths of a deeply recessed doorway. She could tell by the strength of the hold that the arms belonged to a man, though the darkness veiled his face from her view.

This is it, I'm gonna die, she thought.

"Stay here, and remain very quiet," the stranger instructed in a hushed voice. "Don't come out under any circumstances until I tell you to. Okay?"

Nathalie nodded, and the mystery man was gone, vanishing into the dark confines of the alleyway as if he was an apparition.

CHAPTER 18

Beneath a feeble, sputtering light that cast a dim glow, a pair of well-built Caucasian men in suits stepped into the murky Kowloon alleyway, their eyes scanning the vicinity. Wearing the standard CIA uniform of black suits, matching tie, crisp white shirts, and rubber-soled shoes, they seemed as if they walked right out of the pages of the "How to Dress Like a Secret Agent" handbook.

Slightly out of breath, the brown-haired man, whom Charles Hu recognized as Scott Tucker from the photograph, stopped when Hu obstructed his path forward.

"You there," Tucker called out in English. "Did you see a girl running this way?"

Stepping away from the flicker of the overhead light, Charles pulled down the brim of his hat. He replied in slightly accented English, "Now, what would a *gweilo* like you want with a pretty girl at this hour? I'm imagining that the reasons can't be honorable."

In response, Tucker flipped open one side of his jacket, revealing a Glock snugly secured in a shoulder holster.

"We don't have time to be playing around," he said. "Have you seen a girl come this way or not?"

Without answering, Charles slipped a hand into his own blazer, prompting Tucker and his partner, Grant Bricklin, to reach for their weapons. They collectively exhaled when they realized that he had taken out a pack of cigarettes. Casually, Charles lit one and gracefully stepped to the side, motioning the two agents to proceed unimpeded.

"You need to fix your attitude, punk," Tucker growled as he strode forward. "If I had the time, I'd beat some manners into you."

Just as Tucker brushed past him, Charles delivered a roundhouse elbow into the agent's midsection with intense force, momentarily winding him. With lightning speed, Charles extracted the Glock from the agent's holster, instantly training the weapon on Bricklin before the CIA agent could reach for his own gun. He followed this with a precise kick to the side of Tucker's knee, forcing him to the ground.

"You've got two options," declared Charles. "One, I put the two of you down right here and now. The other, you do exactly as I say. Make the right call because I prefer to eliminate only those I've been expressly ordered to, and you two are not on that list."

Bricklin reached for his gun.

"Grant, no," Tucker shouted, but his words arrived too late. A lone gunshot reverberated through the narrow alley.

With a sharp cry of pain, Bricklin collapsed to the ground, clutching his bleeding ankle. The bullet had shattered his talus, destroying the entire joint.

Charles kept the gun trained on the downed agent.

"Take out your gun slowly," he instructed. "Place it on the ground and slide it to me, or the next bullet will be in your head."

"Do as he says," Tucker exclaimed. "He's MSS, aren't you, punk?"

Not responding to the agent's inquiry, Charles watched intently as Bricklin, still grimacing in pain, produced his gun and slid it on the concrete. Charles then took out two pairs of plastic cuffs from his blazer and tossed them toward Tucker.

"Bind your partner's wrists. Then do the same for your own ankles, now," Charles ordered.

Tucker kneeled next to Bricklin and secured his partner's wrists with the cuffs.

"You okay?" he asked.

"No, man. My ankle is shot to hell," Bricklin replied.

After securing Bricklin, Tucker wrapped the cuffs around his own ankles, before glancing at Charles.

"You satisfied?" he asked.

Producing a fresh set of cuffs, Charles moved quickly to the rear of the men. With their backs turned, he stayed out of their line of sight. In one motion, he bound Tucker's wrists behind his back, and after double-checking that every restraint was cinched tight, he replied, "I am now."

"What do you want? Why are you doing this?" Tucker asked.

Charles picked up Bricklin's pistol and left the two agents behind, his only reply coming in the sound of his footsteps that echoed against the alley walls. Charles made his way back to Nathalie. When he approached, the dim glow of the light revealed her pretty face.

Natalie's eyes opened wide upon seeing Charles's face. "Handsome?"

"Are you all right?" Charles asked.

"That was incredible. How did you... Who are you?"

Helping her to her feet, he said, "I work for the government. I'm sorry you had to witness this. Go home and forget everything you've seen, and definitely forget you ever saw me. Oh, and it'll probably be a good idea to quit your job at the bar."

Charles turned around and darted out of the alleyway. He was fully aware that taking this unplanned side trip was not a wise move, but he was a sucker for a damsel in distress. Seizing the scooter that he had conveniently "borrowed" earlier—a Honda Elite 50—he kick-started its two-stroke engine and rushed toward his destination, fully intending to finish his crucial mission in time.

CHAPTER 19

In the back office of Lo Peng's Café Americain, Nigel McKeen paced nervously, his restlessness earning a disapproving scowl from Kai.

"How long does it take two agents to catch a damned girl?" he muttered, casting an impatient glance at his watch.

"Why don't you sit and calm down," Kai said, relaxing in a lounge chair. "You're wearing out the floor."

A knock reverberated on the door, followed by the appearance of Lo Peng.

"All the customers have cleared out," he said.

"We need to move now," McKeen declared with urgency. "That girl, she could be a spy."

The comment drew a chuckle from Lo Peng. "You mean Nathalie? She's no spy. She's just a sweet girl who wants to become a singer. Completely harmless."

"Still, we can't take any chances. There's too much at stake here. We need to move now."

McKeen assisted Kai to his feet and guided him out of the office. Crossing the dining room, the three men stepped into the open air through the main exit. McKeen opened the rear door of the

Mercedes-Benz 560SEL, gesturing Kai to step into the rear cabin. Once the former Chinese leader was seated, McKeen slid into the driver's seat and fired up the car's powerful V-8 engine.

Lowering his window, he said to Lo Peng, "When Tucker and Bricklin return, tell them we went to the safe house, the one on Lantau Island."

Lo Peng nodded. "Will do. Godspeed, Nigel."

Sliding the shifter into "D," McKeen guided the Benz out of the parking space, but he immediately slammed on the brakes when he noticed a lone headlight approach. McKeen leaned on the horn to coax the scooter out of the way, but it continued to come right for him. As it drew nearer, McKeen noticed a gun in the rider's hand.

Without a moment's hesitation, McKeen floored the accelerator, propelling the Mercedes-Benz forward like a juggernaut.

In response, the rider of the scooter executed a skid turn, halting abruptly, leaving a wide rounded rubber tire mark on the tarmac. Unfazed, McKeen maintained full throttle.

Suddenly, three rapid explosions flashed from the rider's firearm. McKeen instinctively ducked beneath the dashboard, only to feel an unexpected lightness in the steering wheel that caused the car to veer uncontrollably. Desperate, he stomped on the brakes, sending the large German sedan into a spin, its side ramming the scooter, sending it flying to the edge of the road in a heap of metal and rubber. McKeen pulled the steering wheel left, but then one of the car's tires struck something solid, launching the vehicle airborne.

To McKeen, the car seemed to float for an eternity, until the harsh metallic crunch of it landing upside down on the concrete snapped him back to reality. Cobwebs danced in his head as he fumbled with his seatbelt, managing to unbuckle it and leave the vehicle by crawling through the shattered driver-side window. Every movement sent waves of pain through his body—his arm throbbed, and he was sure his collarbone had snapped. Blood trickled down the side of his face. Propping himself against the side of the overturned car, McKeen struggled to sit upright. Then, raising his gaze, he saw the man riding the scooter approach slowly on foot. He wore tinted glasses and a large hat, making it difficult to discern his face. All he was sure of was that the assassin was young, perhaps a teenager.

"Who sent you?" McKeen asked in Mandarin, pain in his voice.

"You're alive," noted the gunman.

He stopped before McKeen, his gaze devoid of any discernible emotion.

McKeen, bracing himself for a bullet to be discharged into his skull, met the assassin's stare head-on, but to his surprise, the young man simply shoved him out of the way, sending him to the ground on his side.

"Didn't know the MSS recruited kids. How old are you?" McKeen asked, his head resting against the ground.

Ignoring McKeen, the young man shifted his attention to the overturned car. With a swift motion, he yanked open the rear door and pulled the unconscious Kai from the rear cabin. He then pointed his pistol at the forehead of the elderly figure.

"Do you know who you're about to kill, son?" McKeen asked. "He was one of the leaders of your government, and now he's forced to flee for his life from the country that he loves. Do you know why?"

The young man kept the gun aimed at Kai's head.

"I don't care," he answered in a cold, unemotional tone.

"Well, then I'll tell you regardless," McKeen growled. "It's because he risked his life to make life better for the likes of you."

"Not my concern," was the killer's reply.

Realizing the futility of his appeal, McKeen decided to shift his tactics, adopting a tone of entreaty.

"I'm with the American government, and I'm asking you to let us go. You'll be rewarded."

The young man shook his head. "Sorry, no deal."

"You're the one they call the 'Phantom Assassin,' right?" McKeen asked.

The young man said nothing, but gave the CIA agent a hard look, in essence, a confirmation to his query.

McKeen let out a disappointing grunt. "Okay, but know this, Phantom Assassin. Kill him, and you'll be doing your government a disservice. His death may start a revolution, the likes your country has not seen in decades."

The words seemingly had no effect on the killer, as he placed the tip of the gun barrel onto the forehead of the former government leader. But before he could pull the trigger, the sound of approaching footsteps caused him to pause.

"Handsome?" the waitress from the nightclub called out.

The Phantom Assassin turned around. "Nathalie, what are you doing here? I told you to go home."

"So, you gonna kill her, too?" McKeen asked. "She's seen your face."

McKeen detected a fleeting moment of uncertainty in the young man's eyes. He reached for his breast pocket, causing the assassin to shift the gun's attention toward him. However, the only thing McKeen extracted was a business card, which he nonchalantly tossed in the hitman's direction.

"You can always come work for us," he said. "We'll say that your mark went over the side of the boat in the harbor. Or that he died of a heart attack. We'll make it public, then your bosses will still think you completed your job."

"My scooter," Nathalie exclaimed, seeing her beloved runabout lying mangled on the side of the street.

The young man lowered his weapon, then took Nathalie's hand. "It's not safe here. We need to go now."

As he led her away from the wreckage, she cried out, "What about him? He's hurt."

"He's fine. We need to disappear before the police arrive."

And as quickly as they arrived, they vanished into the night.

McKeen hoisted himself up to a sitting position and slowly crawled to where Kai lay. He checked for a pulse, then his gaze dropped to the spot where he had thrown the business card. It was no longer there.

CHAPTER 20

The following years saw Charles Hu and Natalie Chow become deeply entwined in each other's lives, nurturing a long-distance relationship while keeping their affair hidden from his superiors at the MSS and her parents. With Charles headquartered in Beijing, their meetings were scarce, limited to only a few times a year. But they maintained their connection through secret emails and phone calls— a sophisticated network methodically crafted by Charles.

In 1997, the handover of Hong Kong to China was finalized, and the Chinese government saw an opportunity to leverage Charles's skills in the newly acquired territory, so, they transferred him back to Hong Kong, tasking him with the mission of tracking down dissenters and revolutionists. This included weeding out a network of pro-democracy activists, lawmakers, and journalists who threatened to disrupt the policies of the Chinese regime.

Once settled in the city, Charles, who had just turned thirty, spent nearly every evening with Nathalie, at his apartment in Tsim Sha Tsui or at hers on Hong Kong Island. Their intimacy deepened amidst the chaos of the city's unrest, while he witnessed the Chinese Communist Party's pledge to uphold Hong Kong's autonomy for fifty years begin unraveling at the seams. With each brazen move by the government, he felt the weight of his missions bearing down on him. Caught between his allegiance to his duty and a growing disillusionment with the party's actions, he grappled within the blurred lines of morality.

"I want to leave this place," Nathalie said one morning as Charles was getting dressed. "And our relationship must end."

"What? Why?" asked Charles.

"I can't ignore who you are. It goes against everything I believe in."

Charles had revealed to Nathalie he worked in law enforcement for the Chinese government, but stopped short of disclosing that he was an MSS hitman. He harbored no shame for his profession; every kill was a duty. Regret never clouded his judgment when eliminating enemies of the state, but he never took a life unnecessarily. If they weren't his targets, he always chose to let live, unless his survival or the success of the mission was at stake.

"Please give me some time," Charles said. "I promise things will change."

"How can I believe you? Are you asking me to be the wife of a Chinese government agent? Is that what you want? Well, I can't, and I won't. And neither will our baby."

The last two words caused Charles to freeze. He gazed at Nathalie for a prolonged moment, his brain processing what he'd just heard. He finally murmured, with a mix of shock and apprehension, "You're pregnant?"

Silently, Nathalie affirmed his query with a nod.

Taking her into his arms, he held her close and whispered into her hair, "You don't know how happy this makes me."

Somewhat taken aback by his joyful reaction, Nathalie pulled away, tears flowing freely down her cheeks.

"I need to go home. I need to leave now," she said.

Charles's heart sank as he watched her anguish. Gently, he reached out and held her shoulders, his gaze locking with hers.

"I didn't want to tell you this just yet, but I reached out to Nigel McKeen yesterday," he said.

"Who?" asked Nathalie.

"The CIA agent we left by the wrecked car when we first met. I told him I wanted out of the MSS and out of China, and I asked if he could help. Finding out that I'm about to be a father has only strengthened that resolve."

Nathalie's eyes widened with genuine surprise.

"Oh, Charles. You're saying we will be able to leave here?" she asked, her voice tinged with hope.

"We're supposed to meet soon. I just need to wait for him to reach out," Charles said.

Nathalie couldn't contain her relief and excitement. She threw herself into his arms.

Holding her tightly, Charles glanced out the window and noticed a black Volvo sedan pulling to a stop outside his apartment building. He quickly fetched Nathalie's robe.

"You need to hide. They'll be coming up the stairs, so go to the roof. I'll contact you when the coast is clear," he instructed, handing her the robe.

"Do you think they found out about your call to the Americans?" she asked.

Charles shook his head. "I can't imagine how. I took every precaution. Even if someone had been listening in, they would've had no idea it was me, but you need to go now."

Slipping into the robe, Nathalie gathered her scattered clothes and snatched up her Motorola cell phone. She quietly slipped out of the room. No sooner had she disappeared when the front door burst open.

Standing in the doorway was Yuan Sheng, the Deputy Minister of the MSS. Clad in a tailored suit, the fifty-two-year-old government officer stood squarely in the doorway, his sturdy frame filling the open space. His tufts of gray hair, trimmed close to his scalp, lent a softness to his otherwise imposing presence. Beneath heavy lids, his eyes drooped, giving him the air of perpetual drowsiness. Positioned behind him was Guo Jianlian, his personal secretary.

"*Fù bùzhǎng* (deputy minister). What are you doing here?" Charles asked in Mandarin, pretending to be startled by their unannounced arrival.

Yuan waved a piece of paper at him. "What is the meaning of this? It says here you're requesting a transfer to the Second Section. You want to leave Operations?"

Charles discreetly exhaled a sigh of relief. His secret was safe. "Deputy minister, you didn't have to come all this way to discuss that. I would have happily reported to you."

"I had other business to attend to here," Yuan said. "But the minister and I have given your request much thought, and we agreed that with the imminent passing of Article 23, things here will be under the control of the National Police, and your resources would be better served elsewhere. Thus, I have personally come to escort you back to Beijing where you'll be trained and prepped to serve as an operative in America. We intend to take full advantage of your knowledge of science and English."

Charles's mind whirled with disbelief as the words sank in. Contemplating defection, he had only just reached out to the CIA the day before, and now he found himself being reassigned to America? The timing seemed almost too perfect, too serendipitous to be mere coincidence. It was as if Fate itself had intervened. *Was it a trap?* His mind raced with the possibilities, but there was no turning back now. His options were few, and he steeled himself to see it through to the end.

"Deputy minister, I would be honored," Charles declared with conviction.

Yuan nodded. "Good. We plan to set you up with a wife. There will be photographs of several candidates for you to choose from."

"Sir, forgive me for saying, but I feel that it would be more effective and beneficial if I found my own wife once I'm there," Charles said. "It would draw much less suspicion."

Yuan rubbed his chin.

"You have a point. A proper wife, one with no ties to China...it would be more convincing, especially if she were an American," he said to himself. "Do you think you have the charms to win one over, Agent Hu Qiang? And to keep her in the dark?"

"I will certainly give it my best," Charles replied, intending to propose to Nathalie once the CIA arranged for her to receive American citizenship.

"Then, I'll discuss it with the minister. Now, start packing because we depart for Beijing in three hours."

Without another word, Yuan opened the door and walked out of the apartment, with Guo following closely behind.

After their car departed, Charles called Nathalie on his Nokia phone.

"All clear," he said, then hung up.

Within moments, she returned to the apartment, concern showing on her face.

"What happened? Is everything all right?" she asked anxiously.

Charles covered his mouth to keep his smile hidden. "Better than all right. I'll tell you as I pack."

ACT THREE
THE YAKUZA'S LAIR

黑幫的巢穴

CHAPTER 21

Osaka, Present Day

NESTLED IN WESTERN JAPAN, Osaka, the country's third largest city, was a quick two-and-a-half-hour ride on the *shinkansen*—bullet train—from Tokyo. It played a vital role in the country's history, its age-old landmarks whispering tales of an era marked by samurais who fought viciously to gain control over the nation. In more recent times, the city had transformed into a formidable center of industry and was now known as the country's food capital, its bustling streets filled with the tantalizing aromas of *takoyaki* and *okonomiyaki*. After sundown, an endless array of glittering lights transformed it into a colorful dreamscape, awakening the city's entertainment districts that provided tranquil havens for those seeking drink and company.

Hidden in the underbelly of the Minami district was one such sanctuary. Furnished with felt-covered sofas and glass tables—the air inside reeking of tobacco smoke and hard spirits—Gyaru Gakuen could best be described as a seedy bar attempting to appear upscale.

It was well past the customary closing hour and only one of the plush sofas within the establishment was still occupied—Sho Aikawa sat surrounded by four attractive women, all of them in their early-twenties and dressed in provocative school-girl uniforms. Sporting a meticulously tailored pin-striped Italian wool suit that cloaked his stocky physique, he sipped Cristal champagne from a Waterford flute while friskily placing his hands around the women's waists and upon their thighs. His jet-black hair was swept back, outlining a carved face with a square jawline. On his tattooed wrist sat a diamond-encrusted Rolex GMT. Despite his clean-shaven face, a scar near his temple—partially hidden by gold-framed aviators with tinted lenses—hinted at his rough upbringing. Rising through the ranks of the Yamaguchi-Gumi, he eventually charted his own destiny, breaking away from the notorious gang to establish his own clan. Now, at sixty-three, he stood atop the Aikawa-Gumi, one of the most powerful crime syndicates in the land.

Aikawa gently bit the earlobe of a hostess named Rikako.

"*Oyabun* (boss), you're so naughty," Rikako purred.

"Oh, then, I suppose I'll have to give you an extra-large tip tonight," Aikawa replied with a crooked smile, producing a wad of cash from his wallet.

"Wait, I want a big tip, too. I'm your favorite, right?" pouted another girl, this one named Chie, draping herself over Aikawa's shoulders.

"Be careful with the suit," Aikawa scolded. "This thing costs more than your apartment."

The after-hours debauchery was interrupted by the presence of a slightly older woman, dressed in a pink, sleeveless business suit that revealed a vivid peony tattoo on her left shoulder. Although of average height, her aura transcended that of any other woman in the establishment. She had a captivating face that was highlighted by large, dreamy eyes and thick lashes. Her straight brown hair was neatly pulled into a bun at the back of her head, providing a touch of sophistication to her overall demeanor.

Shiori Nagoya bowed to her boss and spoke with a slight western

Japanese dialect. "Excuse the interruption sir, but we have a major problem in America."

"I told you I don't like to be disturbed when I'm here," snapped Aikawa.

Undeterred by his tone, Shiori continued. "The FBI raided our Little Tokyo office in Los Angeles and arrested Joe Nakajima. Two of our men were injured."

Aikawa shoved aside the girls on his lap and leaned forward in his seat. "The FBI? I thought we had an agreement with them. Are they reneging on our deal?"

"It seems to be the case, boss," Shiori replied.

Reaching into his breast pocket, Aikawa produced a box of Seven Stars cigarettes. With a deliberate motion, he plucked one from the pack. Immediately, one of three well-dressed bodyguards strategically stationed around the room rushed to his side with a lighter in hand. The gangster took a knee and promptly lit his boss' cigarette with practiced efficiency. Aikawa indulged in a long, hard drag, allowing the string of smoke to ascend before exhaling.

"Find out what's going on," he ordered. "Call our contact at the FBI, the African-American guy. I want to know what the hell they're up to."

"Right away, sir," Shiori answered emphatically. "Oh, and someone who claims to have the Dragon Coin has contacted us."

The words propelled Aikawa to his feet, his momentum knocking a glass of champagne from one of the girls' hand. "The Dragon Coin? Are you sure? How credible is this claim?"

With a deliberate stride, Shiori advanced toward the table and delicately placed a photograph upon its surface. Retaking his seat, Aikawa lifted his glasses and studied the image intently. It showed the Dragon Coin perched atop a recent edition of *USA Today*.

"This seems to have been taken yesterday," Shiori said. "And, as far as our analysts can tell, the photo is genuine."

"And who's the seller?" Aikawa asked.

"They wouldn't disclose that information, but whoever it is, they're saying that they will only deal with you directly, face to face."

Aikawa crossed his arms. "I see. Find out more about this mysterious seller, and make sure the offer is legit. If so, I'll only agree to meet if I get to choose the time and place."

"Yes, sir," replied Shiori.

She bowed, executed a graceful turn, and walked toward the store's exit.

As the door closed soundlessly behind her, Aikawa leaned back into the sofa, taking a more relaxed posture. With a mischievous glint in his eye, he pulled Rikako and Chie onto his lap, eliciting a playful giggle from them.

"Now, where were we? I'm in the mood for celebrating tonight," he said. Then, turning to one of his bodyguards, he shouted, "Bring us more champagne."

CHAPTER 22

The jolt of the Boeing 787 touching down onto the tarmac of Kansai International Airport roused Dalton Lang from a deep slumber, one that had consumed most of the eleven-hour plane trip from Los Angeles. Gazing out of the window, a gentle rainfall greeted him to Japan. As the plane taxied toward its designated gate, he recalled reports of how Kansai International was slowly sinking into the ocean. Serving most of western Japan, "KIX" was constructed on two artificial islands in Osaka Bay. Unfortunately, the foundations for those islands were gradually degrading. Scientists predicted that the facility could be entirely submerged by the year 2060.

Traveling under the guise of a Chinese-American businessman named Winston Lee, Lang breezed through customs and headed directly outside the terminal where Max Koga was waiting for him next to a Toyota Alphard.

"How was your flight, Mr. Lee?" Koga asked, holding an umbrella over him.

"Not as nice as yours," Lang replied.

"Well, we did ask if you wanted to join us in the private jet, but you refused."

"I didn't want to take any chances in case I was being watched, and besides, Business Class is just fine with me."

"I feel the same way," Koga said, loading Lang's suitcase into the Alphard.

Lang stepped into the spacious rear cabin of the luxurious mini-van, while Koga jumped into the front passenger seat. Once the Toyota pulled away from the curb, Koga turned in his seat.

"Allow me to introduce you to our team," he said. "Sitting next to you is Raja Singh. He's our computer guy. No one better."

With jet black hair and dark complexion, Singh sat with an air of rehearsed detachment. His attire, reminiscent of a typical computer programmer, consisted of a forest-green hoodie and beige cargo pants. He was thin and appeared to be around thirty years old, with alert brown eyes peering from behind rimless spectacles. Leather sandals adorned his feet, indicating his preference for comfort over style.

"Call me Raj," Singh said, extending a hand.

"Nice to meet you," Lang responded, shaking it.

Koga continued. "And performing the driving duties today is the newest member of Argon Securities, Greg Cosworth, fresh out of Delta Force."

Cosworth glanced into the rearview mirror, locking eyes with Lang.

"Nice to meet you, sir," he said.

Lang gave him a subtle nod. "The pleasure's mine."

Lang didn't need a dossier to discern Cosworth's background; it was written in the contours of his physique and the steely glint in his green eyes. He exuded an unmistakable air of someone well-versed in dealing with danger. His sandy blond hair was trimmed tight like his beard, and he was thick, which was apparent in the way his body filled his sport coat and jeans. Koga, too, bore the marks of a man who could navigate himself through trouble, though his aura lacked the raw intensity that emanated from Cosworth.

"So, where are we headed?" Lang asked.

"We're making a quick stop at the CIA's base here in Osaka,"

Koga replied. "We were asked to check in with the CIA boys there. Then, we'll gear up and go pay Mr. Aikawa a visit."

As the Alphard entered the highway, Lang found himself gazing out the window, captivated by the ever-shifting tableau of urban and rural landscapes. Rolling past open fields, clusters of homes, and quaint towns, he couldn't help but feel a hint of melancholy with the view. Perhaps it was a sense of familiarity with a long-lost chapter in his life.

"You know, my mother was supposedly from around here," Lang commented out of the blue.

"You have Japanese blood in you?" asked Koga.

"That's what they told me at Langley."

Koga rubbed his chin. "Interesting. If that's true, that means Beth might be a quarter Japanese..."

After a quiet hour on the road, the radio booming with American hits hosted by a Japanese-speaking DJ, the Alphard pulled up to a tall building on a busy road in the Kita Ward, in the northern part of Osaka.

"We're here," Cosworth announced, stopping the van. "The U.S. Consulate-General Osaka. Good luck."

"You're not coming with us?" Lang asked.

"Greg is picking up a few reinforcements," Koga said. "Aren't you buddy?"

"Two ex-Delta guys who happened to be in this part of the world," Cosworth replied. "Guys I can trust."

"That's good to hear," Lang commented. "I was hoping it wasn't going to be just the four of us."

"Oh, I think us four could have pulled this off, but it always helps to have extra guys who know what they're doing. See you back at the hotel, Greg," Koga said, stepping out of the van and heading toward the front entrance of the consulate building.

Lang and Singh followed. Together, the three men passed through the security checkpoint, then escorted to the fifth floor by a young lady in a blue dress. At the elevator, they were met by an older

Asian gentleman, clad in a dark suit that struggled to hold his body-builder-like physique. Although shorter than average, the fluidity of his movements, the subtle confidence in his demeanor suggested he was no ordinary civil servant—he was definitely an operative.

"My name is Kenji Ota, Osaka Station Chief," the man said, extending his hand.

Koga shook it. "Nice to meet you, Kenji. We're here to collect some intel on the Aikawa-Gumi."

"Director McKeen gave me the rundown. Please follow me," Ota instructed.

Ota ushered them through a dimly lit corridor, his steps sounding softly against the cold, tiled floor. Stopping in front of an unassuming door, he punched a six-digit code into an adjacent keypad where, after a soft click, the door swung open. He then beckoned his guests to follow him into a large meeting chamber. At the heart of the space was a large rectangular conference table that held a sophisticated workstation with an array of monitors and scanners.

"Please take a chair," Ota directed.

Once everyone was seated, he slid a manilla folder to each of his guests. "In there, you'll find what we have on the Aikawa criminal organization. They have remote offices all over Osaka, but I'm quite sure your meeting with Sho Aikawa will take place at the clan's HQ, in the Tennoji Ward, just a few minutes south of here. That's where he keeps his Chinese relics; the coin you're after should be there."

"I would imagine it's heavily guarded," Koga said, studying a blueprint of Aikawa's facility. "I mean look at this place. It's walled on three sides, with only the front gate providing a means into and out of the place. The only saving grace is that it's a one-story building."

Ota nodded in agreement. "It's basically a fortress. Six armed men patrolling the perimeter, and another six inside, all rotating every five hours, meaning it's constantly guarded. Plus, there's always a bunch of low-level mobsters—usually twenty or more—hanging around outside the compound. And, of course, there are cameras watching your every move, everywhere you look."

Singh rubbed his chin. "I may be able to hack into their system and take out the cameras."

"The cameras aren't the problem. It's the number of armed guards," Lang said. "With the element of surprise, we should be able to get in, but the challenge is getting out. Any suggestions?"

"Here's what I propose," Ota said with quiet confidence. "The Tennoji chief of police owes me a favor, a big one. I'll see if I can have him bust the guys hanging around outside the compound on some b.s. charge while you penetrate the facility. He can probably hold them for an hour or so."

"Which means we need to worry about the six guys around the perimeter and the six inside. Twelve people," Lang observed. He then glanced at Koga. "Well?"

"Shouldn't be a problem. We'll have the element of surprise to our advantage," Koga said.

Ota held up a hand. "Promise me no dead bodies. The yakuza are a vital component of the intricate ecosystem here in the Osaka community. If we upset that delicate balance, it could yield unwanted consequences. They'll seek revenge, then other gangs will get involved—it'll be an absolute mess, and I'll be shipped out to Siberia...if I'm lucky."

Lang placed a hand on the station chief's shoulder.

"No dead bodies. You have my word," he said. "But I can't guarantee that it won't get a bit messy."

CHAPTER 23

Dressed in an impeccably tailored, dark brown Brioni suit, Sho Aikawa reclined behind his grand walnut desk, his legs casually propped atop its polished surface. His office exuded an aura befitting a head of state, with dark maple floors, walls adorned with framed Chinese calligraphy, and a pair of plush Herman Miller sofas situated in the middle of the room.

Engrossed in a phone discussion with a rival boss, Aikawa's conversation was disrupted by a knock on his open door. In the doorway stood Shiori Nagoya, his ever-efficient personal assistant. With a subtle wave, Aikawa signaled for her to enter, promptly concluding his call.

"That bastard wants to renegotiate our boundaries. Like hell I will," he grumbled in Japanese to Shiori, who took a few tentative steps into the room. "So, why are you here?"

"There's an FBI agent, Melvin Patterson, here to see you," she said. "He wants to discuss the events in Los Angeles."

From behind his gold-framed, tinted spectacles, Aikawa expressed surprise. "The FBI agent is here? In Japan?"

"He's waiting outside."

Aikawa felt uneasy at the sudden, unannounced appearance of Patterson. A series of disconcerting events had unfolded around his clan in the past few weeks, and although he couldn't definitively link them, his instincts—honed through years of navigating the landscape of organized crime—told him to exercise extreme caution. They whispered of unknown dangers lurking in the shadows.

"I wish he would've given us some notice, but very good," he said. "There are things I'd like to discuss with him as well. Send him in."

"Yes, boss," Shiori answered with a bow, then exited the office.

Within moments, she returned with Melvin Patterson at her side. "Boss, I present Agent Patterson," she announced in Japanese before taking her leave.

"Melvin," Aikawa greeted in English, a cordial smile gracing his face. "It's a pleasure to finally meet you."

Patterson flashed him a sour glance.

"Yeah? Well, the feeling's not mutual," he grunted.

"I'm sorry to hear that. Please have a seat," Aikawa stated calmly, gesturing toward one of the sofas.

Patterson instead seated himself in one of the single chairs in front of Aikawa's desk. "If you don't mind, I'll take this one."

Aikawa settled back into his own chair behind the desk. "If you prefer. Perhaps you're here to tell me why my men in Los Angeles are in custody?"

"Perhaps you can tell me why they tried to cut me up like a sushi roll?" Patterson countered.

"You talk nonsense. We had a deal, and we Japanese always honor our word. Only when we are betrayed do we unsheathe our swords."

"Sure...honor," Patterson scoffed. "Like how you knocked off Jianlian Guo. What did you do, ambush him in his car? Doesn't sound so honorable to me."

"I assure you, Melvin-san, we had absolutely nothing to do with Guo's death."

"You're a lying piece of shit. And, I suppose you had nothing to do with the murder of Eva Maston."

Aikawa retrieved a cigarette from a small wooden box on his desk, igniting it with practiced casualness. As he reclined in his chair, he exhaled a long wisp of smoke toward the ceiling. "I have no idea who or what you're talking about."

"We had a deal, and you broke it," Melvin exclaimed.

Aikawa leaned forward in his chair and adjusted his spectacles, making sure Patterson could see his piercing eyes. "It is you who broke our deal. We provided you with information on the other gangs working in the Little Tokyo area, and in return, you were supposed to let us run our business there in peace, but you recklessly raided my L.A. office."

A sharp rap on the door interrupted their exchange. Without waiting for an acknowledgment, Shiori pushed it open and stepped into the room.

"I'm sorry to disturb you, but the seller is here," she said in Japanese.

Aikawa glanced at his diamond-encrusted Rolex. "Already? What's he like?"

Shiori hesitated before answering. "He's quite um, normal. Seems like a nice old man."

"And what about the item?" asked Aikawa excitedly in Japanese. "Did he bring it with him?"

"Not to my knowledge, sir. He's waiting in the treasure room. I will stay here with Agent Patterson until you return."

Watching the exchange with amusement, Patterson asked, "What the hell is going on? I'm still not finished yet."

The yakuza boss rose from his chair. "This doesn't concern you. Please excuse me for a moment."

Aikawa exited his office, leaving Patterson in the company of Shiori. The yakuza boss strode briskly down a lengthy corridor, passing by a succession of rooms until he reached a pair of double doors, where one of his bodyguards waited. Ignoring him, Aikawa pushed the doors open and entered his cherished "treasure room," a sanctuary housing his collection of ancient Japanese and Chinese artifacts.

Along the grand chamber's walls stood refurbished suits of samurai armor. In the middle of the room were ornate *katanas* and vases from various Chinese dynasties displayed proudly upon their stands.

Observing a quintet of ancient scrolls under a glass case was an elderly man, perhaps in his seventies, with a thick mane of white hair and a bushy beard that obscured half of his face. Wearing a light brown sweater and loose-fitting sweatpants, he stood with a slight stoop, his physique supported by a wooden cane.

Aikawa greeted him with a smile. "*Omatase shimashita,* he announced in a warm voice.

"English, please," countered the old man. "I heard that you speak it well."

"My apologies," Aikawa responded. "I'm sorry to keep you waiting."

The old man's weathered gaze settled squarely on Aikawa's bodyguard.

"My instructions were to speak with you, and you only," the old man said firmly. "It was bad enough I was patted down on the way in."

Aikawa directed his attention to the bodyguard.

"*Soto de mattero,*" he commanded.

The heavy-set figure bowed respectfully before retreating from the room, his departure marked by the heavy thud of the doors closing behind him.

"Well, then, shall we get down to business? Where may I ask is the Dragon Coin?" Aikawa asked.

"Oh yes, the Dragon Coin," the old man replied. "It is outside, but may I ask where the Monkey Coin is? It doesn't seem to be here in this room."

"You're very perceptive. I keep that in my office, behind a secure case. Now, the Dragon Coin, if you don't mind?"

The old man nodded and grasped his cane firmly in both hands. He curiously twisted the ends of it in opposing directions, eliciting a low creaking sound, until it separated into two pieces.

Watching in rapt fascination, Aikawa realized too late that the cane was in fact a disguised blowgun, one end of it already aimed directly at Aikawa. Before the yakuza boss could react, a sharp projectile struck his neck, injecting a paralyzing agent into his veins. With a sudden loss of sensation, Aikawa collapsed to the ground.

"What...who..."

As the world faded to black, the last image Aikawa could recall in the room was the sight of the old man lifting off a wig, revealing a chilling smile under his fake beard.

CHAPTER 24

Through an open rear window of the Toyota Alphard, parked on an adjacent street about three hundred yards away from the Aikawa compound, Max Koga surveyed the facility through high-powered binoculars from the rear seat of the vehicle. He counted two dozen *chinpiras*—low-level gangsters—lingering in front of the main gate, a bothersome presence even in their apparent idleness.

Ota had briefed Koga on these men, describing them as the foot soldiers of the organization who were more than eager to prove themselves to move up the chain of command. While their presence provided an added layer of protection to the property, they were there mainly awaiting orders from the higher-ups within the syndicate. Koga watched in quiet amusement when Sho Aikawa made his grand entrance earlier that day in his chauffeur-driven Toyota Century; the gangsters fell into formation, lining up on either side of the car, their bodies leaning forward with a hand resting on one knee, like a baseball infielder ready to take a ground ball. The salute was an age-old yakuza sign of respect reserved for their leader.

Inside the Alphard, Koga's team was strategically positioned and ready to go. Next to him sat Greg Cosworth, while hired guns Frank

McLaren and Bruce Williams—former Delta Force operatives turned mercenaries—sat up front, the former designated as the getaway driver manning the steering wheel.

Two minutes had passed since Dalton Lang had entered the facility disguised as an old man with a bad knee. Koga tapped Cosworth's shoulder.

"It's almost showtime," he said, stowing the binoculars into the center console.

Just as Koga's sentence trailed off, four Nissan NV350 police vans hurtled past them and screeched to a halt in front of Aikawa's property. With the sirens conspicuously turned off, the gangsters outside expressed visible surprise at their sudden appearance. Before they could muster any sort of response, a contingent of ten officers spilled from the vans, donning riot gear and brandishing steel batons. Tensions escalated with a flurry of heated exchanges between the police officers and the gang members. Yet, in the face of the law, the gangsters relented, allowing themselves to be cuffed and herded into the waiting vehicles.

When the Nissan vans drove away, McLaren wasted no time in firing up the Alphard's engine. He steered the vehicle toward the Aikawa compound, stopping it in front of the closed gate. With earpieces snugly fitted and custom dart guns firmly gripped, Koga, Cosworth, and Williams leaped out of the Toyota in perfect unison and immediately scaled the high gate.

Within four minutes, all six yakuza guards stationed at their posts around the perimeter lay on the ground incapacitated, each one subdued by a well-aimed dart containing Argon's potent prototype knockout drug.

The three men regrouped at the front entrance of the building, when Koga's gaze caught the surveillance camera perched beneath the eave of the building. A smirk played on his lips when he noticed the absence of the blue recording light. *Leave it to Raj*, he mused. It was confirmation that Raja Singh had infiltrated Aikawa's security system from his workstation back at the consulate, rendering it null and void.

The man is a wonder.

Turning his attention back to his two companions, Koga's voice cut through the tension. "Let's see how Mr. Lang is faring inside, shall we?"

~

WITH SHO AIKAWA'S limbs secured by plastic restraints, Lang shuffled to the door, pressing his ear against its frame to discern any signs of activity in the hallway. Finding it eerily quiet, he glanced at his watch, noting the dwindling seconds ticking away in anticipation of the Argon team's imminent breach. With only moments to spare, he hurried to one of several *katanas* on display, removing it from its stand. He then proceeded to the next phase of the operation.

Gently pushing open the door, Lang saw the hefty bodyguard standing a few feet away, oblivious to the danger lurking behind him. Lang silently approached him and sent the butt of the sword handle into the back of the guard's neck, knocking him forward. He then sent the blunt end of the blade to the burly man's jaw, breaking the mandible and knocking him unconscious.

Moving with fluidity, Lang navigated the dimly lit corridor until he reached the threshold of the main receiving room near the front entrance. There, he saw three armed guards, sitting in plush lounge chairs. Quietly, he made his way forward, the *katana* tightly gripped in his hand. The balance of the weapon, the impeccable craftsman-ship...he truly felt that the samurai sword was the most elegant weapon ever created.

He burst into the room, swinging the blade with deadly precision. The blunt side of the sword smashed into the first man's clavicle, shattering it like brittle glass. Before the other two could even blink, he had broken their ribs with fast, brutal strikes. All three men collapsed to the ground, writhing in agony. Had he used the sharp edge, the floor would have been awash in blood and littered with severed limbs.

Just then, Koga and his team burst through the front door, their dart guns poised and ready. They relaxed when they saw Lang standing among three downed hostiles.

"You certainly don't mess around," Koga said. "Do you even need us?"

"I'm going after the Monkey Coin. You guys take care of the rest of the yakuza," Lang instructed.

"Take this," Koga called out, tossing a dart gun to Lang, who caught it in mid-air.

With a silent nod exchanged between them, Koga, Cosworth and Williams dispersed, each vanishing into a different part of the building, while Lang, feeling a bit remorseful about leaving the sword behind, headed for Aikawa's office, dart gun in hand.

Reaching the end of the hallway, Lang's steps grew cautious, his senses heightened to the slightest hint of danger. He pushed open Aikawa's office door, bracing himself for whatever awaited inside. Suddenly, a presence to his left caused him to whirl around, his dart gun leading the way. His heart skipped a beat when he saw the familiar face of Melvin Patterson, holding a large golf trophy, ready to bring the thing down onto his head.

"Phantom?" Melvin asked with a mixture of surprise and confusion.

"Patterson? What the hell are you doing here?" asked Lang.

"I'd like to ask you the same thing."

"Unbelievable. You followed me all the way here," Lang mumbled as he headed directly to a glass-cased display mounted prominently on the far wall of the office. Inside the case gleamed the coveted Monkey Coin, ensconced within a crimson velvet setting. On its door was a numerical keypad.

Grasping the dart gun tightly, Lang delivered a forceful blow to the glass, but to his dismay, it failed to even scratch the surface. Undeterred, he discarded the weapon and swiped the golf trophy from Melvin's grasp. He then slammed the solid wood base against the glass, but it was the trophy that succumbed to the pounding, breaking apart into two pieces after a couple of blows.

"This damned thing is shatterproof. It can't be opened without the code," Lang said to himself.

As Patterson watched in silent curiosity, Lang made a beeline for Aikawa's desk. He began systematically checking each drawer, casting piles of papers and files aside with little regard; however, any clue to the PIN that opened the case was nowhere to be found. For a brief moment, silence reigned in the office, until it was broken by Max Koga's entrance.

"We're out of time," Koga announced. "Ota just notified me that Aikawa's other reinforcements will be here in a matter of minutes. And they're heavily armed. We need to go, now."

"I can't get to the coin," Lang admitted dejectedly. "We need to take Aikawa with us."

Making a quick adjustment to his earpiece, Koga addressed his team through its built-in microphone. "Greg, did you catch that? Get the big boss into the vehicle."

"He's in the treasure room, down the other hallway," Lang said.

Koga departed the office, leaving Lang to follow. However, before he made it halfway out the door, he was stopped by Patterson's firm grasp on his arm.

"What the hell is going on?" Melvin asked. "Where are you going?"

Lang gazed at him with a curious look. "It doesn't concern you. Now, please let go of me."

Patterson held his ground vehemently. "Not until I get some answers."

Koga returned with a sense of urgency written on his face. "Greg and Bruce have loaded Aikawa into the van. Dalton, we need to leave now. Who is this person?"

"He's FBI, here investigating the Aikawas for Guo Jianlian's murder, I assume," Lang replied.

Koga turned to Patterson. "Well, Mister G-man, we're here on behalf of the U.S. government, and we need to get out of here in a hurry, so if you don't mind..."

Patterson's jaw dropped in surprise. "The U.S. government?" He then turned to Lang. "You're working for us now?"

Lang yanked his arm away. "It's a long and complicated story, one that I don't have time to get into now."

Koga led the trio out of the office. He then held up a fist, the military hand sign for "stop."

"Greg just informed me they just passed a bunch of Aikawa's reinforcements. We can't use the front entrance," he said.

"But that's the only way into and out of this place," Patterson exclaimed.

No sooner had he spoken than the high-pitched squeal of tires sounded outside, signaling the arrival of an army of gangsters.

"They're here," Lang muttered grimly, noticing five black sedans through a front window—a mix of BMWs and Audis—driving onto the property. "And there's a whole bunch of them."

CHAPTER 25

"This way," Max Koga ordered, motioning for Dalton Lang to follow him back to Sho Aikawa's office.

"What the hell are we doing back here?" Melvin Patterson asked. "We're lambs waiting for the slaughter. They will kill us, you know."

Without wasting another moment, Koga began carefully surveying the grand office.

"A bigshot like Sho Aikawa has a lot of enemies, so he must have an emergency exit in case his compound is raided by rival gangs or the police," he explained. "There's no way, this place has only one way in and out."

"Yes, some sort of hidden door," Lang nodded in agreement. "There must be a passageway."

"Oh, that reminds me," Patterson interjected. "Aikawa's assistant was here with me when all hell broke loose. I was distracted by the commotion outside, but before I knew it, she was gone, and I know for damn sure she didn't leave this room through the door."

Koga turned to Patterson. "Do you remember the last place you saw her?"

"Here," Melvin replied, walking next to a display of a magnificent red samurai armor in a sitting position. Atop the *kabuto*—helmet—were deer antlers that formed the *maedate*, sprouting like horns in front. Under the display were the kanji characters, 真田幸村 —Sanada Yukimura—a famous samurai during Japan's feudal era.

Both Lang and Koga joined Patterson at the display.

With intuition guiding his actions, Lang reached out and pulled on one of the antlers on the *kabuto*. It swung down like a lever, locking in place with a muted click. Suddenly, the entire display lurched forward, revealing a concealed passageway behind the armor.

"I knew it," Koga exclaimed, pulling the display forward and revealing a hidden path that led underground.

Activating the flashlight app on his smartphone, he descended a flight of stairs to the dark depths below. Lang and Patterson followed. At the bottom of the steps, a narrow tunnel stretched before them, barely wide enough for them to walk side by side. Koga took the lead, his smartphone's flashlight illuminating the way forward.

"I traveled in an underground tunnel just like this in Mexico a few weeks ago," he said.

As they walked, Patterson bombarded Lang with a relentless stream of questions. Lang answered only a few, the crucial one being his admission that he had been a CIA operative for the past few decades.

"I would have never dreamed it," Patterson said, his face showing genuine shock. "The Phantom Assassin turned on his own country and joined us."

"Trust me, I have a difficult time believing it myself," Lang replied nonchalantly.

When they reached the end of the line, a ladder materialized, its metallic rungs ascending toward what seemed to be a manhole. They scaled the ladder, lifted aside the heavy steel lid, and emerged within the serene confines of a nature park, one with lush green trees and a large pond.

Koga checked his map application on his phone.

"This way," he instructed, heading along the walkway.

As they exited the boundaries of the park, they were immediately engulfed by the vibrant chaos of a bustling metropolis. All around them, skyscrapers towered overhead, casting long shadows over the throngs of people navigating the crowded streets. The air hummed with the sound of cars, while just across the way loomed Tsutenkaku Tower, an Osaka landmark.

"Where are we going?" Lang asked.

"Just in case we needed a place to regroup, I secured an apartment before we left L.A., but it's still a mile or so away," Koga answered.

Patterson's voice sounded from behind. "Hey fellas, I think we have company."

Spinning around, Lang saw three sleek black BMWs hurtling toward them at breakneck speed.

"This way," Koga shouted, hastily darting into a narrow alleyway too tight for a car to follow.

Behind them, the BMWs came to an abrupt stop, their doors flying open and spilling a swarm of gangsters into the alleyway. Some wielded firearms, while others brandished long knives, but all of them wore sunglasses and sported tattoos up to their necks—that is, except for the alluring woman leading the charge. Clad in a form-fitting business suit that accentuated her lithe figure, she sported a delicate peony tattoo on her left shoulder. Lang remembered seeing her face in the brief provided by Mitch Snowhill. If he remembered correctly, she was Shiori Nagoya, the chief secretary for Sho Aikawa and essentially the leader of the syndicate when the clan boss was absent.

By quickening their pace, Koga, Lang and Patterson only encouraged the gangsters to double their efforts, as they steadily closed the gap between them. After rounding a corner, Koga made a split-second decision to enter a semi-crowded ramen shop, gesturing for the others to follow him in. Ignoring the surprised stares of patrons huddled over steaming bowls of noodles, they entered a small kitchen in back, moving so quickly and deliberately that the shop owner was too stunned to voice a protest. They busted out the rear entrance, into the relative safety of another alleyway. Without pausing, they navigated through a maze of small streets and alleyways through the Namba ward and into the Doton-bori district, until they reached a bridge that Lang immediately found familiar.

Spanning a narrow canal, the short pedestrian bridge was surrounded by the glow of countless neon signs, casting a mesmerizing array of colors onto the rippling water below. Large crowds of youthful revelers congregated along its expanse, their laughter and chatter mingling with the hum of the city. Phone cameras flashed as tourists snapped photos, capturing memories of their visit, preserved forever in the digital cloud.

Slowing to a walk, Lang said, "I know this place."

Checking for pursuers behind him, Koga also slowed his pace.

"Well, it is one of the hot spots in Osaka. This is Ebisubashi, or Ebisu Bridge. Our safe house isn't far on the other side."

Bringing up the rear, Patterson leaned against the bridge wall, his breath coming in ragged gasps. "Can we rest for a bit? I think we lost them. I don't see any of those guys behind us."

"I think so, too. This crowd should provide..." Koga began, but his words trailed off as he lifted his gaze skyward.

"What is it?" Lang asked. Then, he noticed it too—a faint buzzing that seemed to emanate from overhead.

Directly above them, hovering in the purple-tinged sky above, were two state-of-the-art DJI drones.

"They've been tracking us from above," Koga said. "We need to keep moving."

"I think I'm about to have a heart attack," Patterson blurted.

With a renewed sense of urgency, the trio pressed on, making their way across the famous bridge. Nearby, the iconic Glico running man on the side of a building silently observed their passage, perhaps trying to tell them to go faster.

On the other side of the bridge, Koga observed the crowd of people splitting open down the center like the parting of the Red Sea.

Through the gap, the yakuzas marched forward, pushing aside anyone who was too slow to move out of their way.

Adjusting his earpiece, Koga spoke urgently into the mic.

"Raj, there are drones tracking us. Can you do anything about them?" he asked.

Raja Singh's voice cracked through the earpiece. "Negative, Max. They're not using the computer at the compound, so I have no idea who's controlling them or from where."

Koga cursed. "That's what I figured. Greg, do you read me?"

This time, it was Greg Cosworth's deep voice that responded in his earpiece.

"What do you need, buddy?" he asked.

"Extraction. How long before you can get to the apartment?"

"We're just unloading the package now at the warehouse. The nav in the car says forty-five minutes," Cosworth replied.

"Forty-five minutes? You're only six miles away, for crying out loud."

Overhearing the conversation, Lang offered his two cents.

"Traffic is probably worse here than it is in Los Angeles," he said.

"We'll still need to be picked up, so come as soon as you can," Koga blurted into the mic. Then, turning to Lang, he said, "The apartment's right up ahead. How are you holding up?"

Lang answered with a thumbs up. Behind him, Patterson struggled to keep pace. Sweat streamed down his face, his breaths uneven and labored.

"I swear, I'm gonna quit smoking," he wheezed between gasps as he pushed himself to keep within shouting distance of the other two.

After entering a residential block, Koga ran up to the entrance of a new apartment complex, stopping in front of a large glass entryway. He entered a six-digit code into a nearby keypad, the door responding with a soft click as it unlocked. He pushed it open and stepped into the building, gesturing to Lang to follow him in.

Behind them, Patterson's voice echoed, "Wait for me."

With a final burst of effort, he reached the door just before it swung shut, narrowly avoiding being locked out. To the right, a trio of elevators loomed. Koga wasted no time entering the one whose doors were already ajar. Lang followed him in.

Once Lang stepped inside, Koga moved to block Patterson's path, positioning himself as a barrier at the elevator entrance.

"Hey, come on, man. We're on the same side," Patterson pleaded between labored breaths.

Koga glanced back at Lang.

"Your call," he said.

Logic dictated that Lang keep Patterson away, for it was entirely possible that the FBI agent was the informant who had exposed his location to the MSS. However, something inside of him told him that Melvin Patterson was a decent man, steadfast in his commitment to upholding the law and not one to be swayed by the allure of wealth. A man like that could be a benefit down the road. He sighed heavily and gave a nod of approval, prompting Max to step aside and allow the FBI agent to join them in the carriage.

As the elevator doors glided shut, the three of them watched in silence as the yakuzas—led by Shiori Nagoya—gathered at the entrance of the apartment complex.

Chapter 26

Nestled in the heart of Osaka's Minami Ward, an unassuming three-story building bore the modest signage: "Shibata Lending." Despite its nondescript appearance, the edifice was one of many in the city owned by the Aikawa crime syndicate. Its facade of legitimacy masked the true nature of the business within—it was in fact a *sarakin*, or private money lender that offered unsecured loans to those desperate for cash, but with exorbitant interest rates that entrapped borrowers into a web of debt.

For those unable to repay their loans, many *sarakins* often employed ruthless tactics to ensure compliance. Women, if deemed desirable enough, found themselves coerced into the illicit world of massage parlors controlled by the syndicates, where their earnings slowly paid back the loan. Meanwhile, men were forced to take out life insurance policies, with the lending company named as the sole beneficiary. If they failed to honor their contracts, their "accidental" deaths would bring in more than what they owed.

The Shibata Building served another purpose as well. Deep within its bowels was a hidden tech hub, a labyrinth of computers and sophisticated equipment, operated by an elaborate AI system whose algorithms executed intricate hacks into the accounts of high-profile figures that included politicians, celebrities, and rival gang members. It scoured the digital realm, monitoring their activities and seeking any morsel of information that could be exploited as leverage when and if they were needed.

In a dimly lit corner of this underground chamber were four control pods that served as the nerve center for a fleet of drones. Each pod possessed a video monitor and an intricate control panel. On this day, two of the pods were occupied by Takuya and Tsutomu, whose faces were obscured by virtual reality goggles and thin headsets.

While attending Kyoto University, Takuya and Tsutomu spent their off-campus time as IT specialists for Aikawa Tech, where they received a generous wage, which not only covered their tuition but also afforded them a surplus of wealth. In addition to their computer expertise, their sole obligation was to maintain secrecy—they were strictly forbidden to divulge any information about their work to anyone. And they knew, all too well, that betraying this pact would invite lethal consequences.

Through their goggles, they immersed themselves in a virtual landscape of Dotonbori, provided by the drones' state-of-the-art camera systems. Using joysticks on the control pads, they guided the flying machines with precision and finesse, swooping between and over the area's tall buildings, tracking the movements of the three foreign men.

"They just headed into the Tokuyama Luxury Apartments a few blocks ahead on the right," said Takuya into the headset.

"What floor are they heading to?" responded Shiori Nagoya.

"Hard to tell now. I'll fly by and see if I can spot them through one of the windows. Hold, please," Takuya replied, tilting his joystick back, causing his drone to leap skyward.

Through his virtual goggles, Takuya zoomed in on the various floors of the apartment complex. He seamlessly transitioned from one room to the next, then shifted his view to thermal imaging, revealing the various heat signatures inside the building. Taking the drone even higher, he saw three figures stepping out of an elevator—their bodies highlighted in a bright orange and yellow, indicating high body temperatures.

"*Mitsuketa-zo* (found you)," he murmured to himself, a satisfied smirk forming on his lips.

~

THE ELEVATOR CHIMED as it reached the fifteenth floor. Max Koga wasted no time stepping out, motioning for Dalton Lang and Melvin Patterson to follow. Hurrying along the corridor, he halted in front of Room 1567, retrieving a card key from his pocket. With a swift swipe, he activated the reader, allowing entry into the apartment. Once everyone was inside, he bolted the door behind them.

The apartment was modestly appointed, featuring a leather sofa on a plush carpet, while a flat-screen TV adorned the wall. A large, square balcony at the far end of the room offered a glimpse of the courtyard beyond.

"Do you live here?" Patterson asked.

"It's a temporary rental, just in case we needed a place to lay low," Koga replied.

"Pretty nice," Patterson responded approvingly. "But as far as safehouses go, something a bit more secluded would've been nice."

"It was just constructed, so most of the units are still vacant," Koga said.

"But Patterson is right. We can't stay here for long," Lang noted. "It'll only be a matter of time before..."

His words were interrupted by a loud bang on the door.

"Speak of the devils," Lang said, moving toward the balcony and noticing two drones hovering in the night air. "It's the drones. They're relaying our position."

"You're armed, right?" Patterson asked Koga. "Just shoot the damned things out of the sky."

"I have my Sig, but if I miss, the bullet might catch an innocent bystander across the way or on the ground," Koga replied. "Dalton, do you still have your dart gun?"

Lang nodded, already gripping it and moving to the side of the balcony door. He unlatched the lock, keeping himself hidden from the view of the drones' cameras. Koga and Patterson engaged in casual chatter to divert attention away from Lang's position; however, despite their efforts, one of the drones seemed to detect something amiss and immediately departed, leaving its counterpart hovering alone in the air.

In a flash, Lang slid the glass door open and stepped into the doorway. He fired two rounds, one dart striking a camera lens on the drone and the other clipping a propeller. The damage sent the mechanism spiraling downward, breaking apart upon impact with the ground.

"Nice shot," Patterson exclaimed.

Another loud bang on the door ended the celebration.

"Just a matter of time before they decide to shoot their way in," Koga said as he pulled open a closet door. From within, he grabbed a black Oakley backpack. "Follow me."

After slipping the backpack on, Koga stepped outside, onto the balcony, and vaulted over the railing, landing on the terrace of an adjacent apartment. Lang and Patterson followed suit, silently grateful for the proximity of Japanese apartments, a testament to their efficient way of maximizing living space in crowded areas.

On the fourth balcony, Koga stopped.

"We'll enter through that door. It's open," he said.

With one final leap onto the adjacent landing, Koga led the way into a residence where a young couple sat on the sofa, their attention fixed on the television. They recoiled in shock, too stunned or frightened to utter a word, when three figures clad in black intruded upon their living quarters.

"Sorry for the intrusion," Patterson uttered, his palms pressed together. "*Gomenasai.*"

They exited the room through the front door, then hurried down the interior hallway, away from the echoing sound of the yakuza banging on doors.

"We're never gonna get to the elevators," Patterson said. "And please don't make me take the stairs. I'm still winded from running through town."

"The problem with the stairs is that they're outside, so we'll be spotted by that drone," Koga countered. "We need to find another apartment."

Koga stopped suddenly in front of Room 1581. On the door, a sign read "工事中　立入禁止."

"I can't read kanji. Do any of you?" he asked.

"It says, 'Under construction. Do not enter,'" Lang replied coolly. "Or at least that's what it means in Chinese."

"Then it's probably vacant," Koga responded enthusiastically, his hand emerging from behind his back gripping a Sig 9mm.

He speedily affixed a suppressor to the barrel, taking aim at the door lock before squeezing the trigger. It took two shots to completely disintegrate the RFID lock system. With a firm shove, he pushed the door open, then placed the sign over the mangled remains of the door handle, hoping to hide it from view. Once Lang and Patterson walked in, he quietly closed the door behind them.

The apartment was dark—the only furniture present was a large, wooden worktable resting on a sheet of canvas that covered most of the floor. Against the half-painted walls stood a ladder, while several buckets of paint and a paint gun sat next to it. The three men maneuvered the table against the front door, barricading it securely, then gathered in the kitchen, seeking refuge in the darkest part of the apartment. However, their secret huddle was interrupted by the buzzing of a drone emanating from outside the balcony.

"They are persistent, aren't they?" Lang said.

"Can you take it out with your dart gun like before?" asked Koga.

"I'm all out of darts," Lang replied.

With an emphatic huff, Patterson walked to the spray gun resting on the floor.

"I've just about had enough of this shit," he said, affixing a filled bottle of paint to it.

Ensuring that the device was powered on, he held it at the ready and turned to Lang. "Open the door on three, will ya?"

Lang nodded, stealthily positioning himself next to the balcony door.

"One, two, three," Patterson called out.

As Lang pushed the sliding glass door open, Patterson stepped into the doorway, unleashing the spray gun's torrent of white paint into the air, most of it finding its mark on the drone, effectively obscuring its camera lenses. The sheer force of the paint sent the flying mechanism reeling backward, disoriented. Flying blindly, it collided with the building's side before plummeting to the ground, defeated.

"That's how we do it in America," Patterson beamed jubilantly.

"Well done," Lang said, clapping lightly.

At that moment, a resounding bang echoed at the door. Although the large table served as a barrier, it began to yield, inch by inch, under the force of the yakuza men who pushed against it.

"Time to go," Koga said, peeling off his backpack and pulling out two sets of rappelling gear.

"You're not suggesting..." Lang uttered.

"We're seriously outgunned and outmanned. This is the only way we're going to lose them, but I only have two..."

"You guys go on," Patterson said. "I'll stay behind. I'm unarmed, and they know I'm FBI, so they'll think twice before hurting me."

Lang put a hand on Patterson's shoulder.

"Thank you, Melvin," he said.

Koga added, "If they don't let you go right away, we'll exchange Sho Aikawa for you after we get what we want."

"Can I get that in writing?" Patterson responded jokingly. "Oh, and Phantom, thanks for saving my arm from being cut off in Little Tokyo. I know that was you. Great shooting."

"I have no idea what you're talking about," Lang replied with a smile.

"Yeah, sure you don't. Now, get the hell out of here," Patterson said.

With a nod, Koga stepped onto the terrace and secured one end of the rope of the rappelling gear to the railing, allowing the other end to cascade down fifteen stories to the ground. Lang mirrored Koga's actions on the opposite side of the terrace. After fastening themselves into their respective harnesses, they exchanged a brief salute with Patterson, then disappeared over the ledge.

Once they were safely on terra firma, Patterson quickly unhooked the ropes from the railing, allowing Koga to gather the gear and stow it back into his backpack.

From below, Lang observed Patterson raising his hands in surrender as the yakuzas surrounded him. Then, from within the swarm, a familiar figure emerged. Shiori Nagoya leaned over the railing and stared down at Lang and Koga, a look of disappointment etched on her face, like that of a predator who had just let its prey escape.

CHAPTER 27

Sho Aikawa's eyelids fluttered open, the world emerging from a haze, slowly revealing itself in gradual clarity. Grogginess gripped him, and he struggled to piece together the events that led to this moment. A face loomed into view, triggering a sudden rush of recognition. It was the man from his office, the one previously disguised as an elderly gentleman. With each passing moment, fragments of memory coalesced, piecing together the puzzle of his drugged state. He attempted to move, but he found that he was seated on a tatami mat, his legs folded under him, and his arms bound behind him by thick rope.

"What's the meaning of this? Where am I?" Aikawa demanded.

"Good morning, *kumicho* (boss)," said the man claiming to possess the Dragon Coin, but without the disguise and now dressed in a neat gray suit. He sat on a foldable metal chair.

When his senses had fully returned, a fresh sense of recognition gnawed at Aikawa. Although he couldn't place where or when, there was an undeniable familiarity to the man that stared back at him. Images flashed in his mind—photographs, fleeting glimpses on television screens—but none offered a definitive connection. And then, like a bolt of lightning, it hit him. The man in front of him was none other than the legendary Chinese assassin, the one known as the Phantom Assassin—reputed to have taken out several heads of states, including China's Hu Yaobang before the Tiananmen Square protests and the Panchan Lama during the Tibet unrest. His status had become legendary in the underworld, even in Japan, until his sudden and mysterious disappearance more than a decade ago.

"Under different circumstances, I would say it's an honor to meet you. I had no idea you were still alive," Aikawa said with grudging respect.

"I'm flattered that you know me."

"I've only seen photos of you, shown to me by members of the Blue Dragon many years ago. They said you took out half the gang bosses in China."

"That was a lifetime ago. And, please call me Lang."

Lang kept his gaze fixed on Aikawa. "Now that I've told you my name, you understand what happens to you if you don't answer a few simple questions?"

Surveying his surroundings, Aikawa guessed he was in some sort of empty warehouse or garage. The air lingered with the cold, metallic scent of industrial machinery. Rows of towering crates were stacked against the walls, while dust danced in the beams of light that shone through the overhead windows. Two men stood behind Lang, one of them an Asian of steely countenance who exuded an aura of discipline, and the other, a Caucasian figure who radiated a quiet intensity, his eyes sharp and vibrant. It was clear to Aikawa that there was no escaping his current predicament.

"I'm as good as dead, so why should I comply?" Aikawa said defiantly.

"You may still live if you do as I say," replied Lang.

"Do you realize what you're doing? You're starting World War III between our two countries."

With a cold, serious expression, Lang asked, "Why did you kill Eva Masten?"

"I have no idea who you're talking about," Aikawa replied.

Lang wrapped a hand around the gang boss' throat. "Don't play dumb with me."

Unfazed by the hostility, Aikawa responded coolly, "For what reason would we want to kill a woman I've never even heard of? As I mentioned before, I didn't know you were even alive until I saw you just now."

"Then, let's try another one, shall we? Why did you kill Guo Jianlian?"

Aikawa let out a tiresome sigh. "Again, not me. I have nothing to do with the things you're accusing me of. As for Guo Jianlian, his death was an unfortunate, or should I say a fortunate, accident. Ever since he took control of the Blue Dragons, things had become very difficult."

Releasing Aikawa, Lang rubbed his chin. "So, it's true. Jianlian was involved with the Blue Dragons."

"He had the former head of the Blue Dragons murdered by his MSS disciples, and then he took control of the gang," Aikawa explained. "He then threatened to shut down our operations in Shanghai if I didn't hand over the Monkey Coin to him."

"And you knew he had the Tiger Coin, so you killed him. Two birds with one stone, right *kumicho*?"

"You're talking nonsense."

"If it wasn't you, then who?" asked Lang.

"My guess is as good as yours."

Lang gestured with his head to prompt the two burly men into action. They strode over to a towering stack of stone blocks resting in the heart of the warehouse. Their hands then closed around a hefty block of granite. Together, they hoisted the massive slab, carrying it toward Aikawa's seated form. They placed the heavy stone upon Aikawa's lap, its bulk pressing down on his legs with crushing force. Agony seared through his thighs and knees, the weight of the granite bearing down like a relentless vise, threatening to crush his bones from its pressure.

"Do you recognize this form of torture?"

Aikawa nodded. "It's the Ishidaki Kneeling Torture, employed by the samurais many years ago."

"Very good," Lang responded with a smile. "I think that four of these stone plates placed on your lap will crush the femur bones, correct?"

A cold sweat broke out across Aikawa's brow as panic set in. "I keep telling you that I know nothing of your murdered friend or Guo's death. That I want the Coins of Wei is no secret, but I would never betray my allies for it. That isn't the samurai way."

"You do know that the coins are counterfeit, right?" Lang said.

"Rubbish. I have it on good authority that they are real. Do you know the legend of these coins, Phantom Assassin?"

"Enlighten me."

"Whoever brings together all three can unlock the hidden power of the Eight Immortals. The last known person to have done this was Kublai Khan. With their help, he accomplished what was thought to be impossible, becoming the first non-Chinese emperor of China," Aikawa said.

Lang shook his head in disappointment. "You're a fool. I would've never taken you to be a believer of fairy tales. However, I do believe you about Eva and Jianlian. I have little doubt now that someone else is responsible. They only wanted me to think it was you. So, what I now need from you is a favor."

The two men lifted the stone block from Aikawa's lap and returned it to the pile.

Feeling a wave of relief, Aikawa responded emphatically, "After what you did to my me and my men, I think not."

"Bring me the Monkey Coin. I saw it in your office." Lang said.

Aikawa laughed loudly. "Now, why would I do that?"

"I can always have my associates place more of those stones on your lap."

"Torture me all you want. I'd rather die a painful death than hand you that coin. Weren't you the one who just said that it was fake?"

Lang smiled. "I'm impressed. You have some courage after all. And besides, my colleagues here don't condone torture, and neither do I, so you can rest easy."

"Then, you're letting me go?" asked Aikawa with a shard of hope.

"Not exactly. I knew you wouldn't simply hand over the coin freely, so I shot you with a special potion, an old Chinese concoction made from the venom of a rare snake and a plant found only in Mongolia. In twenty-four hours, it'll shut down all your organs, killing you quite gruesomely. And only I have the antidote."

Lang held up a vial filled with green liquid.

"Shooting me up with a poison that kills me slowly and miserably. You don't consider that torture?" Aikawa asked.

"Not if you bring me the coin."

"I will never comply."

Lang shrugged. "Suit yourself, *kumicho*, but if you change your mind, call the number on this piece of paper. I'll provide you with instructions on how to retrieve the antidote and deliver the Monkey Coin to me. But I advise you to do this sooner than later because this potion makes you sicker and sicker as time passes. And after twenty-four hours...well, you know."

Shoving the piece of paper into Aikawa's breast pocket, Lang rose from his chair. Simultaneously, one of the men shifted behind the yakuza boss and sent a sharp blow to the side of his neck. In an instant, the world once again dissolved into an abyss of darkness.

~

AIKAWA BLINKED INTO CONSCIOUSNESS, the memory of his conversation with the Phantom Assassin still fresh in his mind. He was still in the same warehouse as before, but this time, he was alone and free to move, sprawled on the tatami mat with no restraints whatsoever. His head throbbed, but a sigh of relief escaped his lips when he confirmed that all of his limbs were still intact. Noticing his smartphone nearby, he snatched it up and checked the map app for his location. He was in Kobe, a chic city famed for its exquisite beef and about a half-hour drive from Osaka. He then dialed his trusted assistant.

"*Kumicho*, I'm so glad you're all right," Shiori Nagoya greeted.

"Pick me up. We have much to discuss." Aikawa instructed and promptly ended the call.

Within a half hour, his prized Toyota Century glided to a stop beside him on the roadside. When Shiori flung the door open for him, he slipped into the plush rear seats, settling in next to his assistant as the hybrid V-8 engine purred softly, propelling the magnificent sedan forward.

Turning to Shiori, Aikawa said in Japanese, "You're not going to believe this, but it was the Phantom Assassin who attacked us yesterday."

Shiori shot back a puzzled look. "I beg your pardon?"

"I suppose he was before your time. About thirty years ago, he was the most feared assassin in Asia. Rumor had it that he was bred by the Chinese government to kill their most difficult targets, but after several years, he disappeared. Some say he escaped to America, while others believed he was killed on a mission. I know now that he's alive, and he isn't working for the Chinese government any longer."

"Well, I'm so glad you're still with us. We were all very worried," Shiori said.

"That bastard shot me with some grotesque poison, but the fool doesn't know that, like my ninja forefathers, my body has been conditioned to resist all types of toxins," he declared proudly. "Track this phone number, and when we find him, the Aikawa-Gumi will end the legacy of the Phantom Assassin once and for all."

Aikawa produced the piece of paper given to him by Lang, when he noticed Shiori's gaze fixed on his face.

"What's wrong?" he asked.

"You have some marks on your..." her words drifted away as she touched her cheek with her hand.

Puzzled, Aikawa activated the mirror app on his phone. Expecting to see his usual reflection staring back at him, he saw a face covered with green, pimple-like dots. Before he could fully comprehend the situation, a creeping sense of dread washed over him, each breath becoming more labored than the last. Nausea gripped him tightly.

"Stop the car," he demanded. "Right now!"

Careening across two lanes, the Toyota Century cut off three other cars before screeching to a halt on a narrow road. The rear door flew open, and Aikawa staggered out, a hand clamped over his mouth in a desperate attempt to contain the rising bile. He sought refuge behind a nearby vending machine, his stomach lurching violently. Bent over, he emptied the contents of his stomach onto the ground, retching until his knees buckled beneath him, his body trembling and coated in a sheen of sweat.

Shiori emerged from the car, quickening her pace to catch up with her boss.

"Are you okay, sir?" she inquired, a show of concern on her face.

"Call that number," Aikawa barked between heaves. "Give him whatever he wants, but get that antidote now."

CHAPTER 28

Alone in the rear seat of the Toyota Alphard, Dalton Lang observed the blur of Kobe City rushing by outside the window. It marked his first venture into western Japan, his third journey to the Land of the Rising Sun, and he still couldn't help but be pleasantly surprised by the region's pristine cleanliness and orderly demeanor. Unlike other Asian locales marred by pockets of decay and rampant crime, Osaka and Kobe presented an immaculate setting, devoid of any graffiti or vagrants.

His thoughts were interrupted by the ring of his burner phone, drawing the attention of both Max Koga in the front passenger seat and Greg Cosworth, who steered the Alphard on the Hanshin Expressway.

"*Moshi moshi*," Lang greeted. Hello.

The voice on the other end belonged to a woman.

"Name the time and place," she demanded in English, her tone devoid of any emotion.

"I'll text you the location. Two hours. Come alone. Bring the Monkey Coin or no deal," Lang asserted firmly.

There was no response, only the click signaling the end of the call.

Lang returned the phone to his pocket with a satisfied nod.

"Well, that was quicker than expected," he announced.

Koga turned in his seat to face Lang. "Was that Aikawa?"

"It was his assistant. It usually takes a full day before that concoction kicks in, but in his case, it was a lot quicker."

"So, the plan worked," Cosworth said.

"I knew he would call. He's a warrior like me, and a warrior's death should either be in battle or alone with no one else present," Lang stated. "Sho Aikawa couldn't risk such a humiliating end."

"You sound like a Klingon," Cosworth noted with a chuckle. "As for me, I think I'd go with the poisoning if that fine assistant of his was at my side."

"She is attractive," Koga agreed, "in a femme fatale sort of way."

"Has the exchange location been arranged?" Lang asked.

"We're all set. Everything's in place," Koga affirmed.

As the Alphard breached Osaka's borders, it headed straight for the heart of the city, eventually halting near the Nanba train station. There, Koga disembarked alone, while the van continued to a three-story building across the street whose facade was adorned with a gaudy paint job that screamed for attention. A bright red sign hung from its awning: "Ruby Lips Hotel."

Taking a seat on a roadside bench with the hotel entrance in clear view, Koga casually pretended to read a newspaper while listening to music through his earbuds. A half hour passed when a black Toyota Century pulled to a stop in front of the hotel. From the rear cabin emerged Shiori Nagoya. Max noted that she was alone and clutched a small briefcase in her hand. His Tag Heuer timepiece confirmed what Lang had anticipated: She was an hour ahead of schedule.

Sho Aikawa must have been in quite a hurry to get his hands on the antidote, he mused.

"The package has arrived," Koga relayed discreetly through the microphone.

~

LANG RECLINED on a plush love seat within the opulent confines of the Ruby Lips Hotel's master suite. The room exuded tacky luxury, boasting a king-sized bed adorned with sumptuous silver-colored linens, soft mood lighting, and a compact jacuzzi in the corner. The entire suite was themed in a cosmic fantasy motif, transporting guests to a realm beyond the stars.

Lang had heard of these business establishments before. To locals, they were known as "love hotels," which offered private and sometimes themed rooms where couples could spend intimate time together. They offered short-stay accommodations, typically by the hour. With his curiosity piqued, he reached for a cardboard menu resting on the nightstand beside him. Its offerings tantalized with a selection of adult-themed accessories available for rent, including astronaut costumes suited to complement the room's theme.

"Wow, these Japanese are kinky," he murmured to himself, returning the menu to the nightstand.

He selected *Celeste Aida* by Giuseppe Verdi to play softly through his smartphone speakers, the rich, melodious tones offering a soothing contrast to the bizarre and somewhat uneasy atmosphere of the room. The song was soon interrupted by the ring of the doorbell. He lowered the volume on his phone and announced in a loud voice, "Come in."

The door slowly swung open and Shiori Nagoya, carrying a briefcase, stepped inside. She surveyed the room.

"Very tacky," she said. "So, you're the Phantom Assassin?"

"That was a long time ago," Lang replied.

Hesitating before entering the room, she asked, "Do you always conduct your exchanges in such perverted settings?"

"My sincere apologies. It wasn't my idea, but we're assured complete secrecy here. No cameras outside the facility or in the rooms, unless of course, you rent one from the front desk."

"The antidote," Shiori demanded.

Lang reached into his front pants pocket and produced a vial of green liquid. He held it up for her to see.

"And the coin?" he asked.

She gracefully crossed the room to a small table with crystal champagne glasses. She set her briefcase down and unfastened a couple of latches. Lifting the lid, she revealed the briefcase's sole content. Beneath a protective felt covering lay the gleaming prize— the Monkey Coin—its luster mesmerizing in the soft pink light of the suite.

"Satisfied?" she asked.

Lang nodded.

"I do have an additional request that I'm hoping you can fulfill," he said.

"What's that?"

"Release the FBI agent. He's not involved in any of this."

"Already done," Shiori replied. "We had no need for him."

"Then our business is concluded," Lang declared, placing the vial of green liquid on the table. "Make sure he drinks that in one gulp."

Shiori swiped the vial and placed it in her handbag. Pausing before making her exit, she stole a lingering glance at Lang, carefully studying the features of his face.

"You know," she said, a blush creeping across her cheeks, "I would've liked to have met you here on a more personal nature. You're definitely my type."

"I'm old enough to be your father," Lang said. "However, I appreciate the compliment."

A playful smile graced her lips, while her eyes shimmered with a seductive allure. "Age doesn't matter to me. I've always been attracted to older men, and I haven't met one as dandy as you in quite some time."

"Perhaps we'll meet again in another lifetime," Lang dismissed her gently with a comforting tone.

"Another lifetime, then," she replied.

With a wink, she gracefully strode out of the room, the door closing softly in her wake.

Lang gave her a minute to clear the premises before casting a final glance at the cosmic-themed setting. A smirk played on his lips, finding amusement in the kinky setup of the room and the flattery of being hit on by a woman nearly half his age. Clutching the briefcase tightly to his side, he made his way out of the hotel.

CHAPTER 29

Dalton Lang dropped into the backseat of the Toyota Alphard, joining Max Koga and Greg Cosworth inside the vehicle. He retrieved his burner phone from his pocket and tapped his fingers softly against the screen, activating the speakerphone app to ensure Koga and Cosworth could listen in on the impending conversation.

After a single ring, an electronically disguised voice crackled through the line. "Yes?"

"I have the merchandise," Lang said.

"Both coins?" the voice asked.

"Affirmative."

"Excellent. Bring them to Chop Suey Restaurant in Chinatown, Los Angeles. The day after tomorrow, three a.m.," the voice instructed.

The connection then faded into silence.

"Looks like we're going back to L.A.," Lang noted, stowing his phone back into his pocket.

Koga glanced at his Tag Heuer timepiece "Two days. That doesn't give us much time. Greg, step on it."

"Yessir," Cosworth replied crisply, his foot pressing down on the accelerator pedal and propelling the Alphard down the fast lane.

In a mere twenty minutes, the Toyota van pulled up to the U.S. Consulate-General building in Osaka. Wasting no time, Lang and Koga exited the vehicle, making a beeline for the elevator. Entering the CIA station office on the fifth level, they headed to a small office in a secluded corner of the floor, where Raja Singh worked fervently away on his laptop.

Koga placed the briefcase he received from Shiori Nagoya on a table and opened the lid. Without uttering a word, Singh slipped on a pair of cloth gloves, and with great care, lifted the Monkey Coin from inside, holding it up under the overhead light to study it from every angle.

Watching him with keen interest, Lang observed the image of a crouching monkey on one side of the coin and the character "李" on the other. As a history buff, he deduced that the original coins were presented by the Qin emperor to his generals, Wang Jian (dragon), Meng Wu (tiger) and Li Xin (monkey). He wondered where the authentic ones were hiding...if they existed at all.

"Have you found anything with the fake Dragon Coin?" Lang asked.

"The CIA lab rats have been examining it back in Los Angeles, but so far, nothing," Singh replied. "No hidden messages in the inscription, no secret compartment, no data drive. The metal on these bad boys is solid."

"Well, they need to try harder. People are dying because of them," Lang said.

Rising from his office chair, Singh walked to a gray machine stowed in an extra-large Pelican case on the far side of the office. After placing the Monkey Coin inside it, he pressed a button, prompting the contraption to whir loudly. He then returned to his desk, where his fingers once again worked his laptop keyboard.

"I'm running a complete scan of it—CT, X-ray, MRI and other

imaging programs you've never heard of," he said. "This machine breaks down everything. I designed it myself."

"How the hell did you manage to fit an MRI machine into a Pelican case?" Lang asked.

Singh simply smiled and responded with a playful wink.

A few seconds passed when a multicolor image of the Monkey Coin gradually materialized on his laptop monitor.

"Nearly pure gold, 24K," Singh affirmed, studying the readout that appeared next to the image. "And the stone in the monkey's eye is high-grade ruby."

"Then it's probably worth at least a few thousand bucks just for the materials," Koga noted.

Suddenly, Singh's facial expression morphed. Leaning in toward the glowing computer screen, he narrowed his eyes. "What's this?"

"What's what?" Lang asked.

Without answering, Singh entered several keystrokes on his laptop. The hum of his special machine filled the room once more when a new image materialized on his monitor. It focused on the ruby stone, capturing its essence in pixels and various colors of light, revealing intricate details previously hidden from view.

"I've magnified it five hundred times, this time using laser technology," he said. "There seems to be unnatural creases inside the ruby. That thin line is actually a fine cut made to look like a miniscule imperfection in the stone. When I magnify the image even more, there, can you see that? The line hides what looks like a small chip— it's the smallest microchip I've ever seen. Impressive."

"Is it a data storage chip?" asked Lang.

Singh shook his head. "Way too small for that. I'd guess it was some sort of RFID chip or a PKE."

"A what and a what?" Lang asked.

"An RFID chip is an electronic device that uses radio waves to identify and send information, like you see on some credit cards. PKE stands for 'Passive Keyless Entry,' like the ones used for cars these days. I've never seen one this small. Man, the Chinese have upped their game," Singh said.

"Not the Chinese, but Professor Linghu," Lang corrected him. "He was one-of-a-kind. So, what you're saying is that there's no data stored in this chip, but it might function as some sort of key?"

"That's exactly what I'm saying," Singh replied.

"But doesn't a remote-controlled key need electricity to function? There's no power source here," Koga pointed out.

"Not necessarily," replied Singh. "Many keys today can start a car, even without a battery installed, but back when this thing was produced, it utilized a simpler device. So, the coins probably fit into a housing or slot that supplies electricity to the chip through the gold. Gold is highly conductive."

"You think they unlock a secret lab or storage facility where his research might be hidden?" Koga asked.

"Not likely, Max," Lang answered. "Professor Linghu was under constant MSS surveillance. They would've known if he had any secret lab or storage space. But I heard he was known to be quite the car enthusiast, and that he often spent his free time restoring old classics. I wonder if this chip operates a vehicle?"

Koga's gaze darted to Singh.

"Raj," he called out.

"Already on it," Singh responded, his fingers flying across the keyboard. "Got something. It's on a Chinese site. Let me run the AI translator. Give it a sec."

Singh rotated his laptop so the monitor faced Lang and Koga. The text on the Chinese-language webpage instantly transformed to near perfect English.

"Wait a minute," Lang remarked. "This is China's Traffic Management Bureau's records page. That isn't a public website; it's very private. It took you five seconds to hack into their system?"

Koga slapped Singh on the back with a grin.

"No black site or protected content is safe from the Raj," he declared. "It says here that Linghu Ning purchased a used Kamita Empire four months before his disappearance."

"Can this coin be used as a key to unlock a car?" Lang asked.

"You mean unlock like a hidden data drive in the car's computer system?" Singh asked.

Lang nodded. "Something like that."

"For sure," Raj said, pressing a button on the keyboard, prompting another web page to appear. "It says here on the *Japanese Nostalgic Car* website that the Kamita Empire was the first vehicle in the world with AI software, so there's plenty of computer space to hide a ton of information inside. And wow, it also had solid state EV batteries. This thing was thirty years before its time. That's why it was discontinued after only two years. The technology around it hadn't caught up yet."

"The Empire, huh? The name's kinda on the nose for all kinds of reasons," Koga noted.

"Can you locate the car now?" Lang asked Singh.

Turning the laptop back toward himself, Singh once again went to work.

"That's odd. No records of this particular car exist presently," he said. "It wasn't sold or involved in any accident. Not even a traffic violation. It just disappeared, and its registration was never renewed."

Lang rubbed his chin. "Then the car was either destroyed deliberately or secretly stashed somewhere."

"Being the company's flagship luxury crossover back then, the Empire had a state-of-the-art antitheft tracking system built into it," Singh said. "And I have the car's VIN number here. Let me see if I can track it by satellite."

Koga turned to Lang. "Do you think Linghu hid a nuclear fusion reactor in the car?"

Lang laughed. "I can't imagine that's the case. An actual fusion reactor would take up a lot of space. You can't just fit one under the hood of a car."

After a few keystrokes, Singh slumped in his seat. "Damn. The tracking system's been deactivated, but maybe, just maybe, I can switch it back on remotely by going through Kamita's main server in Tokyo. It might take a while, though. Their systems are highly advanced and complicated."

"What's a while?" asked Koga.

"A few days," Singh replied.

"You've got one," Koga said. "Get back to me as soon as you find the car. And Dalton sir, we have a plane to catch."

CHAPTER 30

"I can get used to this," Dalton Lang proclaimed, running his hand over the armrest of his leather chair inside Argon's chartered Gulfstream G-650. As it leveled off at its cruising altitude, the roar of the jet engines mellowed into a steady hum, filling the cabin with a sense of calm.

Max Koga approached the back of the cabin, settling himself into an empty seat across from Lang.

"You being the international man of mystery, I would've thought that you'd be used to this kind of travel," he said.

"I wish," Lang responded with a chuckle. "It's my first time on a private jet, if you can believe that."

Changing the subject, Koga's expression turned serious. "I have to address the elephant in the room, Dalton. What do I tell Beth?"

Closing his eyes, Lang took a deep breath before answering. "Elizabeth is the most important thing in my life. She'd already started college when I was forced into hiding, so I consider myself fortunate that I was able see her grow up, but I didn't expect in my wildest dreams that she would go into law enforcement."

"I guess the apple doesn't fall far from the tree. She has a very strong sense of justice. That's why she'll never give up looking for you."

"Then, what do you propose we do?"

Koga's response was quick. "We tell her right away. I can't imagine what she's been going through, not knowing if her father was dead or alive all these years. And besides, Beth is an FBI agent now. She knows how to keep secrets; it's part of her job description."

Lang clenched his eyes, battling to contain a tear threatening to escape. Despite his efforts, it slipped free. With a heavy sigh, he retrieved a handkerchief from his breast pocket and casually wiped his cheek dry.

"In hindsight, perhaps my wife and I should have revealed my true profession to Beth earlier, but we thought we were protecting her by not telling her." He leaned against the window and gazed out into the vast expanse of the clear blue sky. "But you're right, Max. We need to tell her, but can I ask you for a small favor?"

"Name it."

"Say nothing to her until we finish this job. Once we get the Coins of Wei and punish those who killed Eva and abducted Ruth, let's tell her then. And to be honest, I can really do without the distraction right now."

"You got yourself a deal," Koga replied, rising from his chair. "We still have a long flight ahead of us, so I suggest you get some sleep."

With a friendly pat on Lang's shoulder, Koga walked past Greg Cosworth, who was already fast asleep in his chair, and returned to his seat in the back.

Lang slipped in his earbuds and queued up *Das Rhiengold* on his playlist, letting the opera's majestic prelude fill his ears. He chuckled at the prospect of Richard Wagner's Ring Cycle lasting the entire flight. His gaze returned to the blue sky, his mind drifting to his wife. He missed her.

After shipping out of Hong Kong in 1999, Lang was assigned by the MSS to live in a modest house tucked away in the Charlestown neighborhood of Boston. A few weeks later, the CIA arranged for

Nathalie Chow to move into an apartment just a few blocks away. With the agency's influence, she was expedited through the process of gaining U.S. citizenship, and once completed, they immediately filed for marriage, but there was no wedding or celebration, only a mutual understanding that they would always be watched and secretly scrutinized due to the nature of Lang's business. Less than a half-year had passed when they welcomed a baby girl into the family, christening her Elizabeth after the British Queen.

The MSS positioned Charles as a technical engineer at Raytheon, where he handled three low-level assets, provided by the CIA, who fed him intelligence veiled as valuable yet ultimately inconsequential. Amidst walking the dangerous tightrope as a double agent—a mantle Charles wore with unsettling ease—he attended several classes at MIT to hone his science skills, later securing a position as a guest lecturer there.

His primary concern had always centered on the well-being of his daughter, Elizabeth. Nathalie knew the true nature of his business, and she was always prepared for the consequences it could bring. Yet, they decided to shield their daughter from his real occupation, maintaining secrecy for the sake of her safety. From the onset, Lang had been careful, and he was confident that his cover would never be blown, but in case the unimaginable did happen, he demanded that he would be placed into hiding with his entire family. But the analysts at Langley pointed out that while the CIA's Witness Protection Program was good, it wasn't foolproof.

They calculated that the chances of the MSS tracking down a single individual were less than ten percent. For a married couple, the odds spiked to 20 percent. Introduce a third person to the mix, and the likelihood of being discovered soared to more than 40 percent —turning it into a virtual coin toss on whether they all lived or died. Therefore, he made the hard decision to vanish instantly and alone if he were ever compromised, leaving his family uninformed. It was a brutal choice, but one he had to make to ensure their safety.

It took a while, but Lang eventually came to grips with how

things turned out. He couldn't help but reflect on his time spent in Boston with a sense of gratitude, considering himself fortunate that his elaborate charade had endured for so long—nearly twenty years. Despite concern for his family's welfare, reassurances from McKeen that they would be closely monitored and guarded provided some solace. In the initial year and a half after his disappearance, there were reports of suspicious MSS operatives lingering about his old neighborhood, but as time passed, the presence of these figures gradually waned, until they disappeared altogether.

As the Gulfstream jet descended toward its destination, a soft chime echoed through the cabin, signaling the imminent conclusion of the flight. One more job left to do, and perhaps then, he could be reunited with his family.

CHAPTER 31

L.A.'s Chinatown slept under the glow of evenly spaced streetlights that cast long shadows onto the area's empty roads. Several rough-looking Chinese men lingered in front of one of the area's most popular eateries, Chop Suey Restaurant. Under a light rain that fell sporadically during the early-morning hours, a solitary figure appeared out of the mist. Clad in a windbreaker, gray jeans, and a newsboy hat pulled over his brow, Dalton Lang took purposeful steps along the sidewalk until he stopped in front of the familiar figure of Detective Albert Barris, dressed in a beige raincoat.

"I see you do a bit of moonlighting, detective," Lang said, raising his arms, inviting Barris to search him for weapons.

The corrupt detective patted him down in a practiced manner.

"Got to pay the bills," he replied.

From inside the building, a trio of *xià di*—low-level Chinese gang-sters—holding firearms emerged. One of them reached into Lang's jeans pocket and confiscated his smartphone.

"So, it was the Blue Dragons all along," Lang said in Mandarin. "I take it you're part of the American chapter? Who's calling the shots for you here?"

"You'll find out soon enough," a gangsters replied.

Satisfied that Lang was unarmed, Barris swung open the front door of the restaurant, inviting his guest to step inside. With a curt nod, Lang entered the premises. With his senses heightened, he scanned the interior, taking in every detail.

The main dining area was bare, its usual array of tables and chairs were neatly stacked against the walls. To the side, a flight of stairs ascended to an indoor balcony, offering a vantage point overlooking the main floor.

Suddenly, the lights of the balcony flickered to life, revealing Ruth Nguyen standing behind the railing, her arms bound behind her back.

"Dalt," Ruth exclaimed.

"Are you all right?" Lang asked.

Before she could answer, a tall male figure emerged alongside her, dressed in a black business suit and wearing a Kabuki mask.

"Did you bring the coins?" the man inquired, his voice muffled by the wooden mask.

Lang met the man's gaze straight on.

"Once Ruth's safe, I'll hand them over to you," he replied coolly. "But why hide behind a disguise, sir? Are you afraid of revealing yourself to me?"

A tense silence hung in the air as the man hesitated. He then reached up and peeled away the mask, revealing the unmistakable face of Guo Jianlian.

Lang's eyes widened, caught off guard by the unexpected revelation of his longtime acquaintance standing before him. But he quickly regained his composure.

"Aren't you supposed to be dead?" he asked nonchalantly.

Guo smiled. "To quote Ernest Hemingway, 'reports of my demise have been greatly exaggerated.'"

"Wrong author," Ruth interjected.

Guo shot the girl a hard stare.

Lang quickly redirected Guo's attention back onto himself. "But Jianlian, they recovered your body, even the MSS confirmed that it was you."

"Ah, the advantages of having a body double," Guo replied. "And, as you know, DNA and dental records can easily be manipulated by someone in my position. Now, where are the coins?"

Lang chuckled. "Did you really think I would bring them here, so you can kill me as soon as you got a hold of them? I may be old, but I'm not stupid."

From behind his back, Guo produced a Glock 9mm and held it to Ruth's head.

"Okay, okay, no need to get overly dramatic," Lang said, raising his palms in a surrendering gesture. "They're in my car, but I've rigged them with a bomb. Any attempt at retrieving them will blow my precious car, and the coins, to kingdom come."

Guo's laugh echoed throughout the room. "I've got to hand it to you. You don't miss much, although I would've expected no less."

"Let Ruth go, and I'll deactivate it," Lang said.

Guo turned to one of the gangsters.

"Patrick," he called out. "Go see if what he's saying is true." He then turned to Lang. "Where's your car parked?"

"Three blocks north of here, on Bernard Street. Old model GT-R," Lang answered.

"*Shì de, lǎo dà,*" the designated underling responded. Yes, boss.

After performing a quick bow, Patrick exited the establishment through the main door.

"While I have him check out the validity of your words, I must tell you, I'm quite impressed by how fast you retrieved the coins."

Lang took a step forward but was stopped by a sudden blow to the back of his head. He staggered forward, dropping to a knee.

"Don't you even think it, buddy," Barris warned, a small stick clenched firmly in his hand.

"Dalt," Ruth exclaimed.

Lang let out a painful grunt, raising himself to his feet and rubbing the back of his neck.

"I'm all right," he said.

"I'm curious. Where was the Dragon Coin?" asked Guo.

"It was in my possession from the beginning," Lang replied.

"I knew it. And all this time."

Readjusting his hat, Lang asked, "Tell me, Guo Jianlian. Why fake your own death?"

"I don't have to answer you."

"Since it doesn't seem like I have much time left on this earth, why not enlighten me on how clever you are? How did you pull the wool over the MSS's eyes and trick me into doing your bidding?"

A proud smile formed on Guo's lips. "Very well, I'll humor you this one last time. I'm sure you figured out by now that I've secretly taken over the Blue Dragons after I had their leader executed three years ago."

"So, Melvin and Aikawa were right all along," Lang murmured under his breath.

Guo continued: "It's a lucrative business, but little did I know that the minister of the MSS had been secretly investigating my activities for the past year. A loyal colleague informed me that my arrest was imminent, so I devised a plan to stage my death to get the old geezer off my back. It was then when one of my longtime assets informed me of your whereabouts, and it occurred to me that you would be the perfect person to retrieve the coins."

"And these coins? Why are they so important to you?" Lang asked.

Guo's voice turned grave. "They have the potential to start and end regimes. Professor Linghu Ning had been secretly working on a technology that could change the course of humanity, and he hid his findings inside the coins."

"Cold nuclear fusion is a myth," Lang declared. "It can never be achieved, at least not in our lifetime."

Guo's jaw dropped, exhibiting genuine surprise at the comment. "Now, I'm truly impressed. How on earth did you know about that?"

"You'll never get away with whatever you have planned. Not only will the MSS come after you, the Americans will too."

"Then, all the more reason to get out of this accursed country with the coins," Guo said. "Now, where on earth is Patrick?"

CHAPTER 32

Two blocks from the restaurant, Patrick walked briskly toward a sleek, blue Nissan Skyline GT-R, the only vehicle parked on the street. The rain had subsided, leaving a thin layer of moisture on the sidewalk that reflected the streetlights. Positioning himself beside the Nissan, he cupped his hands and peered through the car's passenger-side window, taking notice of a large box on the passenger seat, covered with a tangle of red, blue, and green wires, and a blinking red light on top. Under it sat a leather briefcase. Satisfied with what he saw, he pulled out his smartphone and punched in a number.

"It's me, boss," Patrick said into the phone in Mandarin. "It's as he says. The coins are here, and there's a flashing red light on a big box."

~

RETURNING his cell phone back into his pocket, Guo Jianlian adjusted the position of his gun so that its barrel pointed squarely at Dalton Lang.

"Confirmation just came through. It is as you said. Now, if you don't mind, please deactivate the bomb," Guo said.

On cue, one of the *xià dì* in the room stepped forward and handed Lang his smartphone. Lang snatched it from his hand and gazed up at Guo.

"You've never been a good listener, Jianlian," he said. "The terms were clear: Let Ruth walk, and only then will I disarm the bomb. But tell me, why did you have to kill Eva?"

"You killed mom?" Ruth cried, tears pooling in her eyes.

"That was an unfortunate accident," Guo said somberly. "I had ordered my men to simply abduct her because I was afraid you would refuse my offer. With her in my custody, you would've had no choice but to retrieve the coins for me. But the idiots shot her by mistake."

"So, you took Ruth to take Eva's place. You will pay for what you have done," Lang promised coldly.

Guo let out a sigh. "I understand how you must feel. If it's any consolation, it was that idiot over there who shot her. His name is Yan."

Guo shifted his gun so that its barrel pointed at a long-haired gangster by the stairwell. Without a hint of warning or emotion, he fired. The bullet struck Yan squarely on the cheek, blasting half of his face off. Ruth's scream pierced the air as Yan collapsed, blood pooling beneath his head.

"There, your mother has been avenged," Guo said to Ruth, before turning his attention back to Lang. "The next one will be in the head of this girl unless you disarm the bomb now."

Realizing that Guo was more than capable of following through on his threat, Lang punched in a series of numbers on his phone, then turned the screen toward Guo.

"There, it's done," he said.

Guo then retrieved his own phone from his pocket and spoke. "The bomb has been deactivated. Bring the coins to me now."

~

FROM THE SHADOWS of a nearby building, Yuna Kim watched as a young Chinese gangster gingerly opened the passenger door of Lang's Nissan Skyline GT-R and reached inside, his face glistening with sweat. His fingers closed around the handle of a Tumi briefcase before pulling it free of the car. After exhaling a deep sigh of relief, he sprinted toward the restaurant, his body quickly swallowed by the thick fog.

Two figures silently emerged from behind Yuna, exuding an ominous air in their all-black attire. Max Koga and Greg Cosworth blended seamlessly into the darkness; M4 carbine rifles strapped across their chests, their faces obscured by the camouflage of black paint. They wielded metal batons, the same weapon Yuna herself held—all standard Argon issue.

"That's our cue. Let's do this," Koga said.

The three darted off in different directions, Yuna charting a direct course toward the restaurant. Concealing the baton behind her back, she adopted a casual demeanor, her movements premeditated as she gradually closed the distance between herself and the gangsters guarding the restaurant entrance.

One of them noticed her and barked, "Hēi, piàoliang de nǚshì, nǐ mílù le ma?"

Although she couldn't decipher his exact meaning, the crooked grin on his face made his intentions clear. Yuna responded with a flirtatious smile.

"Do any of you boys want to play tonight?" she asked enticingly.

The gangsters erupted into raucous laughter, their amusement echoing through the dimly lit street. With lustful anticipation, they surrounded her, their gazes hungry as they appraised her from head to toe. Sensing their guard was adequately lowered, Yuna pulled out her baton and swung it as hard as she could. The weighted end of the stick connected with the face of the nearest man, sending him to the ground instantly, knocking him out cold. His companions, taken aback by the sudden assault, instinctively recoiled, giving Yuna time to launch another attack. She followed with a powerful blow that landed square on the forehead of a second gangster, putting him immediately to sleep.

The third man, however, proved to be more agile, dodging Yuna's next strike with a quick sidestep. Several other gangsters from down the street rushed to the scene brandishing combat knives that glinted under the streetlights. They barked orders to each other in Mandarin, their attention solely fixed on Yuna, unaware of the looming danger behind them. Silently, Koga and Cosworth closed in, their movements masked by the cloak of fog and darkness.

Their batons landed with decisive force that took out four men in quick succession.

Chaos erupted among the remaining six gangsters, as they struggled to comprehend what was happening. Amidst the chaos, Yuna, Koga and Cosworth moved with deliberate precision, dispatching the gangsters one by one until only two remained. In desperation, one of the remaining *xià di* drew a revolver, his hand trembling as he aimed it at the intruders. Before he could pull the trigger, his eyes stared into the barrel of Cosworth's M4.

"You might want to think twice about that, buddy," Cosworth warned.

The gangster clumsily tossed his pistol at Cosworth's feet and bolted in the opposite direction. His comrade immediately followed suit, both disappearing into the thick fog.

Tapping the handle of his M4 with a satisfied smirk, Cosworth declared, "Now, that's what I call efficiency. Not a single shot fired."

But before Yuna and Koga could reply, the tranquility of the moment was shattered by multiple gunshots that reverberated from inside the restaurant.

CHAPTER 33

Patrick had returned, a Tumi briefcase clutched tightly in his grip. After pausing at the sight of his dead colleague Yan near the base of the stairwell, he rushed up the stairs, presenting the briefcase to Guo Jianlian.

With a sense of anticipation, Guo cracked open the lid of the case, his eyes scanning through the contents to confirm their authenticity. A wide grin formed on his lips.

"At long last," he murmured.

"You see, both coins are there. Now, let Ruth go," Lang demanded.

"I'll let her go all right, but before I do that, I have one last thing to do. I never said anything about sparing you, old friend. Goodbye, Mr. Dalton Lang," Guo said, aiming his Glock downward at Lang's head.

Lang's instincts kicked in like a predator in the wild, diving for cover behind the makeshift barricade of chairs and tables stacked against the wall before Guo could even pull the trigger. Once out of harm's way, Lang retrieved a hammerless Smith & Wesson revolver hidden under his hat. The compact gun felt comfortable in his grip as he aimed it at the gangsters in the middle of the room. He squeezed off three rapid rounds, each one finding its mark with deadly accuracy. All three men fell to the floor before they could reach for their weapons.

Attempting to flee the scene, Albert Barris rushed to the stairwell, but his bid for escape was halted by a searing bullet that ripped through his calf. He yelped in pain as he fell, striking his head on the steps, knocking himself unconscious.

After seeing the detective fall, Lang's eyes locked onto the balcony. Guo was using Patrick as cover, but Patrick went down and toppled over the railing with a single shot. Lang then shifted his aim to Guo, his finger tensed on the trigger. Yet he was unable to fire, as Guo had cunningly positioned himself behind Ruth, using her as a human shield.

Guo called out to Lang in a booming voice, "Toss your weapon aside and come out, or the girl gets it."

"Have you noticed that none of your *xià di* have come to your aid?" Lang responded. "It's because they're being taken out by my team. So, it's you who needs to drop your weapon and let the girl go. It's over Jianlian."

With a sinister smile, Guo seized Ruth around her waist.

"What are you doing?" Ruth bellowed. "Let me go."

"No. Don't do it, Jianlian," Lang shouted desperately.

"This is your fault," Guo said, lifting Ruth over the railing and releasing her.

Time seemed to slow as Lang watched Ruth fall, her scream abruptly silenced by the harsh impact of her body hitting the floor. Abandoning all caution, Lang launched himself from his hiding spot, his gun spitting its last round as he rushed to Ruth's side. The bullet failed to find its mark for Guo had already vanished, leaving the balcony devoid of people.

Resisting the urge to pursue him, Lang crouched by Ruth's side. She lay on the floor; thankfully, there was no blood. With his free hand, he checked her pulse. Relief flooded through him when he felt a faint beat at his fingertips.

"Ruth, talk to me. Are you all right?" he asked, gently cradling her limp body in his arms.

There was no response.

He hastily retrieved his smartphone and dialed 911.

When he heard the operator pick up, he spoke fast and clear.

"A young girl has had a fall. She's unconscious. Send an ambulance right away to the Chop Suey Café in Chinatown, downtown Los Angeles."

His attention was drawn to the sound of the front door bursting open. Melvin Patterson, with gun in hand, rushed into the room, his expression grim, as he surveyed the scene before him.

"Oh man, what happened?" he asked.

"What the hell are you doing here?" Lang asked, genuinely surprised at seeing the FBI agent.

"I tailed you from the airport," Patterson replied, his eyes scanning the room for any sign of danger. "And then all hell started breaking loose outside."

"She was pushed from the balcony," Lang explained, his voice heavy with emotion. "I called 911. Stay with her, please."

Patterson nodded. "Of course."

"Can I borrow your gun? I'm all out of bullets," Lang said.

Patterson hesitated for a quick moment, then flipped the handle of his Glock toward Lang.

Lang gently lowered Ruth to the floor and quickly made his way to the stairway, Patterson's handgun gripped tightly in his hand. Stepping over the unconscious body of Barris, he raced up the stairs, prepared to shoot anything or anyone in sight.

As he had expected, the balcony was empty. An open window across the floor let the night breeze into the room, fluttering a thin, white curtain in its wake. From the top of the stairwell, Lang noticed Koga and Cosworth huddled next to Ruth and Patterson.

"How is she?" Koga asked.

"She's alive but unconscious," Patterson answered.

"Guo Jianlian got away with the coins," Lang said as he ran down the stairs.

"Guo?" Patterson and Koga responded, their voices sounding in unison.

Their conversation was interrupted when Yuna stepped through the front door.

"Eight men neutralized, and the rest ran off. It's all clear outside," she said.

"The hell it is," Patterson snapped. "The place is going to be swarming with cops and Feds. You all need to get the hell out of here now."

"Yuna, can you stay with Ruth until the ambulance arrives?" Lang asked.

It was more of a directive than a request.

She nodded. "Where are you going?"

"This must end once and for all. Jianlian is alive. It turns out that he's the secret head of the Blue Dragons. He staged his own death, and now, he's out to sell the coins, but to whom, I don't know yet. I'll try to retrace his steps from the window upstairs. Can you two scour the streets?"

"Roger that," Koga responded.

He and Cosworth quickly exited the restaurant.

Lang pointed to Detective Barris lying face first at the base of the stairs and said, "Melvin, make sure this scumbag is properly detained. He's LAPD, and he's as rotten as hell."

"You got it, boss," Patterson replied. "Now go get that slimy sucker."

After returning Patterson's gun, Lang pried a beat-up Beretta 92 from the lifeless grip of one of the gangsters—it was one of his favorite pieces back in the day. He hurriedly ascended the stairs, and upon reaching the balcony, went to the window, squeezing his body through its narrow frame.

CHAPTER 34

Guo Jianlian clutched the briefcase housing the two Coins of Wei close to his chest, as he descended from the roof of Chop Suey Restaurant by ladder. With all three pieces now in his possession, his mission boiled down to delivering the goods to his buyers. He regretted pulling the trigger on Yan, who'd been a loyal soldier since he assumed control of the Blue Dragons, but it was something that needed to be done. As for what he did to the girl, he felt no remorse. Throughout history, he believed that the demise of insignificant individuals paved the path for truly great men.

Calculating his next move, Guo hurried toward his getaway car, a gray Tesla Model Y nestled at the alley's edge, when he detected a lone figure standing behind his electric vehicle.

"Going somewhere?" the man asked, stepping under a dim overhead light.

Guo's tension eased upon recognizing the man's bearded face. It was Grant Bricklin, his prize asset who disclosed to him the location of Dalton Lang, aka Hu Qiang.

"It's you, Sato," Guo said. "I thought you were laying low at the office."

The fifty-something Caucasian man ambled toward Guo, a pronounced limp marking his stride. "Let's stop with the ridiculous names, Deputy Director. No need for role playing anymore. I take it the Phantom Assassin is dead?"

Opening the door to the Tesla, Guo hesitated before replying. "Not exactly. He'll be coming for us, so we must hurry. There's a plane waiting for me at Torrance Airport. The sooner I leave this country, the better."

"But you were supposed to kill him," Bricklin said. "I get his location, and you eliminate him. That was our deal."

"All in good time. For now, we have the coins. That's what's important."

Before Guo could slip into the driver's seat of the SUV, Bricklin had withdrawn a compact pistol from his pocket, a suppressor attached to the end of its barrel. He pointed it directly at the MSS deputy director.

"What do you think you're doing? Put that thing away," Guo said.

"I made a deal with the MSS, not you, and instead of killing Lang, like you said you would, you sent him on your personal wild goose chase for those damned coins. You didn't hold up your end of the bargain."

Showing no concern for the gun pointed at him, Guo replied calmly, "When you decided to work for us—when was that, five years ago?—I wanted nothing more than to hunt down Hu Qiang. But when this opportunity presented itself, everything changed. You should be grateful that I decided to include you in my endeavors. You will be rich beyond belief."

"I never signed up to be part of a Chinese criminal organization. I only wanted Lang dead," Bricklin countered.

"Regardless, you'll receive more money than you can ever have imagined."

"It's not about the money," Bricklin maintained, hitching up his pants to reveal a metal ankle and foot. "After my injury, they stuck me behind a desk, passed me over for promotion more times than I can count. Then, my marriage fell apart, and I lost custody of my kids. The bastard ruined my life, and the only thing I have left is to get him back for what he did."

"If you shoot me here, you'll walk away empty-handed, and the entire Blue Dragon network will come for you. Then, you'll never get your wish. Do the right thing here, Grant."

Bricklin slowly uncocked the hammer of his gun and lowered it to his side. "I've stopped doing the right thing ever since that night in Hong Kong. I better be paid good, pal."

Letting out a sigh, Guo tossed the briefcase into the rear compartment of his car. "I'll need you to hold down the fort here. Make sure our men keep a low profile until the money is transferred to our account. I've told them that you're in charge here for the time being."

Bricklin quietly turned and melted into the shadows, his form vanishing into the recesses of the alley.

It's always about the money, Guo thought.

He jumped into his Tesla, the electric hum of the engine barely a whisper as he sped away, leaving the dark alley and Los Angeles behind.

CHAPTER 35

From the roof of the restaurant, Dalton Lang scanned the alleyway that bled out onto North Hill Street. He made his way to the edge of the roof, where he discovered a ladder that dropped along the side of the building. Quickly, he climbed down, searching for any sign of Guo Jianlian.

Upon reaching the ground, he meticulously checked three nearby dumpsters, but there was no sign of him. Then, from the corner of his vision, he noticed a dry patch of concrete on the damp ground, its size suggesting that it was left there by a car.

He searched the area for the briefcase, but it was nowhere to be found. He ran out of the alleyway and hurried to his R34 Skyline GT-R, jumping into the driver's seat and firing up its powerplant. With no clear lead on the getaway vehicle or its direction, he knew the odds of finding Guo was slim. Yet, he couldn't sit idly by. He had no choice but to rely on Lady Luck to intervene—perhaps spot him before he jumped on the freeway. But just as he pushed the shifter into first gear, his phone rang. Peering down at the screen, he saw Raja Singh's name.

"Raj, talk to me," Lang answered.

"I've got the entire gang on the line," Singh said. "I found the Kamita Empire."

"Where is it?" Lang asked excitedly.

"In Moscow, sitting in a warehouse with a bunch of new Chinese EVs that were just shipped there."

"Should've figured the Russians would be involved," Lang said.

Entering the conversation was Paul Verdy: "Max just told us about Guo Jianlian. We're pretty sure that he's planning on selling Dr. Linghu's technology to the Russians. He seems to have hid the car inside a shipment of EVs from the Yongcheng Car Corporation. He's probably on his way now to deliver the package to finalize the deal."

Then, Agent Mitch Snowhill's voice broke in: "The important thing is that we cannot allow the Russians to get their hands on those coins. Despite the new regime there, Russia is still very much an adversary, and we can't risk them controlling the world's energy supply. I repeat, they can't be allowed to obtain the coins."

"But they already have the car. Didn't Raj just say it's currently in Moscow?" Lang said.

"It wouldn't be sitting in a Yongcheng warehouse if the car was in the Kremlin's possession. It's being hidden there by Guo Jianlian," Snowhill explained. "And it doesn't seem like the Chinese government has the slightest clue of what's going on either, according to our sources in Beijing. Guo apparently didn't share intel with his MSS colleagues. Therefore, we're still in the game, and speed is paramount."

"Then, why don't you go get them yourself," Lang said.

"You know full well that we can't perform any kind of operation like that inside of Russia," Snowhill said.

"Send in Argon, or another PMC. That's what they're there for, aren't they? Plausible deniability in case something goes wrong?"

Koga interjected, "I had a slight run-in with an FSB agent a few weeks back in Beijing. She knows all about me, so I'm afraid I would compromise any operation in the country."

"Cosworth is still too new to handle a mission like this," Verdy added. "And our remaining operatives are all currently working other assignments."

A long silence ensued.

"Okay, I'll go," Lang finally blurted with a sigh. "That's where this conversation was heading, right?"

"You're doing this country a tremendous service," Snowhill said.

"Make sure to tell your boss Nigel that if I pull this off, he's going to owe me big time."

Singh's voice returned to the conversation. "There's one more thing, guys. We—the CIA scientists and I—did a molecular analysis of the gold used for the Dragon Coin, and I just received the results. It originated in the Shandong Province."

"There's nothing unusual about that," Lang noted. "That place has been a gold-mining site for as long as I can remember."

"That's not the interesting part," Singh said. "Although the gold is nearly pure, we found tiny traces of various foreign elements inside —zinc, mercury, arsenic, and some plant DNA that we can't yet match, which is really weird."

"And the point is?" Lang pressed impatiently.

"The mercury possesses the same quality as the one found inside the first emperor of China's tomb, the one that was sealed more than two thousand years ago. And the gold mined at Shandong today no longer has any traces of this mercury."

"What are you implying, Raj?" Verdy asked.

"I'm implying," Singh said with a brief pause, "that these Coins of Wei are most likely the real deal."

ACT FOUR

The Device

秘審裝置

CHAPTER 36

Moscow, Present Day

DALTON LANG SETTLED into the plush leather seat of a private jet for the second time in as many days. Argon Securities was happy to arrange for him to hop back onto the same aircraft that had flown him from Osaka's Kansai International to Santa Monica Airport only a few hours before. The jet had been refueled immediately upon landing and a fresh crew called in, ensuring a swift departure once Lang stepped on board.

Lang welcomed the fifteen-hour commute as a chance to catch up on some much-needed shuteye, for he hardly had a wink since leaving Osaka. The flight was smooth, allowing the Gulfstream G6 to complete the six-thousand-mile journey without a refueling stop. It was 0100 local time when the plane touched down at Vnukovo International Airport. Soft flakes of snow fluttered from the night sky as he stepped off the plane, an Oakley backpack slung over his shoulder and a small roll-on suitcase at his side. With a Chinese passport belonging to a businessman named Chu Shien—a cover provided by the CIA—he quickly got through customs. After making his way out of the airport, he immediately hopped onto a shuttle bound for the local parking garage.

Stepping outside, he was embraced by the hard bite of the frigid Moscow winter, prompting him to don his North Face snow jacket. After navigating his way to the rooftop of the four-story concrete structure, his gaze settled on a black Mercedes-Benz C200 parked in the northwest corner of the lot, precisely where Snowhill had said it would be.

Lang found the key to the car taped to the inside of the front suspension. He stowed his personal suitcase in the trunk, tossed his backpack onto the front passenger seat, and slid his body into the C-Class' driver's seat. The cabin was still warm, indicating that the car had been left there a short time ago. His hands instinctively reached for the glove box, where he discovered a portable police light and siren neatly tucked away among the car's registration documents. Attached to it was a note: "Mobsters use this all the time to break traffic laws and avoid being pulled over. The local police hesitate to stop them out of fear it could be a legitimate government vehicle. So, use it at your own discretion."

With help from Snowhill, CIA agents headquartered at the U.S. Embassy ensured the vehicle was equipped with what they deemed as "the essentials;" however, they were keen to point out that their assistance would extend no further. They gave strict instructions for Lang to steer clear of the embassy and make no contact with any Americans in the country.

Snowhill told him earlier on the phone, "The embassy's constantly under surveillance by the FSB. Stay away unless you want a tail for the entirety of your trip."

Lang then reached beneath the passenger seat, where he found a large envelope. Inside were several injection pens filled with Argon's knockout drug and a compact Sig Sauer P38 automatic pistol. He held it lightly, its mass feeling reassuring in his palm. *The essentials,* he said to himself.

Stowing the pistol in the inner pocket of his jacket, he fired up the C-Class's engine and punched in the address of Yongcheng Car Company's warehouse into the navigation system. Once it calculated the driving instructions, he sped out of the parking garage and onto Moscow's Ring Road, heading north to the industrial city of Vimski. It was imperative that he get there before Guo Jianlian.

Rush hour traffic was still a few hours away, so he breezed into the city in less than thirty minutes—without the need of the police light. It was his inaugural visit to the city, and from what he could gather, it lacked the charisma one might expect from a Russian town so close to the capital. Under the cloak of night, Vimski presented itself as an unassuming residential and industrial hub, devoid of the grandeur of historic landmarks or the allure of tourist hotspots. Following the guidance of the navigation system, Lang steered toward the northeast quadrant of the city, where he found a large sign that displayed the characters: 雍城汽車公司.

Painted in a dull shade of yellowish beige, the warehouse was smaller than Lang had anticipated. Nestled at the eastern edge of the city, it was one of several warehouses in the area belonging to foreign car manufacturers. In the ever-evolving landscape of Russia's car industry, the Chinese had emerged as a formidable presence, their combination of competitive pricing and good quality solidifying their dominance in the country.

Lang brought his Mercedes-Benz to a halt roughly a hundred yards away from the front gate of the property. He retrieved a DSLR camera from his backpack and surveilled the compound. Encircled by a towering chain-link fence, the facility boasted a single sliding gate for entry and exit. A lone guard with dirty blond hair and pasty skin sat bored at a wooden sentry station, while a duet of surveillance cameras recorded every visitor who passed through the gate. Otherwise, the overall security of the facility was surprisingly light.

Reaching into his backpack, Lang's fingers grazed past a pile of scattered papers and a jumble of gadgets before he pulled out a radio earpiece, which he pressed into his ear. Next came the compact handheld satellite transceiver, which he flicked on with his thumb.

"Testing, one, two," he said into the mic. "Can anyone hear me?"

"Raj here," sounded Singh's voice, loud and clear from nearly five thousand miles away.

"I'm in position," reported Lang. "Just waiting for the package to show up. I noticed a couple of surveillance cameras. Can you take them out?"

"Maybe, but it'll take a few minutes," Singh replied.

"By the way, any change in Ruth's condition?" Lang asked.

"Nothing yet," Singh answered. "Last we heard, she was out of surgery, but still in a coma."

"Got it. Thanks," Lang said.

In an instant, he removed all thoughts of Ruth from his mind and focused his attention back on the perimeter. His gaze landed on a trio of Audi Q7s approaching the warehouse gate on the main road. When they reached the sentry station, all three vehicles came to a hard stop.

"They're here," Lang said, taking a closer look with the DSLR camera.

Zooming in on the driver of the lead SUV, his gaze locked onto an Asian gentleman in his mid-thirties manning the steering wheel. Occupying the rear seat was Guo Jianlian. The mere sight of him sent a wave of hatred surging through his veins, the overload of emotion nearly consuming him. He took a deep breath, forcing himself to calm his nerves.

With a firm press of his index finger, he activated the shutter of his camera, capturing the face of every man in the three vehicles. The images were automatically forwarded to Singh.

"I just sent you a few headshots. See if you can identify them," he said.

"Roger that," Singh responded.

As Lang watched, the uniformed sentry at the gate approached the lead Q7, prompting the Chinese driver to roll down his window.

In moments, their conversation escalated into a flurry of gestures and words. Then, the driver produced a pistol. The gunshot was silent. The only evidence of it was a quick flash of orange from the end of a suppressed barrel.

As the security guard fell to the snow-covered ground, two figures jumped out of the second Q7 and hurried to the chain-link gate. With a synchronized effort, they pulled on the heavy metal door, their muscles straining against the resistance as they forced it open, granting passage to two of the three Audis; one of them remained behind.

"I'll be radio silent for a bit," Lang said softly into the mic.

"Roger that," replied Singh. "Be careful."

Quietly, Lang stepped out of the C200, slipped the backpack on, and closed the car door softly behind him. Beneath the layers of his thick jacket, the firmness of the Sig Sauer pressing against his side provided the reassuring comfort of an old friend. As he neared the warehouse, he headed directly for the Q7 that remained at the gate. His gaze narrowed as he observed its two occupants, both unmistakably Asian, exit the vehicle and drag the sentry's lifeless body out of sight. Once their task was finished, they remained outside, their presence a deterrent for any unwelcome visitor that dared to encroach upon their territory.

Taking a deep breath, Lang walked up to them with a smile on his face.

"Ni hǎao," he greeted in Mandarin. "Are you from the head office? I keep telling you guys everything is fine here."

His sudden presence elicited a moment of confusion between the two gangsters. It gave Lang all the time he needed. In a single motion, he whipped out his firearm, unleashing two precise rounds, each bullet striking the chests of the men with lethal accuracy. They collapsed onto the snow, their expressions frozen in shock as their bodies succumbed to the force of the impact. Lang moved quickly, prying an OTs-27 Berdysh pistol from the lifeless grip of one of the men. He checked the magazine. It held eight rounds. The Berdysh wasn't his favorite sidearm, not by a longshot, but in this particular circumstance, it would do.

As he made his way to the warehouse building, Dalton Lang felt a transformation inside of him taking place, a familiar cloak of darkness that he hadn't felt in a long time...and it felt good. A persona he had long buried—one that had been attempting to resurface for ten long years—had been reawakened. The prodigious killer known as the Phantom Assassin was back.

CHAPTER 37

Dalton Lang kept his head down. He exhaled a sigh of relief when he noticed the gangsters had already shot out the security cameras fixed to the warehouse's weathered walls. Under the cover of darkness, he shuffled past the other two black Audi Q7s parked near the side door of the warehouse, his combat boots carving deep imprints in the freshly fallen snow. A bullet-shattered lock dangled from its latch, granting Lang unobstructed access into the building. Silently, with the Berdysh at the ready, he stepped inside.

Under rows of fluorescent lights slept a labyrinth of compact EVs, each car providing an ideal cover for an intruder stalking his prey. The first gangster never saw him coming, as Lang slipped behind him, his hand wrapping around his mouth before he could even let out a cry. With a hard, surehanded twist, he snapped the gangster's neck, sending his body crumpling to the ground with a muted thud.

"Haoyu?" one of his colleagues called out, but Lang was already on the move. He emerged behind the second man like a ghost, his pistol gripped and ready to make a lethal statement. With a single bullet, he took down his target, the thud of the body hitting the ground echoing through the warehouse.

The loud crack of the gunshot caused the remaining gangsters to spin around in confusion. Their panic was evident, as they fired blindly into the rows of parked cars, sending bullets into their metal bodywork, shattering several windows in the process. Using the chaos to his advantage, Lang shifted from the cover of one car to another, picking off the remaining gangsters with deadly precision.

Three shots fired, three men down.

Finally, only Guo Jianlian remained. He wore a mask of desperation as he held his handgun with a trembling grip.

"Who are you?" he called out to his unseen enemy. "What do you want?"

With the barrel of his firearm leveled unwaveringly at Guo's forehead, Lang revealed his position, partially emerging from the protective cover of a compact Yongcheng EV.

"I've come from the depths of hell to punish you, Jianlian," he announced.

That's impossible," Guo uttered when he saw Lang's partially hidden face. "How can this be?"

In a state of panic, Guo unleashed a gunshot at Lang. Amid the "phut" of the muzzled shot, the bullet whizzed well over Lang's head, missing him by several inches.

A surge of raw rage swept through Lang as he locked eyes with Guo, each detail of his face a vivid reminder of the unforgivable wrongs he'd done. Ignoring any concern for his own safety, Lang advanced with reckless resolve, his gun trained steadily on his target.

Guo sent another bullet Lang's way, this one whizzing past his shoulder, but Lang didn't flinch. With a cold, steady hand, he pulled the trigger twice, sending a pair of bullets into each of Guo's shoulders. They were followed by two more shots that tore through Guo's thighs, dropping him to his knees. Lang walked up to him and kicked him in the chest, knocking him onto his back.

"Goodbye, Jialian," Lang said, looking into Guo's terrified eyes. "You should've known better than to start a war with me."

"Have mercy, Hu Qiang. I can make you rich, please..."

The Berdysh spoke for the last time, its final bullet blasting Guo's head.

When Lang had killed before, it was never personal, and it never brought him any pleasure. It was always an order from a superior, just another part of the job. But this time, it was different. As he gazed upon Guo's lifeless body, a fleeting sensation of relief washed over him. Avenging Eva brought a sense of closure, and he firmly believed he had eradicated a true evil from the world. Without sparing another thought for the scoundrel, Lang quickly moved toward the briefcase, his mission was far from over. He unlatched it, confirming its contents—the Coins of Wei sparkled within. Satisfied, he turned his attention to the rear of the warehouse, where the conspicuous presence of the Kamita Empire awaited.

He switched on the communication device in his pocket.

"Raj, get Agent Snowhill and General Verdy on the line. I'm going to the car now," he said.

The time had finally come to find out the secrets it held.

CHAPTER 38

Dalton Lang was fairly confident that the gunshots fired inside the warehouse had gone unnoticed, thanks to the facility's secluded location. Yet, stealing a quick glance at his Hublot timepiece, he realized that the early shift would soon be arriving to begin their workday, and the first thing they would notice would be a dead guard and two shot-up gangsters at the front gate. According to his calculations, he had perhaps a half hour before local law enforcement arrived. The clock was ticking.

Among the sea of compact vehicles packed tightly into neat rows inside the warehouse, the Kamita Empire's imposing size made it easy to locate. Despite its billing as a high-end luxury sedan, the Empire was in reality a crossover—a blend of an SUV and a sedan. It was powered by a solid-state battery that operated four electric motors, one at each wheel—truly a car ahead of its time. It only lasted two years in the marketplace, so seeing one in the flesh was rare. The Empire's exterior was characterized by a retro body style, one inspired by luxury vehicles from the 1920s and 1930s. Its bulging front fenders mimicked those of a Delahaye Roadster, and its elongated long hood and squared-off roofline gave it the silhouette of an elevated station wagon.

With the briefcase containing the coins clutched firmly in hand, Lang approached the luxury car, his mind already concocting plans to gain entry. The windows of the Empire were tinted, making it difficult to peer into the cabin under the dim warehouse lights. Anticipating the need to shatter a window, he tentatively grasped the door handle, and to his surprise, the door opened with a soft click. Peering into the spacious cabin, he saw the key fob nestled innocuously in the cup holder.

Lang delved into his backpack and extracted a laptop and cable, plugging the latter into a data port nestled beneath the Empire's steering wheel. A series of swift keystrokes launched Singh's hacking program, which immediately displayed the car's computer system on his laptop screen. To his dismay, he noticed nothing out of the ordinary, only the standard-issue software that came with the vehicle.

"I'm not seeing any special folder or files in this thing, Raj," Lang said.

"I'm getting what you're seeing on my monitor here," Singh responded, "and I agree. All standard stuff. Is there any kind of coin holder or coin slot in the car? The coins are supposed to act as some sort of key, remember? They may unlock a hidden drive or something."

Lang examined the dashboard for receptacles large enough to hold the three coins but saw nothing. He scanned the center console, but again, nothing. It was only when he directed his gaze aft that he made a startling discovery—the rear seats had been removed, replaced by a massive gray box crafted from dull metal. It dominated the entire rear section of the vehicle.

Well, what do we have here?

"Did you find anything?" Singh asked.

"I'll get back to you," Lang said, muting his mic.

He walked to the rear of the Empire and opened its large hatch-back-style door. The metal box filled the entire cargo compartment.

His eye caught sight of three circular holders attached to the top edge of the box.

With extra care, he opened the briefcase and removed the coins. He then inserted them into the three slots, but nothing happened. Undeterred, he experimented with different combinations, and when he placed the Dragon Coin in the first receptacle, the Monkey Coin in the middle, and the Tiger Coin into the far-right receptacle, a sudden transformation occurred. The gemstones embedded in the coins—the eyes of the animals—emitted a faint glow, while the box itself reverberated with a powerful hum.

The intensity of the sound escalated, reaching a crescendo that prompted Lang to instinctively take a step back, fearing he had unwittingly triggered some sort of explosive device, but there was no explosion.

He unmuted his mic.

"Raj, I found a huge metal box in the back of the car," he said. "It had three places for the coins. When I placed them inside, they triggered something, but I don't know what."

Singh responded immediately. "Judging by what I can see on the computer, the car battery seems to be charging now. Did you connect the Empire to an outlet?"

"Negative. There are no outlets around here and..." Lang's voice trailed off as a realization struck him, a notion so improbable that it defied explanation.

It can't be.

Lang carefully reexamined the metal box in the back of the Empire, his thoughts swirling with abstract theories and possibilities. He visually scanned its surface for any sign of entry—a door, a latch, anything that might offer a glimpse into what was inside. As his fingers traced its edge, he detected a subtle indentation along its side. With a firm tug, he pulled on a latch, causing the front panel to glide open with a soft hiss. Peering inside, he was met with the unexpected sight of a central core surrounded by an intricate array of turbines, heat exchangers, and generators. Each component hummed with energy.

Removing the physical key from the Mercedes-Benz fob, Lang scratched the surface of the metal box. The mark it left behind indicated that the box was made of a soft metal, likely lead. He sealed the door and raced to the front of the vehicle. He jumped into the driver's seat and powered up the Empire, fixing his attention on the display of his laptop screen. As the vehicle turned on, a variety of gauges and graphs materialized, each monitoring the intricacies of the mysterious device's operation. Words including temperature, pressure, radiation levels, and neutron flux danced across the screen, but it was a graph labeled "Spectrometer" that caught his eye. He marveled at it as it traced the path of isotopes.

"I can't believe it," Lang murmured.

"Whoa," exclaimed Singh. "All kinds of weird stuff just popped up on my screen. What are all these graphs and gauges?"

"As you suggested, Raj, the coins unlocked some type of hidden program in the car's computer, but what you're seeing are monitoring systems. I don't think we'll find any hard data in the drive."

"What are these things monitoring?" Singh asked.

"As impossible as this might sound, I think Professor Linghu succeeded in building a cold nuclear fusion reactor, and it's inside this box."

CHAPTER 39

As Dalton Lang spoke the words, he still struggled to comprehend their meaning. Yet, despite his disbelief, every shred of evidence seemed to lead to the undeniable conclusion that the bulky contraption sitting in the Kamita Empire's rear cargo compartment was a cold nuclear fusion device, or at least a working prototype of one. Having spent years lecturing on radar technology at MIT, he possessed a rudimentary understanding of nuclear fusion, and he knew enough that isotopes were necessary for fusion reactions to occur at lower temperatures.

"I think that Professor Linghu achieved the impossible," Lang said.

"Are you sure?" Singh asked through the earpiece. "Weren't you the one who said that cold nuclear fusion was a pipe dream?"

"I did, and I'm still having difficulty believing it. For cold nuclear fusion to work, one would need highly controlled electromagnetic fields to induce the reactions. That means designing electromagnetic systems that can manipulate and compress isotopes within a confined space," Lang explained excitedly. "If the gauges and graphs on my computer screen are to be believed, this contraption is doing just that.

And the power needed to operate these systems is high, but they're being provided by the car's batteries. Another factor is that the container isn't made from any old steel but lead, which is resistant to radiation, a possible byproduct of nuclear fusion, hot or cold."

"Sorry, but the only part I understood was that the box is made of lead," Singh admitted. "Mitch and Paul are on the line now."

Snowhill's voice broke in. "Dalton, if what you're saying is true, you need to get the hell out of there and deliver that car to us."

"How do you suggest I do that? I'm in the middle of Moscow, for God's sake."

"Does the car drive? Is it operational?" asked Snowhill.

Lang nudged the shifter on the central console into the "D" position and eased his foot off the brake pedal. The car lurched forward.

"Yeah, it drives."

"Go to the U.S. embassy," Snowhill blurted with urgency. "It's off the main highway. Once inside, the Russians will be helpless to do anything."

Paul Verdy's deep voice suddenly sounded in the earpiece. "I wouldn't say helpless. They can surround the embassy and not let anything in or out. They can also make up some excuse to raid the building. You'll need a backup plan."

"What do you suggest, general?" Snowhill asked.

"Dalton, if you're compromised, head to Latvia," Verdy said. "We're on good terms with the Latvian government—they're actually members of NATO, meaning we can go into and out of the country freely. There's a city called Terehova on the Russia-Latvia border. Get to the checkpoint, and we'll have a team to transport you and the car back to the States."

Lang punched in Terehova into the navigation app on his phone.

"It says here that it's about 400 miles away. That means at least five hours on the road. A lot can go wrong in five hours," he said.

"That's why you need to try the embassy first," Snowhill said. "The Russians are still clueless about the device, so they won't be on the lookout for the car. It should be a cakewalk."

"Roger that, I'll..." Lang stopped his sentence when he heard the faint sound of a distant siren.

Shit.

"Gotta go, Lang out," he said and cut the feed.

Stepping out of the car, he hurried toward the large rollup door guarding the warehouse's entrance. With the press of a green button, he sent the door ascending with a mechanical hum. Once it was fully open, he noticed a small cluster of people huddled outside near the main gate, their excited expressions a confirmation to what they had discovered: three dead men, shot at pointblank range.

With added urgency, Lang retraced his steps to the Empire and jumped into the driver's seat. Powering it up, he guided it through a row of EVs until he reached the open doorway. An elderly woman standing among the small crowd let out a sharp cry in Russian when she noticed the vehicle.

Keeping his head low and his face hidden, Lang pressed down on the accelerator, shooting the Empire out of the building toward the open gate and the people. As the crowd dispersed, he squeezed through a small gap between the fleeing bystanders and the open gate, narrowly missing the parked Audi Q7.

More shouts in Russian erupted as a few of the people pointed accusing fingers at the fleeing vehicle. Lang allowed his eyes to peek into the rearview mirror—some of them chased his vehicle on foot, while others held out their smartphones, digitally capturing the unfolding drama.

As the whir of the sirens closed in, a duet of police cars appeared on the far side of the road, their flashing blue and red lights glowing in the muted light of dawn. Lang veered sharply onto the first side street he encountered, hoping the police cars would simply continue to the crime scene, which they were undoubtedly head for.

No such luck.

Lang watched in grim resignation as the flashing lights followed his every turn.

In the snap of a finger, Lang's world had been upended. What was meant to be a "cakewalk" had become a harrowing nightmare. His car was now a beacon in a grisly homicide incident, of which he was the prime suspect. Heading to the embassy now was out of the question as every cop in the greater Moscow area would be on the lookout for his very distinguishable vehicle. As for Latvia, the prospect of reaching the border grew increasingly remote—with only one main highway to Terehova, a single roadblock would signal the end of his escape.

Lang considered his options: He needed to disappear until the heat subsided, preferably somewhere invisible to aircraft. Only then could he covertly head to Latvia or Estonia, but he knew that the odds of even getting close to those safe havens were slim at best. But first, he needed to ditch the cars pursuing him.

While speeding through a maze of multistory office buildings and apartment complexes near Vimski's city center, he surveyed the surrounding area on his navigation app. There, outside of the urban sprawl, he found what he was searching for—a way to rid himself of the growing contingent of police vehicles, which had since multiplied to four. With a deft turn of the steering wheel, he followed the signs that led to the Moscow Canal.

CHAPTER 40

Despite its hefty weight of nearly five thousand pounds, the Kamita Empire's agility and speed defied expectations. Zooming through the snow-covered streets of Vimski, Dalton Lang skillfully maneuvered the large crossover through the heart of the city, running every red light he came across.

According to his calculations, he estimated a fifteen-minute window before the inevitable arrival of air support. Keeping clear of the main highways was crucial—he didn't want reinforcements from neighboring cities joining the chase. The scenery soon shifted from an urban sprawl to one marked by a forest, when he came upon a road that ran alongside the Moscow Canal. Lang continued following it until he spotted his target: a narrow access road that led directly to the canal edge.

Disregarding the signs that indicated motor vehicles were not to proceed any further, Lang floored the throttle pedal, guiding the all-wheel-drive Empire onto a narrow, snowy path. He knew of the inherent risk of driving a large, heavy vehicle onto the ice, with no guarantee that it could bear its weight, but he had once driven on a frozen lake in China where the temperatures were less frigid than those in Moscow, so he was confident that the ice would hold.

As the Empire's Yokohama Geolander tires touched upon the canal's icy surface, the vehicle's traction-control system immediately kicked in, minimizing wheelspin and keeping the vehicle hurtling forward. Although the pace of his vehicle slowed dramatically, Lang was careful to maintain a speed above 30 km/h—any less and he ran the risk of falling through the ice. A glance in his rearview mirror revealed that the police cars had already caught up. The drivers of the standard-issue Ford Focuses seemed more than eager to catch the Empire, speeding recklessly onto the icy canal in hot pursuit.

A smile formed on Dalton's face. This was exactly what he had hoped. He pushed his large crossover vehicle to its limits, navigating the slick ice with precision and finesse. Deliberately breaking the rear tires loose with a sudden flick of the steering wheel, he initiated a controlled oversteer slide, the rear section of the vehicle swinging out in a graceful arc as he negotiated a tight turn.

Looking in the rearview mirror, he noticed that the police's front-wheel-drive cars struggled to maintain their grip on the icy surface, their tires slipping and sliding as they fought against the laws of inertia. Their cars were understeering—meaning, they kept going straight although the front tires were positioned to turn—as the drivers frantically wrestled with their respective steering wheels in a desperate bid to stay on course.

Slowing the Empire, Lang allowed one of the police cars to close in on his flank, letting it draw level with his driver-side door. As it aligned with his vehicle, he took out his Sig and fired out the window, the sharp crack of the gunshot echoing across the frozen landscape. The bullet found its mark, tearing through the police car's front tire. With a hiss of escaping air, the silver-colored Focus fishtailed wildly, its driver unable to regain control, until it ultimately slammed into a snow-covered embankment, the impact sending a cascade of powder into the air.

Back on the throttle, Lang veered the Empire sharply to the right before wrenching the wheel to the left—what's known in drifting as a "feint." His foot delicately tapped the brake pedal, prompting the vehicle to respond with a graceful pirouette, executing a flawless 180-degree turn. Once his vehicle was facing the opposite direction, Lang stomped the accelerator pedal once again, transforming the large crossover into a colossal juggernaut of destruction, speeding in the direction of the three remaining police cars.

The air rang with a defiant crunch as the front end of the Empire rammed into the side of one police cruiser, sending it careening into the path of another. The bone-jarring impact snapped the front suspension arm of the first police car like a twig, rendering it immediately useless, while the other car's engine erupted into chaos, billowing smoke and steam from its mangled hood. The two vehicles spun wildly on the slick surface.

As the frosty mist settled, Lang surveyed the scene with a steely gaze.

Three down, one to go.

With another burst of speed, he closed in on the last remaining police car, his pistol at the ready. But before he could act, the driver of the Focus veered, his car making a wide arc and heading directly toward him. It was as if the officer intended to mirror Lang's own tactics, attempting to ram his car into the side of the Empire. However, Lang executed a graceful four-wheel drift, sending his crossover gliding effortlessly across the frozen lake like a ballerina with wheels.

The Ford Focus missed its target by several feet, flying past the Empire in a blur. Now, it was Lang in hot pursuit.

Changing tactics, the driver of the police car made a desperate dash for the far embankment, perhaps to bait Lang back to land.

Not going to happen.

Lang maneuvered the Empire close to the Focus' rear bumper until it was a mere inches away. Gunning the throttle once more, the tread of the Empire's Yokohama Geolanders took a firm bite of the ice, allowing the crossover to surge forward and bury its nose into the back of the Focus. As the rear end of the police car swung around, the Ford spun wildly out of control until it came to a slow stop. Upon which, Lang retrieved his pistol and unleashed a single bullet that tore through the police cruiser's front tire. He discharged an extra round into the front grille, just for good measure.

All four cars, down and out.

With a satisfying smile, Lang swung his crossover around and headed north on the canal. As he navigated the icy terrain, his eyes scanned the landscape for a path to solid ground. Spotting a boat ramp about a half mile away, he guided his trusty vehicle to it, passing under the bridge of a main highway, toward the promise of land that offered a glimmer of hope and freedom.

CHAPTER 41

The chime of a smartphone disrupted the stillness inside the quaint mustard-colored building on Lubyanka Square, home to a section of Russia's formidable intelligence agency, the Federal Security Service, or the FSB. Dressed in a sleek, dark brown business suit, the fabric hugging her athletic figure, Elena Valentinovna Natase answered the call immediately. With intense green eyes and full ruby lips pursed in anticipation, she expected to hear the voice of her prized asset, the Deputy Director of the MSS, but it wasn't Guo Jianlian on the other end of the line. Instead, it was the FSB director himself, Viktor Olegovich Golovin.

She greeted him in a nervous voice, "*Gospodin Golovin,* what can I do for you?"

After a tense pause, Golovin's hoarse yet authoritative voice resonated through the encrypted connection. "There is a concern, *Ahgyent Natase,* that the MSS got wind of your asset's betrayal and eliminated him before he could hand over the device to us."

"I would have been notified by my contacts in the Chinese government if that were the case, sir," she explained, her shoulder-length brunette hair cascading around her face, gently brushing against her high cheekbones. "But I agree, that he's late contacting us is concerning."

"Could the CIA be involved?" Golovin asked with a tinge of concern. "If the Americans get their hands on the device, we will be locked out of the world energy market altogether. They will use it against us. Mother Russia will be doomed."

"Respectfully, I feel it's a ploy by Guo to create concern and increase his demands."

"If so, then *obeshchat' zvezdy s neba,*" Golovin said. Offer him the stars from the sky. "I don't need to remind you, agent, that we must proceed very carefully here. We can't afford to let the Chinese find out about this—they must remain our friends—but getting that device before anyone else is vital. I'm retaining you as the lead on this delicate situation because you're the one who first brought it to us."

"I will get back to you as soon as I learn something new," Natase said.

Golovin responded by ending the call.

Natase had met Director Golovin in the flesh once—and that was only two weeks prior. But the whispers circulating among her colleagues painted a portrait of a man who embodied both strength and fairness. In a time marked by transition and uncertainty in Russia, where loyalty to the past president lingered in the Kremlin, Golovin stood strong. He wasn't driven by a misguided crusade to resurrect the Soviet Union; instead, his focus, like that of the new president, was firmly set on the future. They were more concerned with transforming the country into an economic world power, similar to what China had done the previous decade. Perhaps that's why they placed such an importance on claiming the "device," as they referred to it.

She first learned of the breakthrough technology while working undercover in Beijing, posing as an executive for a North Korean car company called Song Motors. For reasons that eluded her, Guo Jian-lian had somehow unearthed her true identity and tracked her down to a Starbucks near the Song Motors offices. As she patiently waited for her café latte, he materialized beside her with the quiet efficiency of someone well-versed in the art of espionage. He told her he was with the Ministry of State Security and had something her government would be interested in—a revolutionary contraption capable of achieving cold nuclear fusion, a technology even his own government was purportedly unaware of. In return, he asked for a cool two billion dollars U.S. and sanctuary in Russia, complete with a new identity.

Initially, the words reeked like convoluted rubbish, probably a clumsy MSS attempt to catch her spying on China. But on the remote possibility that he spoke the truth, Elena felt an obligation to at least look into it. As she delved deeper into her investigations, her sources painted a portrait of Guo as a man teetering on the precipice of his own downfall. Rumors swirled of his clandestine dealings with a criminal syndicate, and then there was his connection with the disappearance of a Chinese scientist named Linghu Ning, an expertise in nuclear fusion. Little by little, the details added up, until she was convinced that Guo's offer was legitimate.

Immediately, she saw an opportunity to ascend the ranks within the FSB, to carve out a path toward becoming the agency's first female deputy chief in the esteemed counterintelligence department —and at twenty-eight years old, one of the youngest. The tantalizing prospect of advancement fueled her determination, igniting a fire within her to obtain the technology at any cost.

Not a minute after her call with Golovin, her phone chimed again. It was a number she didn't recognize.

"Natase here," she answered.

"This is Moscow police commissioner, Oleg Alexandrovich Volkov. I was told to inform you of an incident we just had in Vimski. There was a multiple homicide of Chinese nationals in a warehouse leased by Yongcheng Motors."

The words made her stop. Her asset, Guo Jianlian, was known to be associated with a Chinese gang that funded Yongcheng Motors. *It had to be connected,* she thought.

"Tell me more," she demanded, rising from her seat.

Volkov complied. "There were seven victims. One was the security guard. All victims were shot except one, whose neck was broken."

Slinging her bag over her shoulder and securing her Glock 17 to her hip, Natase walked quickly as she spoke, bypassing the elevator and descending the staircase for more privacy.

"Was there anything found inside the warehouse? Some sort of scientific equipment?" she inquired.

"*Nyet*," Volkov replied. "But witnesses there reported seeing a large luxury vehicle fleeing the scene. They couldn't make out the driver, but they think it was a man, dark hair."

"How about the security cameras?"

"The cameras were destroyed," replied Volkov.

"And where is this vehicle now?"

After a prolonged pause, Volkov murmured, "The Vimski station was in pursuit, but the suspect managed to evade all four of their police vehicles. He was last spotted driving across the Moscow Canal, exiting somewhere near the M-11."

"Are you telling me you had four patrol cars chasing him, and he managed to ditch them all?"

Volkov let out a grunt. "We're not proud of it, but this guy isn't your run-of-the-mill murder suspect. He was armed and an expert driver. We can, however, provide positive ID on his vehicle. It was a 2014 Kamita Empire, no license plate. Not many of them were sold in Russia, maybe ten total during those years, so he should be easy to find. We're setting roadblocks up and down the M-11, and our choppers have been dispatched."

"If this man is as crafty and skilled as you say, then he won't show up on any main road. He'll be hiding out somewhere or traveling off the beaten path. Where did you say he was last headed?"

"Toward a township in the northeastern part of Vimski," replied the commissioner.

Natase paused, her mind swirling with a multitude of thoughts. *If you were in his shoes, what would you do? Where would you go?* With her mind made up, she said vehemently, "Mr. Volkov, I believe he's still in that area. Please set up checkpoints on all roads that can be accessed to that neighborhood. Inspect every vehicle going into and out of that township."

"There's only one main road that runs through there, Bilenkin Prospekt," Volkov said.

"Then, your job is a simple one. I'll also require as many of your men to conduct a thorough door-to-door search of each residence in the neighborhood. Check every garage and shed, anything that can hide a large crossover vehicle."

"But there must be nearly a hundred homes in that area," the chief noted.

"Then I suggest you get started immediately. Please notify me as soon as if you find anything."

Natase ended the conversation. Stepping out of the Lubyanka building, she jumped into her ten-year-old Toyota Land Cruiser parked in the back lot and fired up its V-8 powerplant. She had originally intended to head to the crime scene to search for clues, but she had a change of heart. Instead, she charted a course toward the residential community of northeastern Vimski.

CHAPTER 42

The Kamita Empire drove onto firm land, its all-season tires leaving shallow tracks on the one-lane road. Dalton Lang took in the quaint surroundings, his eyes searching for an appropriate hiding place, or better yet, an off-road trail that could lead him well out of the area. Nature flourished throughout the remote hamlet, its wild growth subdued beneath a blanket of white powder. To his right, a line of homes was scattered behind a high wall. To his left stretched a dense thicket of pine trees. As the morning sky brightened with the arrival of a new day, he noticed dozens of parked vehicles scattered randomly along the roadside, evidence that the residents of the tranquil enclave had yet to stir from their slumber and brave the chilly Moscow air.

Lang had initially hoped to find an abandoned garage, shed or an empty mechanic's shop, but while driving from one block to the next, he found that any structure that had the potential to hide his vehicle had padlocks attached to its doors. With the imminent arrival of the police, he needed to disappear quickly. He continued heading north, away from Moscow, his navigation system informing him he had reached a residential district called Zarechny Hills, characterized by increasingly upscale residences with stylish driveways.

As he forged ahead, the narrow road curved to the right, but he kept his vehicle traveling straight, driving off the paved road and onto a makeshift trail, heading into the heart of the woods. The Empire's all-wheel-drive system did a commendable job of powering the vehicle through the deep snow. Lang navigated the large crossover vehicle through a maze of pine trees, exploiting every gap to his advantage, weaving his way deeper into the green. After covering perhaps a mile or so, he finally found a secluded spot, hidden from the prying eyes of passersby, street cameras, and aerial surveillance.

This would do for now.

He stopped the Empire but did not cut the power. If an inexhaustible energy source indeed powered his vehicle, the batteries would never die. A working nuclear fusion reactor would allow him to maintain a warm cabin around the clock, while being able to recharge his phone and laptop as many times as necessary. With ample snow for hydration, he speculated he could potentially survive for two weeks without food; however, time was not on his side. A search party into the woods could soon be dispatched, so he couldn't afford to sit still for too long.

He switched on the transmitter.

"Lang here. I was able to ditch the local police. I'm currently hiding out in the middle of a forest, but I may only have a few hours before they figure out where I am," he said.

Raja Singh's reply came immediately. "Thank God, you're all right. Mitch says he wants to speak with you."

Mitch Snowhill's anxious voice cut through the static. "Dalton, what's going on? What's your status?"

"I'm good, for now," Lang replied calmly. "But I'm a sitting duck. Just so you know, getting to the embassy or the border in this vehicle will be impossible—everyone in Russia is looking for it. You'll need to send somebody to me near these coordinates, preferably one who owns a moving truck or a large SUV. This contraption I'm carrying is cased in lead, so I'll need a couple of guys with a strong back."

"I see. You want to transfer the box to another vehicle. Good plan," responded Snowhill. "FSB surveillance activity around the embassy has spiked in the last hour—no doubt caused by your actions—so we can't send any of our agents to you, but I'll have one of our remote assets there within an hour. Just hang tight."

"I'm not going anywhere, but in the meantime, could you get a hold of Dr. Ferdinand Mezger at MIT? He's a former colleague and leading expert in fusion technology. He's worked with the U.S government before, so he should already have clearance. We'll need his help to determine if this thing really is a cold nuclear fusion reactor."

"Count on it," replied Snowhill. "Keep your comm line open. I'll be in touch."

"Any news on Ruth?" Lang asked.

"No change," Singh answered. "Melvin Patterson and your assistant, Yuna, are with her. They promised to notify me if anything changes."

"Roger that. Lang out."

He emerged from the vehicle and made his way to a nearby tree. Snapping off a branch heavy with bristles, he sauntered back to the trail. With meticulous care, he swept the bristles over the Empire's tire tracks from the deep layer of snow. Fully obscuring the marks was impossible, but only a keen eye would now detect them.

Once he was finished, he jumped back into the driver's seat of the Empire and studied the monitor on his laptop.

"Let's see if you're the real thing," he said, tapping several keys.

CHAPTER 43

When Elena Natase reached the border of northeastern Vimski, the police checkpoints had already been set up. A queue of vehicles had formed, each driver patiently awaiting inspection by Moscow's finest. Maneuvering her Land Cruiser past three weathered sedans and a pair of compact SUVs, she parked her vehicle off the road near the checkpoint. A portable police light affixed to her vehicle's roof granted her all access.

Leaving the engine running, Natase emerged from the Land Cruiser dressed in a faux fur coat and a plain brown beret. She walked up to one of the four armed policemen on duty, each clad in standard black uniform, bulletproof vest, and matching black *ushanka* hat, adorned with the Moscow Police insignia.

"I'm Elena Natase. I take it a similar checkpoint has been set up on the other side of the township?" she said, flashing her identification.

The officer responded immediately. "Yes. No suspicious vehicles yet, but it's still early."

"Pay special attention to vans and trucks. The suspect most likely possesses cargo that he wants to transport out."

"Yes, ma'am," the officer responded.

"If you find anything, contact me on your walkie-talkies," Natase instructed firmly, pivoting back toward her vehicle.

Slipping behind the wheel of the Land Cruiser, she merged back onto the road, proceeding along Vimski's two-lane thoroughfare at a deliberate pace. She scanned the surroundings for any hiding spots that could conceal a large crossover luxury vehicle. She noted several police cars stationed along the roadside, the officers diligently conducting door-to-door inquiries in search of the missing vehicle and its driver.

We have the most efficient police force in the world, she thought.

Then, from the corner of her vision, she spotted a blue and white police cruiser—a Haval Dargo SUV—stopped behind a white Gaz Gazelle cargo van parked on a dead-end street. The vehicles lingered near the entry to an upscale neighborhood called Zarechny Hills. On the van's side was "Служба по очистке бассейнов Алекса"—Alex's Pool Cleaning Service. She stopped her vehicle behind the police cruiser and stepped out. When she did so, a tall, handsome police officer in his mid-thirties emerged from the Dargo.

"What's going on here?" she asked.

Wearing a black beret and a matching Moscow police uniform, the officer turned to Natase.

"You're from the federal police?" he asked.

"*Da*. And I asked you a question, officer..."

"Senior Lieutenant Sergei Georgiyevich Tolkachev, at your service ma'am," he replied with a salute. "I'm inspecting all vans and trucks in the area, as ordered by the commissioner."

"Very good," Natase said approvingly. "Don't let me keep you from your duties."

With a curt nod, Tolkachev walked briskly to the driver-side door of the Gaz van and gestured for the driver to lower his window.

He was a rotund man with a thick salt-and-pepper beard and closely cropped hair. The name "Dmitri" was stitched on his shirt.

Once the window lowered all the way down, the man named Dmitri asked, "What seems to be the problem here?"

Tolkachev stretched his neck, leaning forward to peer into the depths of the van. "An odd time of year to be cleaning pools. Where are you going?"

"Don't you have better things to do?" Dmitri countered with a defensive posture. "You Moscow cops..."

He stopped in mid-sentence, his face registering surprise when Natase approached holding an identification badge of the Federal Migration Service.

"Please answer the officer's question," she said in a low voice that commanded respect.

"I was called to service an indoor pool, but I can't seem to find the location. I think our dispatcher gave me the wrong address," Dmitri said.

"Open the back of your vehicle," Tolkachev instructed.

The pool cleaner responded with a confused look, making no move to comply.

"Now," Tolkachev demanded.

"Okay, okay," Dmitri muttered, opening his door and stepping out onto the street. He gazed uneasily at Natase as he made his way to the rear of the vehicle.

Following the two men, Natase's eyes remained fixed on both of them, watching their every move. Once there, Dmitri reached for the door handle and raised the hatchback door open in a single fluid motion. He stepped aside to show Natase and Tolkachev his cargo— bottles of cleaning chemicals, a skimmer brush and an array of vacuum hoses. Nothing out of the ordinary.

"So, care to tell me what this is all about?" Dmitri asked.

"Just making routine inspections," Tolkachev replied. "Thank you for your cooperation."

Dmitri slammed the rear door of the van shut and returned to the driver's seat. Without uttering another word, he quickly drove away.

Natase patted Tolkachev on the shoulder.

"Well done, senior lieutenant," she told him.

Tolkachev nodded, returned to his own vehicle, and pulled away from the curb. As the Dargo disappeared around the first bend, Natase reached for her walkie-talkie, and in a calm and authoritative voice, relayed instructions to the police officers manning the checkpoints.

"There's a white pool-cleaning van going your way. Detain the driver," she commanded firmly. "There's something suspicious about him."

She noticed the change in his expression when he saw the FMS identification. Only those familiar with law enforcement knew that FSB agents frequently masqueraded under the guise of the Federal Migration Service. It wasn't something a pool cleaner would normally be privy to.

The killer is close, Natase thought, caressing the Glock attached to her hip. *I can feel it. He's close.*

CHAPTER 44

The laptop hummed with activity, its processor crunching through hundreds of thousands of data points every nanosecond. Dalton Lang peered closely, trying to make sense of the readings. Every indication was that the large lead box stashed in the cargo space of the Kamita Empire was actively powering the vehicle's solid-state batteries. It cleverly rerouted some of that energy back into the device itself, creating a perpetual loop that kept the batteries always at full capacity.

"This is amazing," Lang murmured, absorbed in the technological marvel before him.

Just then, a voice cut through his earpiece.

"Dalton, we have a problem," Mitch Snowhill said.

"Not the words I wanted to hear. What's wrong?" responded Lang.

"Our asset just informed us that Moscow police and, we suspect the FSB and GRU, have set up checkpoints on the road going into and out of your current location. They're checking every vehicle carefully. Our asset maintains that there's no way to get that device out unless you can somehow drive it out through the forest."

Lang let out a light chuckle. "That's not going to happen. The trees become too dense from here on."

Snowhill cursed. "I'm afraid we don't have any choice but to ask you to destroy it."

Lang didn't respond immediately. He mulled over the words he'd just heard, then said, "You're telling me to destroy what could be the most important invention of the twenty-first century, if not the millennia?"

"You're no doubt familiar with the ways of the Russian government," Snowhill responded. "What do you think will happen if they get this technology before us?"

"I admit it wouldn't be ideal," Lang answered. "But surely a deal can be worked out at some point, or perhaps the CIA can steal it back —you do have the best thieves in the world. What you're asking me to do is to disrupt human progress—it's like sabotaging the Wright brothers' plane before their maiden flight—and I'm not prepared to do that. And, besides, I don't have the means of destroying it. It's not like I packed C-4 explosives with me."

"Dr. Mezger says it can be accomplished by tweaking the program. He says he can walk you through the process," Snowhill said.

"I'm sorry, sir, but I refuse," Lang declared adamantly.

For a long moment, neither man spoke, the silence stretching between them like a taut violin string. The tension finally snapped with the familiar voice of CIA Director Nigel McKeen.

"Dalton, it's me. I understand your concerns, but Mitch is right. You need to destroy it now. If you don't, the Russians will weaponize it against us...against the free world. With the power this technology grants them, it will not only encourage their pursuit of global dominance, but it will intensify it to the nth degree."

"But what if it doesn't? Who's to say that they won't recognize the benefits it offers to all mankind? They have a new regime in place, after all."

"Don't fool yourself, Dalton," McKeen countered flatly. "No

matter who's in charge, they'll find a way to weaponize it. Need I remind you how they turned social media into a tool for chaos, using it to nearly topple our nation just a few years ago? They spread propaganda among the masses, to those all too willing to believe without questioning. They divided our country from within. We're fortunate they didn't start a second Civil War here, which I'm sure was their intent."

"But what you're asking me to do..." Lang muttered, letting the sentence drift off.

"Dalton," McKeen continued. "I would have loved for the U.S. to possess this technology, but honestly, we probably aren't yet ready for it either. Perhaps in twenty, or fifty, or a hundred years, but mankind isn't prepared to handle the magnitude of power it brings at this time in our history. And besides, it's been done once, so it can be done again. Doing it the first time is always the hardest. We now know cold nuclear fusion is possible, and we have some data recorded by Singh that we can hand off to our best scientists."

Lang pressed his fingers into eyes and grimaced, weighing McKeen's words carefully. He could see the logic in them, hard as they were to accept.

"All right, tell me what I need to do," he said finally.

"Thank you, Dalton," McKeen responded, relief evident in his tone. "I'll leave the rest to Mitch. See you when you get back."

Snowhill's voice sounded through the earpiece again. "We have an exit plan for you in place. Go to the following coordinates and look for this vehicle with this license plate. Sending you the images now."

Lang's satellite phone dinged. He glanced at the screen and did a double take. "You're kidding, right?"

"Not in the slightest," Snowhill retorted without missing a beat. "The code phrase is 'A storm is coming from the north,' and the response is, 'That's why the birds fly south.' Here's Dr. Mezger."

After a brief pause, Ferdinand Mezger' voice sounded on the line.

"Hello Charles. It's been a while," he said.

"Likewise, Ferry. I'm sure Mitch walked you through all the red tape about confidentiality and national security. So, let's get right to it. How do we do this?"

"For the record, I'm on your side—I'm against destroying this thing," Mezger said. "Prototype or not, I really can't believe someone actually achieved what we all thought was at least a hundred years down the road. It's nothing short of a miracle."

"Agreed. While I'd like to keep chatting, I'm a bit pressed for time, so can we get this show on the road," Lang pressed.

"Sorry, yes. I'm with Raja Singh. He's given me access to his computer, and I had a chance to study the readouts. I can see what you're seeing on your monitor. The primary functions can only be executed at your end, so follow my instructions to the letter."

"Roger that," Lang responded.

"Because the device is designed to handle only a certain threshold of energy input, if we can exceed those limits, it could force the thing to shut down," Mezger explained. "So, I've increased the amount of energy from the solid-state batteries going into the core of the device on my end. If you can now hit the "Enter" key on your laptop."

Lang pressed his index finger down firmly on the key. Immediately, the device began humming loudly.

"Whatever you did, the reactor is definitely responding," Lang said.

"Now for the difficult part. Despite this contraption being a *cold* fusion device, I suspect that deliberately manipulating the operational temperatures by removing the isotopes will cause it to overheat. Combine that with the extra energy we just fed into its core, and it should initiate a complete meltdown situation."

"Whoa, hold on there. Am I going to be showered with radiation?" asked Lang. "I thought that cold fusion produced no radiation."

"It's an untested prototype, so who knows what can happen. Raj told me it's housed in a lead box. Make sure the box is secure, no open doors or vents," Mezger instructed. "There's no way of knowing how much energy the reactor is harnessing, so I can't promise you that the thing won't explode. I would get as far away as possible. You'll have about ten minutes after we start the process."

"Can I remove the coins beforehand?"

"Once we initiate the meltdown, it can't be stopped," answered Mezger. "Therefore, removing any type of key or switch will have no effect. I've just inputted the necessary parameters on my end. All you need to do is press the 'Enter' button, and then get the hell out of there."

Lang stared at his laptop, his finger poised above the key, his mind swirling with doubt about the righteousness of his decision. Just as he steeled himself to act, a gunshot rang out, reverberating through the dense forest around him. Birds took flight in a flurry, their scattered forms darkening the already gray sky. Then, another gunshot. This time, the bullet shattered the side mirror of the Empire, scattering fragments of glass and plastic on the ground below.

Instinctively, Lang ducked, pressing his body flat against the center console. He pulled the hood of his jacket over his head and slipped on a surgeon's mask to cover the lower half of his face. Whoever had tracked him down had done it much quicker than he'd expected. It was crucial that he neutralize the threat immediately and escape, knowing a veritable army would converge on him in moments.

He pressed the "Enter" key and pulled his trusty Sig Sauer from his backpack. He was now on the clock—ten minutes and counting.

CHAPTER 45

Elena Natase completed a meticulous sweep of the Vimski neighborhood, her focus narrowing on the affluent Zarechny Hills area. Here, many of the swank residences boasted large garages—a perfect place to conceal a full-size crossover vehicle like the Kamita Empire. Theoretically, the suspect could break into one of these homes, neutralize its occupants, and then settle in quietly until nightfall; however, if it was her on the run, she wouldn't choose to hide in an occupied residence—too many unpredictable elements. The woods offered a far more strategic refuge, shrouded in the natural camouflage of densely packed trees. So, with a sharper eye, she surveyed the area a second time, this time searching for any entry into the woodland—perhaps a discreet trail or a forgotten path frequented by hunters or hikers.

She rounded a curve that led into Zarechny Hills, when a subtle anomaly caught her eye—a slight break in the tree line straight ahead. With her curiosity piqued, she pulled to the edge of the tarmac and stepped out of her Toyota Land Cruiser to investigate. The snow beneath her feet seemed oddly disturbed, as if hastily covered by a broom or rake. Sensing a clue, and with nothing to lose, she jumped back into the driver's seat of her trusty Toyota and steered it off the road. Her Land Cruiser's all-wheel-drive system handled the challenging terrain with ease, efficiently advancing the vehicle through the snowy terrain.

About a hundred meters in, Natase noticed a second anomaly—this one far more noteworthy than the last—fresh tire tracks that cut through the snow, their width and tread suggesting a four-wheel-drive vehicle. Cautiously, she slowed her Land Cruiser to a crawl and unholstered her Glock. The mid-morning sunlight pierced through the gaps in the canopy above, casting a majestic glow across the forest's interior. The serene beauty of the scene belied the tension of the situation. Then, up ahead, she saw it: the red taillights of the Kamita Empire, faintly glowing against the darkened backdrop of the forest. She quickly reached for the walkie talkie.

"Target found. I repeat, target found. I'm in the woods, off the main road that leads into Zarechny Hills," she said softly.

"Roger that," came the response. "We're enroute now."

Ideally, Natase would have waited for backup to arrive before making a move, but she noticed the rear of the Empire bouncing slightly, indicating activity inside the vehicle's cargo area. She quietly stepped out of the Land Cruiser, her Glock 17 firmly in her grip. She positioned herself beside her Toyota for cover, catching a glimpse of the Empire's occupant through the vehicle's window. All she could see was the back of his head—he had short black hair, and he seemed intensely focused on something in his lap—possibly a laptop.

Then, a sudden realization dawned on her—he might try to destroy the evidence. This, she could not allow, for her future depended on apprehending the device.

Natase emerged from the safety of her position and closed the gap on foot between herself and the Empire. Not wanting to get too close, she stopped about fifty meters away. Her plan was to incapacitate the man with a shot to the head before he could complete his task.

Kill first and answer questions later.

Raising her gun and taking careful aim, she unleashed two rounds,, the sharp crack of the gunshots shattering the silence of the forest. Natase's aim was slightly off—neither bullet hit the intended target, although one shattered the Empire's side mirror.

The commotion would surely prompt the man to react, she thought.

Positioning herself strategically with a clear line of sight to the driver's-side door, Natase readied herself for the moment the man would emerge. She was confident that she could take him down before he could retaliate. She held her breath, her finger resting on the trigger, ready to shoot the instant he appeared.

But the situation took an unexpected turn. The taillights of the Empire flashed white—a clear signal that the vehicle's transmission had been thrown into reverse. In the next moment, the luxury crossover was rolling backwards at her at breakneck speed, its large rectangular body jolting violently as it navigated the uneven terrain

"*Chort,*" Natase cursed under her breath.

She pivoted sharply and sprinted toward the safety of her own vehicle. Behind her, the Kamita closed the distance with increasing speed. She reached the Land Cruiser just in time, jumping behind it as the Empire's rear end slammed into the front fender of the Toyota. With a thunderous crash, the impact momentarily lifted both vehicles off the ground, coupled by the crunch of crumpled steel.

Undeterred by the collision, Natase gripped her Glock tightly and moved toward the Empire with cautious steps, but when she came around to the driver's side, she noticed the cabin was empty.

As her mind raced, a sudden, blunt force struck her from behind, sending her sprawling to the ground, her gun flying from her grasp. A significant weight pinned her down, and she felt the cold, hard point of a gun barrel press against the back of her neck. It was at that moment when she realized that her assailant had taken advantage of her focus on the empty vehicle to get the drop on her. With a gun at her neck and her own weapon out of reach, she was now completely at his mercy.

"You're a gifted operative," the man said in broken Russian. "That you found me so quickly is impressive. I commend you."

His words were followed by a sharp, unexpected pain in her right thigh. Glancing down, she saw he had administered a substance using an injection pen. Despite the numbing shock of the drug, Elena summoned every ounce of her remaining strength to turn herself onto her back and look at her assailant directly.

A cloth surgeon's mask obscured his face, revealing only his eyes. They were brown, but they weren't menacing or filled with ill intent; rather, they regarded her with a peculiar warmth that contrasted sharply with his aggressive actions. Natase reached up with her right hand, her fingers slipping under the edge of his mask in a desperate bid to unveil the face behind it. But as her fingers tugged at the fabric, her vision began to blur. The enveloping darkness closed in, and her empty hand dropped helplessly to her side.

CHAPTER 46

The directive was clear, and it reverberated across all police frequencies, issued directly by the Moscow police commissioner himself. "All available officers, proceed to the woods near the Zarechny Hills area. Suspect's vehicle has been spotted. A government agent is requesting backup. Be advised, the suspect is armed and extremely dangerous. Repeat, proceed with caution."

Senior Lieutenant Sergei Tolkachev activated his police cruiser's flashing lights.

"Son of a bitch," he muttered, maneuvering his blue and white Havel Dargo through the Zarechny Hills neighborhood, setting a course for the northern checkpoint. It was a short drive, under five minutes, and just as he expected, a familiar sight awaited him. Parked along the roadside was a white cargo van, adorned with the logo "Alex's Pool Cleaning Service." With his back against the rear tire, Dmitri sat dejectedly with his arms secured behind his back.

Tolkachev approached at a slow pace and pulled up beside the lead officer, a compact man in his thirties with a stocky build and sharp blue eyes. Yuri Ivanov had served under Tolkachev for several years in the Second Regiment before his transfer to the Riot Unit.

Lowering his window, Tolkachev pulled alongside Ivanov and said, "You were able to detain the pool cleaning van. Well done. I was afraid he got away with all the commotion."

"He came straight to us, sir, and he seemed to be in a hurry, too," Ivanov replied. "We're waiting for orders on what to do with him."

Tolkachev glanced over at Dmitri, catching his intense gaze. "I would imagine we're going to take him back to HQ and interrogate him until he cracks, unless the FSB wants to take their shot first."

Ivanov nodded. "But what a joke, using a pool cleaner as cover in the dead of winter. Not so smart, this guy."

Overhearing the conversation, Dmitri shouted, "I keep telling you. The call was for an indoor pool. I've done nothing wrong."

Tolkachev ignored him and turned to Ivanov. "I've got to recharge my vehicle. Almost no range left, so I'll be back in about a half hour."

Before Ivanov could utter a response, a thunderous explosion violently shattered the stillness of the countryside, its source originating from the direction of Zarechny Hills.

"What in God's name was that?" Ivanov asked, his voice filled with tension.

"Whatever it is, it can't be good. Do not abandon your post unless specifically ordered by the commissioner, and do not leave the pool cleaner alone under any circumstances," Tolkachev directed.

"Understood, sir," Ivanov replied crisply.

With a firm nod, Tolkachev raised his window and accelerated away from the checkpoint, his siren screaming a high-pitched whine. The lightbar on the roof pulsated with red and blue flashes, prompting other vehicles to move out of the way. He barreled down Ulitsa Rozhdestvenskaya and onto Bilenkin Prospekt.

Several kilometers later, Tolkachev swerved the Dargo onto a narrow, unmarked road. He stopped his vehicle and killed the siren and police lights. He sat in silence for a full minute, remaining perfectly still, making sure there were no other vehicles around. Then he spoke.

"Did anyone get a look at your face?" he asked in English.

From the confined space of the cargo compartment, a somewhat muffled voice responded, "No, I'm almost positive that no one did."

"Good. Keep your head down and stay under the cover," Tolkachev instructed. "I'll drop you off at the nearest international hotel. You can have the concierge hail you a taxi, and from there, you can disappear wherever you need."

"Thank you," the man under the cover said.

Without responding, Tolkachev resumed driving, recalling when his handler at the U.S. embassy first reached out for his assistance. He initially balked at the request. "Too risky," he protested, but when she offered him a cool fifty thousand dollars for what seemed like thirty minutes of work, he agreed, although somewhat grudgingly.

Now, his sole regret was not negotiating a higher fee, for the assignment was laden with hazards: Covertly moving a man out of Vimski amidst a web of checkpoints and under the watchful eyes of his own colleagues was not an easy task. But Tolkachev, a seasoned international chess master, devised a plan as cunning as any he had ever deployed on the checkered board. By using a pool cleaning company as a diversion, he was able to focus the attention of the FSB elsewhere, while the real play was carried out. It was a classic move of misdirection. Unfortunately, this meant that Dmitri, the unsuspecting and totally innocent pool cleaner, would face some difficult days ahead, but Tolkachev was confident that he could secure his eventual release.

As for the package, Tolkachev did not care who or what it was. However, he couldn't hide his surprise when an Asian man showed up at the rendezvous point. Initially, he suspected a trap, but the man knew the correct code phrase, confirming his identity as the one who needed to be safely escorted out of the area.

After 30 minutes of careful driving and maneuvering, Tolkachev pulled his car to a stop in front of a Holiday Express Hotel.

"We're here," he announced. "*Udachi*." Good luck.

In his rearview mirror, Tolkachev watched the man emerge from under the canvas cover in the rear cargo compartment. After swinging the rear hatch open, the man quickly climbed out of the vehicle—a black backpack secured tightly across his shoulders—and slammed the door closed. He gave the side of the vehicle a couple of firm taps—a clear signal it was safe for Tolkachev to depart.

Easing the police cruiser away from the hotel driveway, Tolkachev's eyes lingered on the figure through the Dargo's side mirror. With brisk strides, the Asian man made his way to the entrance of the hotel, vanishing behind its sliding glass doors, never to be seen in the country again.

~

ELENA NATASE's senses struggled back to consciousness in a disorienting haze. Her eyes fluttered open to the stark, white interior of an ambulance. She found herself lying face up on a gurney, the scent of antiseptic filling her nostrils.

Her temples throbbed with a piercing headache, a reminder of the knockout drug that had rendered her unconscious. She tried to move, but her limbs felt heavy and unresponsive. Inside the vehicle with her was a medical technician who monitored her vitals. The technician, a young brunette in her early twenties, wore a nametag labeled "Margaret."

"How are you feeling?" Margaret inquired.

As Natase tried to speak, her throat felt dry, and her voice came out as a hoarse whisper.

"What happened?" she asked.

Margaret settled onto a small stool next to the gurney and adjusted the bed's backrest, elevating Natase into a reclined sitting position.

"We found you passed out in the woods," she explained.

Feeling a resurgence of strength, Natase pushed herself up from the gurney. Gripping the siderails for support, she climbed out of the back and leaned against the side of the vehicle, steadying herself as she took in her surroundings. The crisp Moscow air felt good on her cheeks, but it was not enough to brace her for the view that unfolded before her eyes.

Near the treeline, the skeletal remains of her beloved Toyota Land Cruiser sat lifeless, its frame charred black beyond recognition. Beside it, the Kamita Empire suffered a similar fate, its once elegant exterior now marred by severe burn damage. A group of half a dozen workers clad in biohazard suits meticulously examined the still smoking wreckage. It appeared like a scene from a Hollywood disaster movie.

"Did a bomb go off?" asked Natase.

Margaret stepped out of the rear of the ambulance, placing a blanket over the FSB agent's shoulders. "There was an explosion. Thankfully, no police officers were near the cars when they blew up. The technicians are saying that while there are low levels of radiation, it's nothing that would be harmful to us."

Trying to piece together her last memories, Natase remembered she had lost consciousness next to the Empire. Yet, as she looked down at herself, there was no evidence of burns or rashes; even her clothes remained pristine and undamaged.

"How am I not injured, or even dead?" she asked.

"You were well out of the blast zone. We found you over there on that flat spot," Margaret replied, pointing to a clearing about fifty yards away.

"How long have I been unconscious?"

Margaret peered down at her Apple Watch. "About two hours."

As Natase's memory came into focus, she pieced together the image of the unknown man who had drugged her. She remembered his warm eyes and realized that he must have been the one to pull her from the blast's vicinity.

"The device," Natase suddenly exclaimed, the memory triggering a rush of adrenaline.

With a quick, apologetic shove, she rushed past Margaret and hurried over to the nearest police officer. To her mild surprise, it was Senior Lieutenant Sergei Tolkachev.

"Senior Lieutenant, do you know what happened to the cargo inside of the Kamita?" Natase asked, still shaky on her feet.

Tolkachev took hold of her arm to steady her.

"Whatever was in there has melted down to a blob. Completely unsalvageable," he replied.

"And the suspect? Has he been captured?"

Tolkachev shook his head. "He seems to have vanished into thin air."

Natase violently pulled her arm away and made her way back to the ambulance. Her lips were tightly pressed together, anger and profound disappointment brewing within her gut. Despite being grateful on some level that the man with the deep brown eyes had saved her life, she seethed internally. It wasn't because he had succeeded in destroying the device, but the reasons cut deeper—she had been outmaneuvered at her own game, on her own turf.

Peering up at the gray sky, she spoke in a hushed tone. "Whoever you are, we will meet again, I promise you that."

CHAPTER 47

Argon Securities' private jet touched down in Santa Monica just after sundown, the sky painted in vibrant shades of purple and orange over the Pacific Ocean. Argon boss Paul Verdy arranged for Dalton Lang to access the company's private terminal, allowing him to skip customs, pausing just long enough for a quick stamp on his fake passport. As he stepped outside, a familiar black Lexus ES awaited him at the curb. Recognizing it instantly, he strode over without hesitancy and swung open the passenger-side door.

"Have a nice trip?" Melvin Patterson asked from the driver's seat.

"Good and bad," Lang answered as he took off his backpack. He slid into the passenger seat, placing the backpack on his lap.

"Ruth's condition hasn't changed." Patterson said. "She's hanging tough, though."

Lang nodded. "I'd like to be with her as soon as possible, so can you step on it?"

"Roger that," Patterson replied with a smile, stomping the accelerator pedal. The ES's tires squealed loudly as he sped away from the curb.

Lang had endured countless life-or-death encounters, and fear was no stranger to him; yet, sitting beside Patterson in the careening Lexus, he felt a visceral terror unlike any he'd ever experienced. Melvin jerked the wheel left and right, narrowly missing more than a few parked cars. The vehicle constantly darted back and forth like an out-of-control missile of death. Every few seconds, they were blasted with the sound of honking horns, accompanied by a barrage of middle fingers from other drivers. For the first time in his life, Lang's palms were slick with sweat as his eyes constantly glanced over at the wildly fluctuating speedometer.

"Melvin, let's get there in one piece, yeah buddy?" Lang commented with a quivering voice.

"What? Now, you don't like how I drive?" Patterson snapped back. "You're the one who wants to get there in a hurry."

Oh, how he regretted uttering those words.

The thrill ride finally reached its end when the Lexus skid to a halt in front of Good Samaritan Hospital. Patterson killed the engine and leaped out. Grabbing his backpack, Lang followed suit, both of them rushing past the sliding glass doors into the building. Once inside the lobby, they were immediately greeted by a nurse.

"I'm sorry, visiting hours are over for today," she said.

Patterson reached into his coat and flashed his identification. "This is an FBI matter."

The nurse's eyes widened in surprise.

"Oh," she said, quickly stepping aside to let them through.

Lang went straight to the patient manifest, where he carefully studied the list of names. He flipped through a couple of pages until he found the one he was searching for. It wasn't Ruth Nguyen.

"This way," Patterson called out. "No need to look her up. I know where her room is."

Patterson led Lang past the nurse's station and into the ICU, the sound of their footsteps clacking through the dimly lit corridor. They moved quickly, until they reached a room at the end of the hall and stepped inside.

On the bed lay Ruth, her eyes closed, her face serene. Lang's attention was so riveted on her that he didn't notice a figure in the corner—Yuna Kim, sitting quietly, her presence almost spectral in the dim light.

"Hi, boss," she said, her face drawn and tired. It was evident she hadn't slept properly.

Lang walked over to her and held out his arms. Yuna, surprised by the gesture, paused for a moment before rising from her seat and hugging him tightly.

"Thank you for everything. I've got it from here, so please go home and get some rest," Lang said warmly, his voice filled with concern.

"I need to get to work," she replied.

"You can leave the bar to your assistant tonight."

"It's a Saturday, boss. I can't leave her alone there. Call if you need me," she said, giving Patterson a curt nod before slipping out of the room.

Lang approached the bed, his fingers trembling as he gently brushed Ruth's face.

"I'm so sorry," he whispered, his voice barely audible. "This is all my fault."

He pulled a chair close to the bed and sat down. Unzipping the main compartment of his backpack, he extracted the Coins of Wei. He held all three of them in both hands, their combined weight formidable, making him struggle to keep them aloft.

"Are those the things that you were looking for in Osaka?" Patterson asked.

Lang nodded. "They're the reason for everything that has happened. They've been the bane of my existence."

"What are you going to do with them?" asked Patterson.

Lang shrugged his shoulders. "I don't know. They were supposed to unlock a device, but that device has been destroyed, so they're nothing but useless relics now."

A sharp knock on the door cut through the conversation. Max

Koga and Mitch Snowhill entered the room wearing expressions of relief and urgency.

Snowhill spoke first: "Dalton, we can't thank you enough for what you did. And to think you even had the wherewithal to bring the medallions back, too. Director McKeen has asked for them. He says he plans to return them to their rightful place."

Lang nodded in agreement. "Well, that's where they belong."

Koga interrupted sharply. "Before you do that, could you hand them to me for a moment, please?"

Lang held out the coins. Koga took them, expressing surprise at their unexpected weight. He scrutinized them carefully, then stacked them up on each other—they clicked into place like three pieces of a puzzle. He then closed his eyes, as if attempting to draw out some hidden, mystical power from within.

"What the hell are you doing?" Patterson asked.

"This is going to sound crazy," Koga said, his voice low and earnest, "but I have this heightened spiritual sense. I won't get into all the details, but when we first brought two of these coins together, I felt some odd power emanating from them. And I thought maybe, with all three together, they can provide Ruth with some life energy, you know, *chi*."

Lang sighed. "And all this time, I thought you were a man of science."

"Don't tell me you don't believe in things that can't be explained by science," Koga retorted, gently placing the coins on a small bedside table.

"I don't believe any of it," Lang replied with a straight face.

"Then how do you explain Dr. Linghu Ning inventing a technology all by himself that every scientist in the world deemed impossible?" Koga countered. "Don't you think these coins might've had something to do with that?"

Lang let out a dry chuckle. "You have a very active imagination, Max. We can't even confirm that the contraption actually worked."

A soft rustling came from the bed, interrupting the conversation.

Everyone froze, their eyes fixed on Ruth. As they inched closer, Lang noticed her index finger twitch.

"Ruth," he called out, his voice trembling.

She drew a deep breath and let out a quiet grunt.

"I'll fetch a doctor," Patterson said, urgently bolting out of the room.

Lang leaned over her, just as her eyes fluttered open.

"Where am I?" she whispered.

"It's me. It's Dalton. Can you hear me?"

Ruth nodded weakly, her voice barely a whisper. "Yeah. My head hurts."

"Stay still and rest. The doctor's coming," Lang said.

He then glanced at the stacked coins sitting innocently on the table.

"Nope. No way," he muttered to them. "Mitch, take these things away. I don't ever want to see them again."

Koga placed a hand on Lang's shoulder.

"It's okay to believe," he whispered, then quietly exited the room with Snowhill, who took with him the Coins of Wei.

CHAPTER 48

"It's quite miraculous, really," Dr. J Rothman, a former army pediatrician with a penchant for Corvettes, told Lang after examining Ruth a second time. "Initially, we feared she had suffered extreme brain trauma. However, the most recent CT scan shows that the swelling has subsided drastically. I expect her to make a full recovery."

Relieved by the words, Lang thanked the doctor and glanced over at Ruth, who was sleeping comfortably.

"Please tell her I'll return in the morning," he told the attending nurse.

"Of course," she replied.

Lang stepped out of the room and found Patterson waiting for him in the hallway.

"You hungry?" Patterson asked. "How 'bout we grab a Tommy's chiliburger?"

Lang shook his head. "I need to visit one more patient."

Patterson shot him a surprised look. "Really, who?"

"Follow me," Lang instructed, slinging his backpack over his shoulder.

They moved briskly through the corridor, slipping past a pair of nurses engaged in hushed conversation. The lobby loomed ahead, and Lang followed the signs pointing toward the general medical-surgical ward, situated on the far side of the complex.

With Patterson trailing silently, Lang stepped into the elevator. The doors slid shut with a soft chime, the carriage beginning its ascent to the fourth floor. Once there, Lang quickened his pace, his eyes scanning the room numbers on each door of the hallway.

Noticing a policeman standing guard ahead, he stopped short of Room 425. The cop's gaze was sharp, his muscular build imposing. Lang tried to sidestep him, but the officer moved to block his path.

"Excuse me, but no one's allowed in here," the policeman stated firmly.

Without missing a beat, Patterson stepped forward, flashing his FBI identification. "It's all right, we're here on official business."

The policeman examined the ID, then nodded. "Yes, sir. I'll be right here if you need me."

Lang casually stepped past the guard and entered the room, Patterson following closely on his heels. The lighting was dim, but Lang ignored the switch, instead, marching straight to a solitary bed occupied by the slumbering figure of Detective Albert Barris.

Without warning, Lang's hand slapped the side of Barris' face. The detective's eyes snapped open.

"What the..." Barris mumbled.

As his eyes focused, the initial confusion on his face quickly gave way to fear.

"Hello, detective," Lang greeted with a devious smile. "I have a few questions for you, and I would suggest you answer them truthfully or things will go very badly for you."

"I've got nothing to say to you," Barris replied.

Lang shot a glance at Patterson and tilted his head, his unspoken message crystal clear.

In response, Patterson glanced at his watch.

"Oh crap, look at the time. I need to go pick up my dry cleaning," he said, hastily exiting the room.

When the door closed behind him, Lang walked to the foot of the bed and picked up a metal clipboard. He began reading the patient report aloud: "A gunshot wound to the leg and a major concussion. Few days' observation needed." He then took the pen attached to the clipboard and began scribbling. "And, a broken finger."

Barris's eyes widened. "A what? I didn't..."

Before he could finish his thought, Lang tossed the clipboard aside and seized Barris' right index finger. He placed his other hand over Barris' mouth, and in one swift, brutal motion, he wrenched the finger back until the sharp crack of snapping bone sounded among the hushed silence of the room.

Barris' eyes opened wide with pain, his scream muffled by Lang's hand.

Keeping his hand firmly pressed onto Barris' mouth, Lang seized the detective's middle finger. Leaning in close, he whispered, "I will give you one chance to answer, or another finger bites the dust. Who gave up my location to the Chinese?"

Lang lifted his hand, allowing Barris to speak.

"You son of a bitch," the detective howled.

Snap.

Barris screamed, his voice again stifled by Lang's hand.

"Let's try this one more time," Lang said, gripping Barris' ring finger.

When Lang's hand lifted, Barris—his face beet red and tears streaming down his face—blurted out in a state of panic, "I don't know, man. I took orders from the bossman, Mr. Fuji. That's all."

"Mr. Fuji? Are you talking about the man on the balcony?"

Barris nodded.

"Well, Mr. Fuji's dead. Did he confer with anyone else?"

"Yeah, some guy named Sato. I think he was Fuji's number-two."

"Was he at the restaurant with us?" asked Lang.

Barris shook his head. "No man. The dude's a white guy, red hair and a thick beard."

"A Caucasian in the Blue Dragons?" Lang asked himself aloud.

"Fuji told everyone to lay low in their crib in the Arts District until he called for them."

"The location, now," Lang demanded.

"Fifth and Seaton...a white building, steel, green door and lots of graffiti on the walls," Barris answered.

Lang released Barris' finger. "If you're lying, I'll be back to finish all ten."

Barris cradled his broken fingers with his other hand. "I'm not lying. Those bastards killed my partner right in front of me."

From his backpack, Lang pulled out an injection pen and jabbed it into Barris' shoulder. Before Barris realized what was happening, his head lolled to one side and slumped into unconsciousness.

After a final visual sweep of the room, Lang stepped out of the hospital room, where he spotted Patterson in a deep discussion with the policeman about the state of the Dodgers and Lakers.

"Did you get what you needed?" Patterson asked when he noticed Lang approach.

"Yeah, I think so," Lang replied. "Thanks for your help, and yours too, officer."

The policeman responded with a mild salute as Lang and Patterson headed down the hall. They stepped back into the elevator and rode down in silence, the hum of the machinery the only sound between them. Once outside the building, Patterson unlocked his Lexus ES and slid into the driver's seat. Lang stopped short of the car, motionless, making no move to get in.

The driver-side window of the car lowered.

"What's wrong? Jump in. I'll give you a lift home," Patterson said.

Lang hesitated, memories of his earlier ride flashing through his mind.

"I'll Uber it, buddy," he replied.

"Suit yourself," Patterson responded, visibly offended by the refusal. "I'll see you soon, Phantom."

He started the engine and sped away, tires squealing as he tore out of the parking lot.

Lang didn't wait long for his ride to arrive. In less than two minutes, a Hyundai Sante Fe pulled to a stop in front of the hospital's main entrance, driven by a pleasant Arabic woman. He quickly scanned the area before slipping into the vehicle's rear seats, his backpack positioned strategically beside him. The Sante Fe accelerated smoothly out of the hospital parking lot, turning onto Wilshire Boulevard, when Lang's smartphone vibrated. Looking down at the screen, he saw an encrypted text from CIA Director Nigel McKeen.

Job well done, it read. *I'll be out of the country for a few days, but I will have some urgent news for you soon. Please do nothing out of the ordinary, including contacting your family, until my return.*

Without bothering to respond, Lang shoved the phone into his pocket. The urge to connect with his wife and daughter gnawed at him, but the danger was still too great. Guo Jianlian's death would trigger a relentless MSS investigation, and Lang's name and location could surface, unleashing the full force of the Chinese agency upon him. For now, however, the shadows concealed his secrets, and the eastern front remained thankfully quiet.

The Santa Fe glided to a stop in front of his home in San Gabriel, pausing just long enough for Lang to step out. Once the hired Uber disappeared around the corner, Lang slipped into his house without turning on the lights. Using his smartphone flashlight to guide him, he quickly made his way to the garage, where he opened a hidden compartment under the floor. After securing his special cache in his backpack and changing into all-black attire, he climbed into his Acura MDX. He wrote a quick text, sent it off and headed toward the Arts District of downtown Los Angeles, his mind busy crafting potential scenarios and strategies for navigating the challenges that awaited him.

CHAPTER 49

Max Koga sat at a dimly lit corner table inside the bar at J.M. Gin—what the locals fondly called Gin's Joint. This place, a popular retreat for weary workers, thrived during happy hour. It was half-past seven, and the bar still buzzed with life. Waiters and waitresses, clad in black, wove through the throngs of customers, balancing trays of drinks and plates of food for the cheerful patrons. Koga, lost in his own world, paid no mind to the surrounding commotion. His eyes flicked to the front entrance every few seconds.

Beth Hu was running late.

He took a deep breath, planning the words he needed to say. With the return of Dalton Lang from Russia, and the affair with the Coins of Wei all but settled, he couldn't delay the inevitable any longer. The secret he had kept for weeks felt like a weight pressing down on his chest, and tonight was the night he decided to unburden himself from it. He replayed the conversation over and over in his mind, of how he would break the news to her, each imagined scenario ending with him as the bad guy. He knew how much she had struggled with her father's disappearance, so keeping this secret had been agonizing.

The minutes seemed to stretch endlessly, as Koga took another swig from his bottle of Asahi beer, his second one in ten minutes. Finally, the bar door swung open, and Koga saw Beth step into the room. Her black hair fell freely onto her shoulders, and her slender form was wrapped in a neat blue and gray business suit. He quietly laughed at her appearance because to him, everything about it screamed FBI agent. He watched her movements closely, noting the practiced precision in every step, until her scanning eyes finally locked onto his.

She smiled as she approached, giving him a quick peck on the cheek before sliding onto an empty barstool next to his.

"Hiya, handsome. Sorry I'm late. Did you wait long?" she asked in a light and cheerful tone.

"No worries. I'm glad you made it," Koga replied casually, although his insides were churning with anxiety.

Beth settled onto the stool and placed her purse on the table. She ordered a glass of cabernet from the waitress, then turned her full attention to Max.

"You look on edge. Is something wrong?" she asked.

Koga reached across the table, taking her hand in his and squeezing it gently. "You do know that I care for you very much, more than anyone in a long time..."

With a terrified expression, Beth pulled her hand away. "No, Max. We've only just met. It's too soon."

Koga paused, trying to decipher what she was talking about. When it dawned on him, he let out a genuine laugh.

"You thought..." he said, shaking his head. "I'm not going to propose."

Beth's face relaxed. "Oh God, you scared me for a moment there."

Koga raised an eyebrow. "Wow, I didn't know the idea of marrying me was so horrifying."

Taking Koga's hand into hers, Beth said in a low sweet voice, "Of course, it's not. It's just... we've only been dating for a short while. I thought you were rushing things."

"I get it. And no, I'm not proposing," Koga reiterated. "But I do need to tell you something very important."

Just then, as if choreographed by some unseen hand, Koga's phone chimed, shattering the tension between them. He glanced down and saw a message from Dalton Lang.

Speak of the devil.

If Lang was reaching out, it was invariably urgent.

"Hold on," Koga said to Beth. He opened the text and scanned its contents quickly.

"Is everything all right?" Beth asked, her eyes narrowing with concern as Max placed his phone back on the table.

He rubbed his chin, a familiar gesture that masked his indecision.

"What the heck?" he blurted loudly, slapping the tabletop with both hands. "It's best if I show you. Can you come with me?"

He pulled a couple of twenty-dollar bills from his wallet, tossed them onto the table and rose from his stool.

"And where are we going, may I ask?" Beth inquired.

"To see your father."

Beth's eyes widened.

"What?" she exclaimed. "Is this some kind of joke?"

"It's not. I'll explain on the way," Koga said, sliding off his stool. "And bring your gun."

With a look of shock and uncertainty, Beth grabbed her purse and hastily followed Koga. Together, they left the bar, stepping into the cool night air with a shared sense of urgency.

CHAPTER 50

Dalton Lang eased his Acura MDX to a halt on Fifth Street, a block from Seaton. His eyes quickly identified the building he sought, yet he couldn't make sense of Guo Jianlian's choice for a base of operations. The building's stark white exterior and the wild graffiti made it stand out significantly amid the drab, nondescript structures surrounding it.

Glancing at his Hublot, Lang noted the hour was nearing eight. It was still early, so he decided to surveil the scene and observe. He turned off the MDX's engine and lights, then lowered himself into the driver's seat, his eyes fixed intently on the building. Aside from several vagrants wandering aimlessly on the street, the area was eerily quiet. Lang wondered if Albert Barris had misled him. Yet, the fear etched in his eyes hinted he was telling the truth—but perhaps that fear wasn't directed at him. Lang speculated on whether the news of Guo's death had reached this outpost. The place was quiet, too quiet. The kind of quiet that signaled danger.

His thoughts were interrupted when two Chinese men exited the building, their voices carrying the sharp tones of Mandarin in the still night.

"What do we do now?" asked the thin one.

"We need to go tell the rest of the gang," replied the other gangster, a larger man wearing a Los Angeles Clippers jersey.

"Where the hell are they?" the thin gangster asked.

"They're celebrating at a Chinese girlie bar in the Bonaventure Hotel," Clippers Fan replied.

The thin man unlocked the doors of a black BMW 5 Series parked in the driveway. They stepped into the car, fired up its turbocharged six-cylinder engine and disappeared into the Los Angeles night.

Time to move.

Slipping out of his vehicle, his personal suppressed Sig Sauer in hand, Lang crossed the street, his eyes locking onto the surveillance cameras affixed to the front wall. Without breaking stride, he raised his weapon and took out each camera with a muffled *phut*. He then approached the house's entrance. After shattering the lock with a single round, he yanked the green steel door open and stepped inside.

The interior of the house was dimly lit, a miniature chandelier hanging from the molded ceiling that cast a soft, elegant glow. He was taken aback by the room's exquisite nature, a stark contrast to its rough exterior. The walls, adorned in rich mahogany, were complemented by ornate paneling, evoking the refined atmosphere of a traditional British gentleman's club.

Silently, Lang delved deeper into the building. He navigated a hallway with four doors, two on each side. Gun pointed forward, he methodically checked each room, finding all of them empty. Returning to the living room, he entered a narrow corridor, eventually reaching a staircase that branched both upwards and downwards. Choosing to go up, he ascended the steps. When he reached the top, he faced a short hallway that ended with a pair of open wooden doors. Ignoring the other rooms on the floor, Lang advanced quietly to the open doors. He positioned himself at the side of the doorframe and peered inside—the room was vast and furnished as an office; however, no one was inside. No sign of Sato.

Something seemed off.

With his alertness intensified, Lang retraced his steps, moving cautiously down the staircase. Suddenly, a loud thump echoed from below, freezing him in place for a split second. Tightening his grip on his Sig, Lang resumed his descent, bypassing the main floor and heading toward what he suspected was the basement. Upon reaching the bottom of the stairs, he encountered a steel door. Beside it, a numeric keypad glowed faintly in the dim light.

"It's five, five, six, three," a voice sounded from behind.

Lang spun around as the sharp crack of a gunshot pierced the silence, but it didn't originate from his weapon. His body slammed against the steel door, pain searing through his right shoulder. He had been shot. Expecting a lethal barrage to follow, he braced for the end, but the anticipated hail of gunfire never came. The silence that followed was both a relief and a puzzle, leaving him to wonder why his assailant had not finished the job.

As Lang's senses slowly returned, his vision cleared to reveal, standing alone on the stairwell, Clippers Fan—the gangster who had earlier sped away in the BMW.

A wisp of smoke curled lazily from the barrel of his Heckler and Koch P30 handgun.

"I have to hand it to you," Lang said in Mandarin. "Not too many people can sneak up behind me undetected."

Clippers Fan showed no reaction. His face remained cold and serious.

"Drop your firearm and punch in the number I just told you into the keypad," he instructed in Mandarin. "There's someone inside who wants to speak with you."

With a concerted effort, Lang pushed himself away from the door, the pain in his shoulder intensifying. He let his gun drop to the floor, recognizing that the man holding him at gunpoint was quite skilled. He quietly turned to face the keypad and punched in the numbers as instructed.

With a sharp click, the door unlatched, swinging open just a fraction.

"Go inside," Clippers Fan ordered.

Clutching his wounded shoulder and feeling the sticky warmth of blood seeping through his fingers, Lang pushed open the heavy door and stepped into the room.

The basement was spacious but drab, lined with cold concrete walls. In the center of the room was a Caucasian man with red hair, lounging with an air of calm in an opulent leather chair. Behind him, a well-built Chinese gangster sat on a stack of large wooden containers, holding an AR-15 semi-automatic rifle with the barrel trained on Lang. A large, steel safe loomed in the far corner of the room.

"It's nice to see you again, Phantom Assassin," the bearded man said. "You're right on time."

Lang's eyes narrowed as he studied the man's face. He sensed a flicker of familiarity in his features, a subtle and elusive reminder of something he couldn't quite place. The nagging sense of recognition tugged at his consciousness—that freckled face, that unruly mop of red hair. They were vaguely familiar. Then, it came to him. They belonged to a CIA operative with whom he had crossed paths in a dimly lit alleyway in Hong Kong more than thirty years prior. If his memory served him right, his name was Agent Grant Bricklin.

But why here, and how?

CHAPTER 51

In the next instant, three more Chinese gangsters, all armed to the teeth, emerged through the doorway behind Dalton Lang, effectively sealing him in the basement. Their appearance was hardly a surprise though—he realized he'd walked into a trap the moment he saw the empty office upstairs. If he could get out alive, Detective Barris was going to pay dearly for setting him up.

Lang faced Grant Bricklin and asked in a casual tone, "Would it be safe to presume that you're the one who ratted me out to the MSS?"

"Do you know who I am?" responded Bricklin.

"Agent Grant Bricklin. We briefly crossed paths in Hong Kong back in the day."

"I'm honored that you remember. That was the day you ruined my life."

Lang scratched his head. "If I recall correctly, I did just the opposite. I spared your life."

The former CIA agent chuckled at the remark. "You would've done me a huge favor if you'd just killed me then."

"I don't know what you've gone through, but I'm pretty sure I'm not the one to blame," Lang said with unwavering clarity.

"I lost my foot because of you," Bricklin shot back. "And my career at the agency was finished. Then, my family left me. I lost everything, and it was because of you."

Lang paused, still struggling to decipher the accusation hurled at him. "Sounds to me like you couldn't deal with the challenges life threw at you. You're just using me as a convenient excuse to justify your shortcomings."

An upwelling of fury flashed on Bricklin's face, his cheeks turning pink with rage. He drew in a steady breath and reclaimed his composure. "I've dreamed of killing you for years, but I'm willing to let you go if you hand over those coins to me."

"What coins?" Lang asked.

"Oh, you're a funny one," Bricklin said with a hearty laugh. "Tell me their location, and you walk out of here alive. If you don't, your life ends here, tonight."

Lang rubbed his injured shoulder. The pain had subsided, but the bleeding hadn't. He needed medical attention fast, but he also knew one thing with irrefutable certainty: Bricklin was not a man to honor his word.

"First, you know as well as I do that those things are fakes," Lang said. "And, I don't have them anymore. Your old boss, Nigel, took them from me already."

Bricklin shook his head in disappointment. "That's a shame. My friends here are going to be very upset they won't get the money Jianlian Guo promised them. Any last words, Phantom Assassin?"

Lang looked Bricklin in the eyes. "You know, Grant. It's not too late to do the right thing here. We can both walk away from this as winners."

"You don't understand, do you? Exacting vengeance on you has been my life's mission. Of course, a billion dollars in my bank account would have been an acceptable tradeoff, but seeing that you don't have the coins, well, I'm left with..."

Bricklin's sentence was cut short by a thunderous bang from upstairs. The noise jolted everyone in the room. Ignoring the searing pain in his shoulder, Lang lunged at the gangster on the wooden container. He drove his fist into the man's jaw and wrenched the AR-15 from his grip.

Lang's actions drew the attention of the other gang members, who immediately opened fire. Crouching low, Lang used the stunned gangster as a human shield. He felt the impact of bullets tearing through the man's body, but fortunately, not a single one reached him. He then swung the AR-15 around and unleashed a dozen rounds at the gangsters near the entrance. The room erupted into chaos as Bricklin dropped to the floor, scrambling for cover amidst the deafening gunfire.

Anticipating more gangsters to burst into the room, Lang sprinted and dove behind the stack of wooden containers. Suddenly, more rapid gunfire erupted upstairs, followed by the deafening boom of a flashbang grenade. Several gangsters spilled into the room, their faces turning to shock when they saw their dead compatriots on the floor, realizing that they had just walked to their doom. Without a gist of emotion, Lang methodically cut them down, the AR-15 spitting rounds with deadly malice. When the sound of gunfire ceased, only he and Bricklin were left breathing in the room.

Bricklin crawled on the floor, his hand fumbling for a gun among his fallen henchmen. He grabbed a Walther PPQ 45, then quickly took cover behind the safe.

"What the hell is going on?" he asked.

"My reinforcements have arrived," Lang replied, his voice a calm contrast to the chaos around him.

"I thought you worked alone," Bricklin shouted from his hiding spot. "Guo told me you never teamed up with anyone, ever."

"Just like back in the day, Grant, your intel was bad," Lang said. "Now, how do you want to play this? You're severely outgunned, and your men upstairs are being taken out as we speak."

"I'm not a fool," Bricklin said. "I know I'm no match for you, especially armed with just this peashooter. Let me walk, and you'll never see or hear from me again. I'll vanish from your life for good."

"You'll have to do better than that," Lang said, "much better."

"Then, what?" Bricklin asked.

"Turn yourself in," Lang replied resolutely.

After a long pause, Bricklin shouted, "Deal."

"Then, we can start by you dropping your weapon and sliding it away."

"Only if you do the same," Bricklin countered.

Lang stretched his arm from behind the wooden containers, providing Bricklin with an unobstructed view of his AR-15. Moving deliberately, he placed the semi-automatic rifle carefully on the floor. "I'll slide it away when I see your piece on the ground."

Remaining crouched behind the safe, Bricklin lowered his weapon and slid it to the far side of the room.

"Your turn," he said.

Squatting low, Lang cautiously slid the automatic rifle away with one hand. He then emerged from behind his cover, his hands raised in a gesture of truce. He walked slowly to the middle of the room.

In response, Bricklin stepped out from behind the safe, moving with a noticeable limp, his hands raised as well.

"Now, let's go upstairs. You lead, I'll follow," Lang said.

As Bricklin took a step forward, a sinister glint in his eyes betrayed his intent. In a flash, he drew a concealed handgun from an ankle holster; however, before he could align his aim, the crack of a .38-caliber round shattered the air. The impact of the bullet detonated Bricklin's skull in a gruesome display of brain and blood, the deadly deed carried out by Lang's hammerless Smith & Wesson 442 revolver, which he had kept hidden under his belt.

Bricklin fell backward onto the floor with a resonating thud.

Peering down upon what was left of Grant Bricklin's face, a fleeting sensation of empathy washed over Lang. Here was a man ensnared by a single mishap, becoming a casualty of his own inability to overcome life's adversities. How a CIA agent working the shadowed alleys of old Hong Kong ended up in the lair of a notorious Chinese crime syndicate, Dalton couldn't begin to guess.

Perhaps deep down, he wanted me to kill him...

Before Lang could turn, the unmistakable click of a gun being cocked behind him registered in his ears.

Damn, I forgot about him.

"Where were you hiding?" Lang inquired in Mandarin, letting his Smith & Wesson fall to the floor.

"You've done me a favor by killing the white devil. With him and Guo Jianlian gone, I can now take the helm of the Blue Dragons," Clippers Fan said.

"How do you propose getting past my colleagues upstairs?" asked Lang.

"There's a hidden door here that leads outside."

"Of course there is," Lang said with a chuckle. "Then, what do you say we go our separate ways and forget any of this ever happened?"

"You really don't have the Coins of Wei?" asked Clippers Fan.

"I'm afraid not."

"Then, it's time to say goodbye. Hell, I may even get a reward from the Chinese government when I tell them I was the one who eliminated the legendary Phantom Assassin," Clippers Fan declared with a cold finality.

Lang reacted instantly, leaping forward and rolling onto the floor, fully aware that he was going to take a bullet. Clippers Fan was too skilled to miss at this range. Lang just hoped that it would strike somewhere non-fatal, and he would have a chance to grab his pistol and fire back.

The sharp boom of a gunshot reverberated through the room, as Lang completed his roll, coming to rest on one knee, the Smith & Wessen already in his grip. As he swung around, he instinctively searched for the telltale sting of a bullet wound but found only the familiar burn of his shoulder injury. Otherwise, he was sure he was unscathed.

With his pistol aimed at the target, Lang saw Clippers Fan standing rigid, his hand holding the H&K P30 still extended. His face wore a blank expression, his eyes staring into nothingness. A small, dark hole had appeared in his throat. Time seemed to hang suspended as he stood there, frozen, before a spurt of blood expelled from the wound, and he collapsed forward onto the hard cement floor.

Then, Lang saw her. There, in the doorway, was the unmistakable sight of his daughter, whom he hadn't seen in more than a decade. The scene took a moment to register in his mind. It was both surreal and dreamlike. Her hands grasped a Glock 19 aimed at the spot where Clipper Fan had been.

"Dad?" she asked.

He didn't notice the tears welling in his eyes until they began falling down his cheeks.

"Elizabeth," he murmured, his voice choked with emotion. No other words came to him.

CHAPTER 52

The winter sun slumbered over Geneva, Switzerland, casting the city in a chilly pre-dawn hush. It would be another hour before the iconic Jet d'Eau would pierce the sky with its powerful spray from Lac Léman, also known as Lake Geneva. Just a few dozen kilometers away, hidden in a tranquil corner of the city, was Parc Solitaire. This secluded private estate had been the backdrop for clandestine meetings over the years by governments from around the world. At this hour, it was deserted, save for the occasional bird perching on a bare tree that stood like a skeletal sentinel guarding the secrets uttered within the park's boundaries.

Nigel McKeen advanced with the silent movements of a veteran operative, his footsteps shuffling softly through a thin blanket of snow. The frigid air nibbled at the edges of his scarf and gloves, each breath producing a fleeting cloud. His leather-gloved hand maintained a firm grip on a leather briefcase. Shadowing his every step was his assistant—a man who doubled as both bodyguard and interpreter, ever watchful and ready to act at a moment's notice.

McKeen paused on the deserted walkway that cut through the middle of the park, stopping fifty yards short of a weathered bench, its wooden slats sheathed in a thin layer of frost. He checked his watch and waited. Within moments, he spotted a figure materializing from the far end of the estate, a dark silhouette against the murky pre-dawn light. The man's short frame was enveloped in a heavy over-coat, and he was not alone. His companion, a much larger man, moved with the lethal grace of a tiger, every step exuding a quiet, predatory confidence.

Although they had never met, McKeen knew more than most of the mysterious Zhou Pengxi, the Minister of the MSS. His reputation was formidable, just as McKeen's own was in the covert circles they inhabited.

Signaling his assistant to stay put, McKeen strode toward the wooden bench alone, his grip on the leather briefcase tightening with each step. Across the park, Zhou did the same, leaving his body man standing guard as they converged on the bench from opposite direc-tions. They sat down simultaneously, maintaining a calculated distance between them.

McKeen broke the silence, his voice low and controlled.

"*Bùzhǎng, nín hǎo,*" he greeted in Mandarin. Hello Minister.

Zhou turned to face his counterpart, the narrow eyes behind his rimless spectacles cold and assessing.

"And you must be Director McKeen. It is a pleasure to meet you," he responded in English.

McKeen spoke in his native language. "I didn't know you spoke English so well. Thank you for accepting my invitation. Just so you know, the President of the United States has granted me full authority to negotiate as I deem necessary."

"It must be important," Zhou said, "to suggest a secret meeting like this on neutral ground. Can you imagine what the press would say if they found out the head of the CIA and MSS were meeting in secret?"

"The conspiracy theorists would have a field day," Lang said with a chuckle.

Zhou slid closer to McKeen. "So, why have you called me here?"

McKeen lifted the briefcase and snapped open the lid. He turned it toward Zhou, revealing its contents. The Chinese minister's eyes widened with surprise as he took in the sight. Slowly, he extended his right gloved hand, reaching forward with a mixture of curiosity and caution.

"May I?" he asked.

"Of course," McKeen replied.

Zhou grasped the Dragon Coin and lifted it toward the feeble light of a nearby lamppost. The gold surface emitted a muted brilliance, while the green gem set in its eye shimmered with an enigmatic sparkle. He studied it intently.

"They are glorious. It's hard to believe they're fake. I'm sure you know that they were fabricated by Professor Linghu Ning," Zhou said, placing the coin back into the briefcase.

"That's what we thought as well, but when we analyzed the coins more carefully, we discovered they were genuine, but I think you knew that. These are the true Coins of Wei, presented by the first emperor of China, Qin Shi Huang, to three of his top generals, Wang Jian, Meng Wu and Li Xin."

Zhou's attention returned to the coins. "You're sure about this?"

"We will be happy to share our findings with you."

Suddenly, Zhou's expression shifted to that of a shrewd spymaster, one who carefully calculated every angle of every situation, of every deal.

"So," he murmured, his eyes narrowing with suspicion, "why show me this?"

"I would simply like to return them to their rightful place. The coins are yours to take with you," McKeen said in an even tone.

"Oh?" Zhou responded with a hint of amusement laced with suspicion. "And you expect nothing in return?"

"Well, there is one thing," McKeen said, his voice lowering to a conspiratorial tone. "I would consider it a great personal favor if you could call off your hunt for Hu Qiang aka Dalton Lang."

Zhou took a long, deliberate breath and shifted uneasily in his seat.

"We've been hunting that traitor for years, and now that we've finally tracked him down... What you ask is difficult. However, given the circumstances and the evolving relationship between our two countries," he said, glancing at the Coins of Wei, "I think we can work something out."

"That is very good to hear, Minister Zhou. *Xièxiè nǐ, wǒ de péngyǒu.*" Thank you, my friend.

Placing the suitcase on the snowy ground by Zhou's feet, McKeen began to rise. However, he was halted by Zhou's voice.

"There is one more matter I'd like to discuss. In fact, it's the real reason I came all this way," the Chinese minister said.

"And what might that be?" McKeen asked, already anticipating the subject.

"The device you left in Russia, or what was left of it."

"What device?"

"Come now, Nigel, we've had a very amicable and fruitful conversation up to this point. Why spoil it now?" Zhou said, his tone carrying a hint of warning.

McKeen smiled. His counterpart was indeed clever and devious, and undeniably astute. He was not a man who indulged in games. McKeen expected no less from the head of what could very well be the most formidable intelligence organization in the world.

"You're talking about the nuclear fusion contraption," McKeen answered with complete transparency.

Zhou nodded.

"Unfortunately, and I'm telling you the absolute truth here, it was destroyed before we could confirm its operation," McKeen said. "I'm sure you know by now what happened. You only need to verify it with your Russian friends."

"The device and all the data associated with it were lost?" Zhou asked, his eyes narrowing with suspicion.

McKeen nodded, maintaining his calm demeanor.

"That means these coins are now nothing more than historical relics," Zhou said.

"If you don't want them, I'll be happy to take them back with me to America."

"That won't be necessary. If they are indeed genuine as you say, then they are part of our long and rich history, and they belong in our national museum." Zhou reached over to take the briefcase and stood. "Have a nice trip back, director."

"You as well, minister," McKeen replied, rising from his seat.

As they prepared to part ways, Zhou stopped and turned, a shadow of something unspoken lingering in the air.

"Is there something more?" asked McKeen.

"Please give my regards to Hu Qiang," he said. "Tell him to savor every minute for the rest of what I'm sure will be a fruitful life, compliments of China."

"I shall, minister," McKeen replied.

With that, both men turned and walked back to the opposite ends of the park, not looking back once. A light snow began to fall, erasing any traces of their presence. By the time the sun came up, the park bore no evidence of the covert meeting that had taken place there, as if it had never happened.

FINALE

The Empire Beyond

神秘帝國

CHAPTER 53

Los Angeles, Present Day

SIX MONTHS HAD QUIETLY DRIFTED by since the notorious Chinese gang incident in downtown—fifteen dead and a veteran L.A. detective implicated—a story that had dominated headlines for a week in Los Angeles. Agent Beth Hu and Melvin Patterson were credited for bringing down the local chapter of the Blue Dragons, earning them the Medal for Meritorious Achievement from the FBI. Meanwhile, Dalton Lang, along with the CIA and Argon Securities, slipped back into the shadows, content to let the accolades pass them by, just as they preferred.

With summer in full swing, Southern California was experiencing the kind of weather that made it a tourist hotspot for sunworshippers all around the world. It was late morning on yet another perfect day when Lang stirred awake in his modest San Gabriel home, drawn from his slumber by the irresistible aroma of bacon and eggs. He stretched, savoring the familiarity of the scent, and made his way to the kitchen.

There, Nathalie moved gracefully around the stove, her presence a comforting vision he'd longed for more than a decade. It felt like a scene out of their Boston days, where she'd cook breakfast nearly every morning, then sent him off to work. Walking slowly toward her, Lang wrapped his arms around her waist from behind.

"Oh, how I've missed your cooking," he murmured, pressing a kiss to her shoulder.

She leaned back into him, a smile playing on her lips. "We're too old to be playing lovey-dovey. Just sit down like a good middle-aged man and eat your food."

"Nonsense," shot back Lang, squeezing her tighter. "This is the age when life begins."

Just then, his smartphone chimed, shattering the playful moment. He picked it up from the counter, recognizing the number. It was the principal's office at Mesa Middle School.

"Dalton Lang here," he answered.

The assistant principal's voice crackled through the line. "Ruth Nguyen says you're picking her up early from school. We'd like to confirm."

"Yes, we have a special family trip planned today," Lang said.

"As you're her temporary guardian, she can be dismissed, but we still need a note from you."

"I'll email it to you now," Lang answered, ending the call with a click.

After crafting a brief letter on his smartphone and sending it off, he and Nathalie sat at the dining table. Their conversation flowed easily. There had been no trace of the awkwardness one would expect after more than ten years apart. Instead, it felt as if the years had never happened. They laughed and chatted about everything and nothing, the comfort of their old familiarity wrapping around them like a worn blanket.

Lang could still remember when CIA Director Nigel McKeen informed him that the MSS had agreed to call off their hunt for him.

Without wasting a moment, he picked up his phone and dialed his wife.

"It's me, sweetheart," he said.

He heard her sobbing on the other end. "It's about time," she replied.

Once breakfast was finished and the table cleared, Lang announced, "We'll leave as soon as you're ready."

"Why are you so mysterious about today? Where are we going?" Nathalie asked.

Lang flashed a devious smile. "You'll see."

After changing into his beige Ascot Chang suit, no tie, Lang headed to the driveway, where he opened the passenger-side door of the Acura MDX for his wife, who gracefully slid into the passenger seat. She was clad in dark jeans and a pink blouse. A quick drive across town, and they pulled up to the front of Mesa Middle School, just as Ruth appeared on the front steps. With a casual wave, she quietly approached and stepped into the rear of the vehicle.

"So, are you going to tell me now what this all about?" she asked as she belted herself in. "You know that I have three tests next week."

"He won't say," Nathalie responded with a shrug.

"It'll be worth it," Lang assured them. "Trust me."

With the morning rush hour behind them, the drive from Mesa Middle School to The Getty Center took a smooth half hour. After parking the vehicle in the parking structure, they took a tram that ascended gracefully to the museum entrance. The brief ride offered a stunning panoramic view of Los Angeles, which shimmered under the late-morning sun, the downtown skyline looming in the distance.

The Getty Center, perched on a hilltop, was a modern architectural marvel. The museum boasted an extensive collection of art, from the masterpieces of Vincent van Gogh and Rembrandt to the revolutionary works of Auguste Rodan. As the tram came to a halt, they stepped out into the open air, greeted by the gentle hum of the crowd and the distant sound of fountains. At the entrance, Beth Hu stood waiting, a warm smile spreading across her face.

"It's good to see you, mom" Beth said, giving Nathalie a hug.

"Oh, sweet daughter," Lang cut in, hugging Beth tightly.

Beth smiled and hugged him back. She then high-fived Ruth.

"So, you're playing hooky today," Beth said.

"It wasn't my idea. Really," Ruth replied.

"Let's not waste any more time. Follow me," Lang said, leading the way to the entrance.

They passed a large banner near the ticket sales counter that read, "The Marvels of the Qin Empire, Courtesy of the National Museum of China and Sponsored by the Automobile Digest Group."

"Are you sure you got your days right, dad? The Qin Empire exhibit doesn't start until the day after tomorrow," Beth said.

"We have a special private preview. VIP only," Lang said proudly.

An attendant, a young man with curly brown hair, asked to see their tickets at the main entrance.

Lang pulled out his smartphone and tilted the screen his way. "They told me to show you this."

"Yes, sir. This way," the attendant replied, leading Lang and his group past the metal detectors and down a flight of stairs.

They entered a sweeping corridor that extended into a private wing. The soft strains of Italian opera played on ancient Chinese instruments filtered through hidden speakers, growing louder as they approached.

Good to see they have good taste in music, Lang thought. *Interesting arrangement.*

At the entrance to the grand room, two burly security personnel stood guard, their presence a silent reminder of the exclusivity of the gathering within. With blank faces, they allowed Lang and his party of four inside.

The main room was filled with ancient artifacts—from vases to silk clothing to an array of weapons. Only about ten people milled about, among them was Max Koga. Seeing him, Beth hurried over, and they exchanged a brief kiss. For Lang, seeing his daughter involved in a relationship still felt strange, but he knew he had to get used to it—she was a responsible adult now, who didn't need an over-protective parent.

On either side of the room, inside thick glass cases, Lang spotted five examples of the famous Terra Cotta Soldiers—discovered in 1974 by farmers in Shaanxi, China. Their lifelike features gave them an eerie quality, as if still standing guard after two millennia, protecting their emperor, Qin Shi Huang, the man who had united the seven kingdoms, establishing the foundation of modern-day China.

Lang's eyes narrowed as he took them in.

"It's hard to believe there were so many of them," he murmured to Nathalie and Ruth, who were equally captivated by the display.

"The actual number is eight thousand," a voice sounded from behind.

Lang turned and saw a man in his early thirties, who appeared to be of mixed Asian and Caucasian descent, with short, dark brown hair and wearing a Gran Turismo 3 T-shirt under a gray blazer. "You don't say? Do you work here?"

"No, I..."

Interrupting the conversation, Koga quickly stepped in. "Dalton, this is Stockton Clay. He's the CEO of the Automobile Digest Group, the main sponsor of the exhibit, and he arranged for us to be part of this private showing."

Lang turned to Clay and shook his hand. "Thank you, Mr. Clay. You must be a big fan of Chinese history to be doing this. It probably cost a small fortune to sponsor this event."

Clay chuckled. "It wasn't that bad. And besides, Director McKeen told me that you have a divested interest in this collection. And, I'm sure you'll be particularly interested in the display at the back of the room, behind the curtains."

Lang shot a tense, bewildered glance at Koga. Their operations with the CIA were supposed to be shrouded in the utmost secrecy, layers of classified information buried deep. So how did this young, rich kid know about Lang's connection to McKeen?

Koga flashed Lang a thumbs-up sign and said, "All good. I'll explain later."

Beth offered her hand to Ruth. "Let's check out those bamboo scrolls. Apparently, they used bamboo for writing because paper wasn't invented yet."

"Funny how we've almost come full circle," Ruth remarked. "We barely use paper now."

She took Beth's hand, and with Koga in tow, the three sauntered toward the scrolls display together.

Lang turned to Clay. "Thanks again, Mr. Clay. My wife and I are going to start by seeing what's behind that curtain."

"Enjoy," Clay said, stepping aside.

Lang guided Nathalie to the back of the room, where they slipped through a gap in the black curtains. The space there was sparse, housing only a single display. In a large glass case, lit by a solitary beam from above, were the Coins of Wei.

The golden medallions, catching and refracting the light, were mesmerizing. Lang and Nathalie stood in awe, their silence heavy with unspoken thoughts.

Finally, Lang said, "You know, people say these things have magical powers, but all they did for me was create a lot of grief."

"That's not entirely true," Nathalie corrected him. "When you had only one of them, you experienced misfortune. But when you brought them all together, they brought us back together, all of us."

Lang replied with a chuckle, "I suppose that's one way to look at it. But they're really nothing more than mere artifacts from a time long past."

Nathalie placed her palms together in front of the coins and incited a soft prayer of gratitude.

"You and Max'll get along just fine," Lang said.

As he leaned in closer to the display for a better look, he found

Nathalie's comments to be amusing, but in the end, he knew it was all just a manifestation of humanity's inclination to believe in higher powers. Examining the coins' meticulous craftsmanship—each line carved into the metal, the amazing detail of the Dragon, Tiger, and Monkey—he had to admit, the level of artistry was otherworldly.

His thoughts were interrupted by the vibration of his smartphone in his pocket. He pulled it out and saw Raja Singh's name on the screen. Ignoring the sign at the entrance that read, "No cell phones allowed," he answered the call.

"Hey Raj, nice to hear from you," he whispered. "I can't talk now, so can I call you back in a few?"

Singh responded in an excited voice. "I just wanted to tell you that when I looked into every Kamita Empire sold in China during 2013 and 2014, the numbers never added up. According to Kamita Motors, twelve were sent to China, but the Chinese government registered only eleven units sold. One was missing. So, I decided to dig deeper and found that one sale had been deleted from the Chinese archives; a car purchased by a person named Wong Liying."

"So?" Lang asked. "It was probably a local politician who snuck one through the system. That kind of thing happens all the time in China."

"However," Singh replied, "Wong Liying is the maiden name of Dr Linghu Ning's wife. I'm thinking that there might be another Kamita Empire that belonged to him hiding somewhere. And who knows, a second prototype of the device might exist..."

Lang let the phone drop to his side, his mind scrambling to make sense of what was happening. With the harmonious tones of *Possente spirto* from Monteverdi's *Orfeo* softly filling the room, he stared intently at the Coins of Wei as they basked in their magnificence from within the case. He glanced over at Nathalie, who continued to softly recite her prayer, then he returned his gaze to the coins.

A sudden doubt flickered in his mind, as if an unseen force from a distant realm was beckoning him into action.

"Find someone else," he said to the coins, taking Nathalie's hand and leading her out of the room.

For the first time in his life, he had found true contentment, and Dalton Lang wasn't going to let anyone—whether mortal or divine—disturb what he had chased after for so long and finally grasped.

Not today, at least.

THE END

ACKNOWLEDGMENTS

This book is the product of many remarkable individuals, who generously contributed their time and expertise to ensure that every scenario and detail was accurate and grounded in reality.

Special thanks to David Lovett and Daniel Charles Ross—exceptional writers in their own right—who scrutinized every word and scene to minimize errors and ensure logical consistency. Their editorial prowess is truly invaluable.

My gratitude also extends to William Y. Chen and Oleg Ivanov for their assistance with the use of Mandarin and Russian throughout these pages. *Xiè xiè* and *Spasibo*, my friends.

This book would have never seen the light of day without Ryan ZumMallen of Carrara Media. His company also published hardcover second editions of *The Prototype* and *Red Mist*—Book I and Book II of *The Prototype Trilogy*. It was during our discussions of releasing these novels when the idea of Book III was born.

In conclusion, I'd like to mention my late friend Jason Michael Gin. I originally crafted this story as a screenplay at his request, but with his untimely passing, I made the decision to transform it into a novel and dedicate the work to him. I hope he approves.

— Sam Mitani, Los Angeles, August 2024

About the Author

Sam Mitani was born in Tokyo, Japan and is best known for his work as International Editor for *Road & Track* magazine, where he was a staff editor for 22 years.

His debut novel, *The Prototype*, was published in 2018, winning the coveted Gold Award in the Thriller Category of the 2019 Next Generation Indie Book Awards. *Red Mist,* Book II of *The Prototype Trilogy,* was released in 2023.

Sam holds a sixth-degree black belt in judo and has previously placed 3rd at the 2007 World Masters Championship International Competition in São Paulo, Brazil.

For more information, visit *sammitani.com.*

Praise for Sam Mitani

The Prototype, 2018

"This zany book plays with science fiction and thriller tropes, resulting in a tale that is oversized, fun, and fast." — *Foreword Reviews*

"Combining the balletic combat of John Wick and the jet-propelled exploits of the Fast and the Furious franchise, Mitani succeeds in absorbing readers into a shadowy, futuristic Tokyo where nothing is as it seems." — *Blue Ink Review*

"Sam Mitani's writing is strong and the author exhibits a gift for plot; the pacing is fast, and the plot structure is brilliantly imagined and executed with unusual skill." — *Reader's Favorite*

"Mitani nailed it on his first try." — *PBS (WFYI Indianapolis)*

Milton Keynes UK
Ingram Content Group UK Ltd.
UKHW022341011124
450602UK00006B/122